The Tetherballs of Bougainville

Also by Mark Leyner

I Smell Esther Williams (1983)

My Cousin, My Gastroenterologist (1990)

Et Tu, Babe (1992)

Tooth Imprints on a Corn Dog (1995)

The Tetherballs of Bougainville

A Novel

by

Mark Leyner

Harmony Books ⚭ NEW YORK

Published by Harmony Books, a division of Crown Publishers, Inc., 201 East 50th Street, New York, New York 10022. Member of the Crown Publishing Group.

Random House, Inc. New York, Toronto, London, Sydney, Auckland

http://www.randomhouse.com/

HARMONY and colophon are trademarks of Crown Publishers, Inc.

Printed in the United States of America

Design by Lynne Amft

Library of Congress Cataloging-in-Publication Data

Leyner, Mark.

The tetherballs of Bougainville / Mark Leyner.

p. cm.

I. Title.

PS3562.E99T43   1997

813'.54—dc21   97-10699

CIP

ISBN 0-517-70101-4

10 9 8 7 6 5 4 3 2 1

First Edition

To my sister, Chase:

International House of Pancakes . . . Cakes! Stanley. Sure, I help you. Monsters in the vents . . . I'm at Liz's. Like my hal-vah? Laura G. *is* fat! Never forget the night Calder fell on you . . . best Christmas ever! Who'd you rather do: Rusty, Eugene, the guys from Trapani's, or Goiter Man? Did I kinda neglect to, like, inform you that you're, uh, my hero? I love ya, hon.

P.S. Yes, the birthday party was a surprise; no, I didn't steal your coat.

When an astronomer observes a galaxy in some distant realm of the universe, what he is actually seeing is light that has traveled incomprehensibly vast distances over vast periods of time before arriving at the lens of his telescope. In the present, this galaxy may no longer even exist. He is quite literally looking at the past.

Theoretically, if we could travel to a point many light-years from the earth and somehow view the light emanating from our planet with the resolution of, say, a spy satellite—advanced photoreconnaissance spacecraft are capable of reading the washing instructions on a black silk chemisette from 22,300 miles in geosynchronous orbit—we could actually observe ourselves in the past.

But until we can outrace light, until we can set up our hyper-resolution telescope on some planetoid 15, 20, 30 light-years from the earth and—by dint of its optical wizardry—watch our youth unfold, we must make due with our memories, our diaries and notebooks, our videotapes, microcassettes, floppy disks, our photo albums, our evocative souvenirs and bric-a-brac—all the various and sundry madeleines we use to goad our hippocampi into reverse-scan.

With only the crude armamentarium of the memoirist at our disposal, it is impossible to portray the past with anything approaching clinical accuracy. Cognitive neuroscientists frequently use the image of hooded convict-drones pumping pink fiberglass insulation into the attic of a sumptuous mansion whose mistress sprawls below caressing the soft down of her belly with a riding crop to describe the way we fill the lacunae in our memories with a meringue of utter fabrication. And we invariably litter the mise-en-scène of our past with the cultural props of our present—Mommy staggers to the table at a Pee Wee Football Awards dinner anachronistically accoutered in an Azzedine Alaïa mummy dress, Great-grandpa, five days out of a shtetl in Poland, washes down Pringles with a 40-ounce bottle of St. Ides malt liquor as he waits in line for an eye exam at Ellis Island.

Wary of these pitfalls, I have tried my best—in the following capsules—to provide an accurate chronicle of my past. And I have tried to confront unflinchingly what were once dirty little secrets buried in the databases of government statisticians, but are now acknowledged as the Three Fundamental Sociological Axioms, the demographic triple pillar upon which our culture stands:

- By the time most Americans have reached the age of 35, they have either killed someone or been accessory to a murder.
- Virtually every American adult habitually engages in some form of sexual depravity that results in the ritualistic sacrifice or mutilation of, or transmission of flesh-necrotizing bacteria to, his or her partner.
- The overwhelming majority of American physicians, surgeons, ICU nurses, air traffic controllers, airline pilots, and school-bus drivers spend their working days in an alcoholic haze, narcotic stupor, or hallucinogen-addled dreamworld.

As you read on, some of you may experience an eerie shock of recognition. You may bolt upright in bed, murmuring to yourself, "I think I actually *know* this guy." Some of you may even say,

"Hey, I think I *dated* this guy." (For female readers who lived in the Dallas–Fort Worth metropolitan area in the mid-eighties—if the droll conversational icebreaker "I'd like to get you real high and eat your pussy for an afternoon" sounds familiar—yes, that was me.)

On the other hand, you may feel as if you're reading your *own* diary. If you feel dirty and ashamed and yet flushed with arousal as if you've been caught in an act of auto-voyeurism, peeping through the bedroom window of your own doppelgänger, or as if you're intoxicating yourself on your own body's fumes and detritus, huffing your own halitosis or snorting a line of your own dandruff from the page, because each page is like a mirror, and you've literally never seen yourself so closely and the pores of your nose have never seemed so gaping, like rabbit holes, and suddenly there's that terror of actually falling down one of them, that terror of interminable free-fall . . . Well, OK, that's cool, that was my intention. In a sense, I've tried to write *your* autobiography. Or perhaps induce you to write mine . . .

Because what I really want is for you to actually inhabit my body, to get into my musculature and fascia, my limbs and trunk and head, to envelop your brain with my brain. I want you to wear my parka of viscera, to string yourself with my organs like a suicide bomber festooned with explosives. I want you to know what it feels like to walk through a Foodtown encumbered by the twitching heft of my 140 pounds and then to try to read a USDA nutrition label on a can of kipper snacks as your mind thrashes against the vortical undertow of my ghastly memories.

I want you to experience what it's like to be four years old and summoned to the school neurologist's office and told that because of hypertrophic dendrite growth in your brain, your head can no longer be supported by your neck—to be told that it's like trying to support a bowling ball on a single strand of uncooked angel hair pasta—and to have to wear a specially built cervical flying buttress—a doughnut-shaped base worn around the waist, from which four thick metal flanges rise up to pinion the front, sides, and back of the head. I want you to experience the instantaneousness with which the uproarious din of a Chuck E. Cheese is stilled when you walk in sporting that device. I want you to feel what it's like to be ten and, while the other kids are frolicking at summer camps in the Berkshires, you're immured in the recesses of a mildewed hovel, subsisting on cigarettes and black coffee and spending twenty hours a day shooting a perverse misanthropic video version of *Pippi Longstocking* using tiny intricate marionettes made of cockroach carapaces, chicken bones, rat vertebrae pried from traps, discarded condoms, foil ketchup packets—whatever you can scavenge from the garbage-strewn halls. I want you to feel what it's like to be in postproduction, your editing equipment darkened by the shadow of your huge head. And I want you to feel what it's like to be suddenly remanded into the custody of a so-called "aunt"—a bushy-haired, pockmarked woman with a lush mustache and tall rounded karakul hat who fills your head with paranoid conspiracies and crackpot theories, including the notion that Jack Ruby didn't intentionally kill Lee Harvey Oswald, that his death was accidental and occurred as the two had rough sex.

In order to wear this garment of a body, you'll need to take the bones out. Bones function essentially as hangers and shoe trees. So filet first, then get in.

Once you're in, I'm out.

My soul is released.

But don't worry. It's cool. This was my intention. It's why I wrote this book.

You see, the soul can outrace light. (They've clocked souls leaving bodies at somewhere around 190,000 miles per second.) So while you're trudging around in my body, my soul will be on that distant planetoid, sitting on a couch in front of the telescope's monitor, drinking a beer, eating a mortadella, prosciutto, and provolone hero—watching the reruns of my past. Laughing, crying, belching.

Some night, when you're all alone and feeling particularly alienated and forsaken, close your eyes and cup your hands to your ears. You'll hear a kind of muffled roar. That's the cumulative sound of 30 billion souls—one from each human body that's ever walked the earth; each now alone on its own individual tiny desolate planet, furnished with couch, telescope, minibar, and self-replenishing hoagie—laughing, crying, and belching as they watch their lives loop endlessly in universal syndication.

The Tetherballs of Bougainville

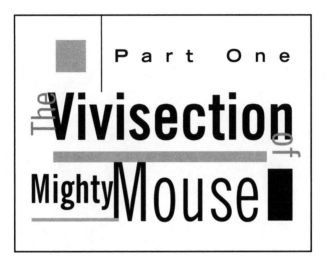

Part One

The Vivisection of Mighty Mouse

My father is strapped to a gurney, about to die by lethal injection, when the phone rings. Everyone—warden, lawyers, rabbi, Dad—looks at the red wall phone. That's the one that rings when the governor calls to pardon a condemned convict. But when it rings a second time, they realize that it's not the old-fashioned tintinnabulation of a wall phone, but the high-pitched electronic chirp of a cellular. I reach into my jacket pocket and answer: "Hello? [It's my agent.] What's up?" Everyone's giving me this indignant glare like, "Hey, we got an execution here," which I deflect with the international sign for "Bear with me, please"—the upraised frontal palm (gesturally closer to the Hollywood Indian's gesticulated salutation than to the traffic cop's "Stop," which is more peremptory and thrust farther from the body). I'm nodding: "Uh-huh, uh-huh, uh-huh . . . That's great! OK, I'll talk to you later." I slip the phone back inside my jacket.

"Good news?" my father asks.

"Yeah, kind of," I reply. "It looks like I'm going to win the Vincent and Lenore DiGiacomo / Oshimitsu Polymers America Award."

"What's that?" the doctor says, retaping the cannula in my father's arm and sliding the IV drip stand closer to the gurney.

"It's a very prestigious, very generous award given every year for the best screenplay written by a student at Maplewood Junior High School—it's $250,000 a year for the rest of your life."

"Jesus fucking Christ!" Dad exclaims.

"Mazel tov," says the rabbi.

"Whoa . . . hold on, folks," I say. "There's one big problem here—there's no screenplay. I haven't written word one. I don't even have a title yet."

The warden—an absolutely stunning woman in a décolleté evening gown—eyes me dubiously. "How'd you win the award if there's no screenplay?"

"That's the advantage of having a powerful agent," I say.

Everyone nods in agreement.

"Trouble is—I gotta get this movie written soon. . . . Shit, I could really use a title. I can't write without a title, y'know, I gotta be able to say to myself, I'm working on *Such and Such.*

"How does *Like Lemon-Lime Sports Drink for Carob Protein Bar* strike you?" the executioner asks.

"I thought of that myself," I say, "but it's a little too close to *Like Water for Chocolate.*"

"Mark, what about *Double Life: The Shattering Affair Between Chief Judge Sol Wachtler and Socialite Joy Silverman?*" the warden suggests.

"Too long."

Dad pipes up. "I've got the title," he says decisively.

"What?"

"*Eventually, Even Mighty Mouse Is Vivisected by the Dour Bitch in a White Lab Coat.*"

There's a long silence.

"I love it," the rabbi finally says. "It's haunting. It's archetypal. It speaks to the collective unconscious. Every culture has, if not a full-fledged myth, than a mythological motif involving the man/rodent—strong, honest, resolute in his convictions, striving diligently to excel in life—who, in the end, is confronted by the merciless, omnipotent giantess—a sort of postpartum, premenstrual proto-Streisand—with opulently manicured and fiendishly honed fingernails, who plucks him up and slices him open from his Adam's apple to his pubic bone. *Eventually, Even Mighty Mouse Is Vivisected by the Dour Bitch in a White Lab Coat,*" he reprises, gesturing as if at a marquee.

"C'mon, that's much too long," I say.

"Bullshit," rebuts my father. "The length is irrelevant. Moviegoers condense titles regardless. They called *One Flew Over the Cuckoo's Nest 'Cuckoo's Nest.' Willy Wonka and the Chocolate Factory* became *'Willy Wonka.' Steroids Made My Friend Jorge Kill His Speech Therapist: An ABC Afterschool Special* was simply *'Steroids.'* So they'll call this *'Vivisected'* or *'Dour Bitch.'* But you want succinct? How about *No Exit Wound.* Sort of Jean-Paul Sartre meets Jean-Claude Van Damme. Or you want a real contemporary, John Singleton sort of feel? What about something like *Yo! You're My Dope Dealer Not My Thesis Adviser. If I Wanted Your Opinion About My Dissertation, I'd Have Asked for It, Motherfucker!*"

I'm starting to get a little impatient. I glance at my watch, a Tag Heuer chronograph. "Listen, I gotta get over to the library and try to come up with some ideas. Can we, uh . . ." I make the international sign for lethal injection: thumb, index, and middle fingers mime squeezing hypodermic and then head lolls to the side with tongue sticking out of mouth.

The executioner and operations officer check and recheck the IV line and make a final inspection of the delivery module, which is mounted on the wall and holds the three lethal doses in syringes, each of which is fitted beneath a weighted piston.

Everyone's being especially punctilious here because of an

accident that occurred recently at an execution over in Missouri, where leaks in the octagonal gas chamber's supposedly airtight seals allowed cyanide gas to seep into the witness room, killing ten people, including members of the condemned criminal's victims' families. Only writer William T. Vollmann, who was covering the execution for *Spin* magazine, walked away unscathed.

Dad beckons me to come closer. "Here, son, I want you to have this," he says, handing me his ring, a flawless oval Burmese sapphire flanked by heart-shaped diamonds.

Something about the way he contorts his body against the leather restraints in order to remove the ring reminds me of my first memory of my parents naked. I must have been three or four—they'd just gotten out of the shower and were toweling each other off. My father's entire body was emblazoned with tattoos of Frank Lloyd Wright buildings.

"What's that, Daddy?" I remember asking.

"That's the Kaufmann house at Bear Run, Pennsylvania, that's Taliesin West in Phoenix, that's the Johnson Wax building in Racine, Wisconsin, and that's the Guggenheim," he explained, pointing, his head twisted backward over his shoulder.

"Why'd you get those?" I asked.

"I was drunk, I guess . . ." he shrugged.

My mom's buttocks were tattooed with an illustration of an 1,800-pound horned Red Brindle bull crashing through the front window of a Starbuck's coffee bar and charging a guy who's sitting there sipping a cappuccino and reading M. Scott Peck's *The Road Less Traveled*. The caption reads: "Life's a Bitch and Then You're Gored to Death."

Lately I've been trying to fix Mom up with the lawyer Alan

Dershowitz, who helped prepare an amicus-curiae brief in support of my father's last appeal. Mom spends most of her time these days dressed in black, fingering her rosary beads, sighing, daubing away tears with a black, lace-trimmed handkerchief, and doing Goldschläger shots—so I thought it might be a good idea for her to start getting out more. My dad's family is really pissed at me because they think Mom shouldn't start dating until after the execution, and they're also mad because I sold some nude photos of Dad to this bondage magazine and they claim to have a right to some of the proceeds, and my position is basically: I tied him up, I took the photographs, they're my property, profits from their sale belong to me, end of discussion.

It's time. The superintendent reads the death warrant.

Everyone turns to the wall phone, giving it one last opportunity to ring.

"If you think the governor's gonna call with a stay of execution, you're nuts," I say. "She's probably not even awake yet. It's only noon."

(They'd lowered the voting age to 15 in order to bring the highest-spending demographic sector into the electorate. This resulted in the election of a 17-year-old as governor. It's been a real joke. At her inauguration, the chief justice had to make her remove her Walkman and spit out a huge multicolored bolus of Skittles so she could hear and repeat the oath of office. And you know how barristers and judges in England wear those white powdered perukes? Our new governor signed an order requiring the lawyers and judges in New Jersey to wear these big-hair wigs—y'know like mall hair. You should have seen my father's trial—I'm telling you, it was a joke.)

■

My father is not an evil person. He just can't do PCP socially. At the risk of oversimplification, I think that's always been his basic problem. Some people are capable of being social phencyclidine users and some people are not, and my father unfortunately falls into the latter category. Normally Dad's a very sweet, patient, benevolent guy, but when he's dusted, he's a completely different person—belligerent, volatile, *extremely* violent.

I remember once he was helping me with some homework— I was in the third grade, writing a report comparing the ritualistic sacrifice of prisoners of war during the Aztec festival Tlacaxipeualiztli (the Feast of the Flaying of Men) with recent fraternity hazing deaths at the Fashion Institute of Technology— and Dad was being just extraordinarily helpful in terms of conceptualizing the theme of the report and then with the research and editing (he was a fastidious grammarian), and at some point the doorbell rang and Dad went downstairs. Apparently it was some of his "dust buddies," because he disappeared for about a half hour and when he returned to my room, he was transformed. Sweating, drooling, constricted pupils, slurred speech—the whole profile.

We started working again, and all of a sudden Dad grabbed the mouse and highlighted a line on the computer screen, and he said, "That's a nonrestrictive modifier. It needs to be set off by commas."

I probably said something to the effect of, "It's not a big deal, Dad, let's just leave it."

At which point he went completely berserk. "It's a nonrestrictive adjectival phrase. It's not essential to the meaning of the sentence's main clause. It should be set off by commas. It *is* a big deal!"

And he grabbed a souvenir scrimshaw engraving tool, which I'd gotten at the New Bedford Whaling Museum gift shop several summers ago, and he plunged it into his left thigh, I'd say at least two to three inches deep.

"All right, I'll put the commas in," I said.

Dad evinced absolutely no sensation of pain, impervious as he was, thanks to the PCP. If anything, impaling his thigh with the scrimshaw graver seemed to mollify him. He certainly made no attempt nor manifested the slightest desire to remove it, and later, while we were trying to come up with a more colloquial way of saying "bound to the wheel of endless propitiation of an unloving and blood-hungry divinity," Dad absently twanged the embedded tool as he mused.

Another fascinating and potentially mitigating factor emerged during my father's trial for killing a security guard who'd apprehended him shoplifting a Cuisinart variable-speed hand blender and a Teflon-coated ice-cream scooper from a vendor's kiosk at an outlet in Secaucus. (The imposition of the death sentence in New Jersey requires "first-degree murder with heinous circumstances." In this case, it was determined that the weapons used in the commission of the homicide were the purloined implements themselves—the hand blender and the ice-cream scooper. The lower torso of the security guard, who'd pursued my father down into a subterranean parking garage, had been almost totally puréed, the upper torso rendered into almost a hundred neat balls.) Unbeknownst to me, Dad had an extremely rare hypersensitivity to minute levels of gamma radiation. An eminent astrohygienist from Bergen County Community College testified that once a day there's a 90-minute gamma-ray burst originating from colliding comets within the Milky Way. She was able to link each of my father's most violent episodes (including the grisly murder of the security guard) to a corresponding gamma-ray burst. My father's intolerance was so acute, she contended, that exposure to as little as 15 picorads of gamma radiation resulted in extreme neurological disturbances.

Unfortunately, the jury in its verdict and the judge in his sentence proved unsympathetic to this theory. In retrospect, I think that the spectacle of my father's attorneys in their big-hair mall wigs leading witnesses through hours of arcane testimony about Gamma-Ray Sensitivity Syndrome tended to damage his cause.

My father has always been a good provider. And in terms of a work ethic, he's been a wonderful role model. He taught me that every morning—no matter how you feel physically and no matter what mood you're in—you have to get yourself out of bed, shower, shave, put on a dark suit, hood your face in a black ski mask, and go out into the world and make some money.

Back when I was in the fifth grade, Dad had just come off one of his best years—he'd been swindling insurance companies by faking auto accidents and claiming nonexistent "soft-tissue" injuries, and also traveling around the country, using a high-voltage taser stun gun to rob Publishers Clearing House Sweepstakes winners—and we all moved to St.-Leonard-de-Noblat in the Limousin region of France. This was supposed to be a very chic place. In the late nineteenth century they'd flooded 50 acres of pasture to create a beautiful lake with three islands. So when Mom and Dad gave me some brochures and I read about the man-made lake, I thought whoa! excellent! swimming, water-skiing, fishing. But the neighborhood had really gone downhill lately. Several large ancien-régime families, all suffering from lead poisoning, had moved in recently. There were two contending explanations for their condition: one, that they'd been eating foie gras from pottery finished with lead glaze (goose liver soaks up lead like the proverbial sponge), and two (this is the one that I believed), that they suffered from congenital pica and had been nibbling away for generations at the peeling lead-based paint and plaster from their dilapidated chateaus. Whatever the cause, they exhibited all the classic symptoms: reduced IQ, impaired hearing, and trouble maintaining motor control and balance. But, worst of all, these lead-poisoned erstwhile aristocrats had developed the unfortunate custom of washing livestock, defecating, and dumping corpses in the lake. By the time we moved back to the States, the coliform bacteria count in the lake was nearly 700 times the permissible limit. (And bear in mind that the French, being far less squeamish than Americans, have much higher acceptable coliform bacteria levels than we do.)

I think that we tend to select certain emblematic images to store in our memories as visual icons representing each of the journeys and sojourns in our lives. And when I remember our year in St.-Leonard-de-Noblat, I think of the topless contessa and her boom box.

Every sunny afternoon I'd go down to the lake and watch the contessa, a voluptuous woman from one of the most severely lead-poisoned families, struggle for 45 minutes to mount her chaise longue and then endeavor spastically for another half hour to remove her bikini top. This finally accomplished, she'd pillow an ear against her huge radio, which was turned up so loud that it literally drowned out the dredging equipment that the sanitation department used to remove bodies from the turbid water.

There I'd loiter, leering, until I'd hear my mother's calls—her voice so shrill that it easily pierced the roar of the dredging equipment *and* the blare of the bare-breasted contessa's ghetto blaster. I'd reluctantly trudge home to find Mom on the veranda, draining her second pitcher of kamikazes.

"Get your steno pad," she'd bark, lighting a cigarette and singeing the ends of a platinum tress that had swung into the flame of her Zippo.

And so each afternoon my mother would dictate yet another revision of her "living will." And although all sorts of frivolous codicils were continuously appended—often to be nullified the following day—the gist of the will remained constant: "In the event that I ever become seriously ill and my ability to communicate is impaired, please honor the following requests. No matter how onerous a financial and emotional burden I become to my family and no matter what extraordinary means are necessary, I want to be kept going. I don't care about mental lucidity, dignity, or quality of life, I don't care how flat my EEG is or for how long, I don't care if I'm just half a lung and a few feet of bowel—I want to be kept alive."

"Do you understand?" she'd snarl.

"Yes, Mom," I'd nod.

I'd file the latest version in a strongbox in her lingerie drawer, and then scamper back to the lake, hoping that I'd hadn't missed the departure of the contessa, a sad and beautiful spectacle. Her lead-suffused flesh luridly burnished in the gloaming, she'd attempt to free herself from her folding chaise, which would have collapsed around her like a Venus' flytrap enclasping some engorged and lustrous bug.

The warden reads the death warrant. The doctor daubs my father's limbs and chest with conductive jelly and attaches five EKG electrodes. He then gives him a pre-injection of 10 cc of antihistamine to minimize spasming.

"Do you have a final statement you wish to make?" the warden asks.

"Yes. I'd like to direct my last words to my son.

"Mark . . . Mark?"

"Just a sec, Dad," I say, my head bowed, eyes glued to the Game Boy that glows in my hands. "I'm on the brink of achieving a new personal best here."

I'm playing a game called *Gianni Isotope.* It's pretty awesome. The ultimate object is to enable the hero, Gianni Isotope, to save as many rock stars as possible from being turned into edible breaded nuggets at a space-based processing plant in the Lwor Cluster. You earn the opportunity to attempt the Lwor rescue mission by scoring a requisite number of points on the two preceding levels.

First, before beginning play, you have to choose the outfit that Gianni Isotope wears throughout the game. I usually just put him in what I wear to junior high every day—no shirt, Versace leather pants, and Di Fabrizio boots.

In Level One, you manipulate Gianni Isotope as he flies a helicopter into a city whose skyline comprises cylindrical and rectilinear towers of deli meats and cheeses. You/Gianni have to fly upside down and, using the whirring rotor blades of the heli-copter, slice these skyscrapers of bologna, salami, ham, liverwurst, American cheese, muenster, etc., as thinly as possible. The object is to slice the city's entire skyline down to ground level. Points are awarded based on speed and portion control. You need 5,000 points to advance.

In Level Two, Gianni Isotope works for a private investigator in Washington, D.C., who's compiling scurrilous information about Supreme Court justices. You/Gianni can pick any of the eight optional sitting justices, or you can play the default set-ting—Clarence Thomas. If you choose Justice Thomas, for instance, you're given the following five stories:

- Thomas's fascination with breast size is well established. But he is also intrigued by more-arcane aspects of the female anatomy. His standard interview queries—proffered to job applicants when he chaired the Equal Employment Oppor-tunity Commission—were gynecological in their scope and specificity: 1. Objectively describe your urethral meatus. 2. Is your perineum very hairy? 3. How violent are the contrac-tions of your bulbocavernosus and ischiocavernosus muscles when you experience sexual orgasm, and how might that affect your performance at the EEOC?

- Thomas delights in sharing his frisky frat-house humor with fellow Supreme Court Justices. Recently, while the high court was hearing arguments about the constitutionality of a statute regulating interstate commerce, Thomas was seen scribbling a note and passing it to Ruth Bader Ginsburg, who read it, became slightly red in the face, and then shrugged back at a grinning Thomas. Sources with access to several of Ginsburg's clerks contend that the note read: "How big was Felix's frankfurter?"—a reference, of course, to Felix Frankfurter, the distinguished Austrian-born jurist who was appointed to the Supreme Court by Franklin Delano Roosevelt, and who served as an associate justice from 1939 to 1962.

- Thomas's self-titillating fear of pubic hair has been immortalized in his legendary entreaty "Who has put pubic hair on my Coke?" Ever attentive to the requirements of politesse and protocol, Thomas can couch his scatological solecisms in more delicate terms when he deems it appropriate. At a recent Embassy Row cocktail party, Thomas was overheard asking his hostess, the patrician wife of an ambassador, "Who has put a tuft of epithelial cilia on my Chivas?"

- Seated in the first-class section of American Airlines Flight #3916 en route from O'Hare to Dulles, Thomas, thoroughly engrossed in Willa Cather's *My Antonia,* suddenly looks up and exclaims, "Antonia's gotta be at least a 34C"—speculating upon the bra size of the novel's plucky protagonist.

- As a college undergraduate, Thomas submitted a final term paper for his American Literature of the Nineteenth Century class which was titled, "Hester Prynne, Spitter or Swallower?"

You/Gianni Isotope have to track down leads, interview witnesses, and unearth documents that will corroborate these anecdotes before rival investigators from the tabloids and liberal media elite do it first.

Then an indignant Justice Thomas, black judicial robes billowing in his wake, pursues Gianni Isotope through an aquatic labyrinth on jet skis.

During the labyrinth chase, Thomas's and Gianni's energy supply can become low. To replenish, Gianni can buy Citicorp stock from surfing Saudi princes in matching madras trunks and kaffiyehs. Justice Thomas can refuel by snaring Big Gulp Cokes from vending machines on buoys. If either character's energy supply becomes too depleted, he is engulfed in a large cloud of greenish incandescent gas and can only jet-ski very, very slowly.

If you/Gianni Isotope are able to scoop the Fourth Estate with Supreme Court scandal, elude the avenging Justice through the aquatic labyrinth, and then, finally, negotiate a creature with the upper torso of a Dallas Cowboy cheerleader and the lower torso of a coatimundi without being shredded by its claws, you advance to the ultimate level.

Welcome to the Lwor Cluster in the Goran H47 Helix.

Rock musician is the protein of choice for the typical Lwor creature. Certain parts of the musicians are considered delicacies. Their burst eardrums are eaten by Lwors like popcorn while they watch movies. Their alcohol-ravaged cirrhotic livers are especially delectable to the Lwor palate and are mashed into a paste and served on flat bread and Wheat Thins.

At a processing plant, the live musicians are emptied onto a conveyor belt that leads to a darkened room, where Lwor workers hang them upside down from U-shaped shackles on an assembly line. The rock stars are stunned with an electric shock, their throats slit by machine, and they move through boiling water to loosen their scalps and tight pants. Machines massage off the hair and trousers, eviscerate and wash the musicians inside and out, and slice them into pieces. Seventy rock stars a minute move down the line. Nothing is wasted. Studded jewelry, latex underwear, blood, internal organs, even the decocted tattoo ink is collected and sent to a Lwor rendering plant to become ingredients in cattle feed and pet food for export to other planets. Processed rock musician is Lwor's most lucrative commodity. They debone it, marinate it, cut it into pieces, press it into patties, roll it into nuggets, bread it, batter it, cook it, and freeze it.

You/Gianni Isotope attempt to save the likes of Dave Mustaine of Megadeth; AC/DC guitarist Angus Young; Def Leppard drummer Rick Allen; Tony Araya, the bassist from Slayer; Joe Perry of Aerosmith; Eddie Van Halen; Terence Trent D'Arby; Jon Bon Jovi; and, inexplicably, Val Kilmer. (The updated version, *Gianni Isotope II: The Final Dimension,* includes Pantera, Rivers Cuomo of Weezer, and David Roback of Mazzy Star.)

For each rock star you rescue from the processing plant, you're awarded 1,000 points.

The highest score I'd ever gotten was 30,000. I'm about to pluck Metallica frontman James Hetfield from the deboning machine—which would give me a record-shattering 40,000 points—when my father breaks my concentration. Hetfield's filleted and flipped into the fry-cooker and time runs out. Game over.

"Fuck!" I mutter, flicking off the Game Boy.

I take a deep breath.

"What is it, Dad?"

"Did you bring your camera?"

"Yeah, but they won't let me take any pictures in here."

"That's too bad. I thought you could get a shot of me dead on the gurney and sell it to Benetton and maybe they'd use it in an ad."

There's a pause.

"Are those your last words?" the warden asks.

"No, that was just an aside."

"OK. We don't want to start administering the drugs if you're not finished. Unfortunately, that's happened before."

"You've killed people in the middle of their last words?"

"Well, if a person pauses for an extended period of time, we might just assume that he's finished, and execute him. We had a guy recently who ranted for a while and then he sighed and said nothing for about a minute, so we administered the drugs. But then the next day, when we went back and read the transcript and parsed the sentence, we realized that, having finished this long string of subordinate clauses and prepositional phrases and appositives, he'd apparently just paused in anticipation of introducing the main clause. So, as it turns out, unfortunately, we did execute him in mid-sentence. In mid-ellipsis, actually. So if you could give us a general idea of what you're going to say and about how long you think it might take . . ."

"You mean like an outline?"

"No, just a rough idea of where you're going. And that'll make it much less likely that we kill you *in medias res.*"

"Well, I don't know . . . I was thinking of maybe starting off with some maudlin and desultory reminiscing—that should only take a couple of minutes—and then I thought I'd tell a brief impressionistic anecdote about hair, and then I figured I'd finish off with some sort of spiritual or motivational aphorism for my son. I think we're looking at about four or five minutes, tops."

"Excellent," says the warden.

"It's very nice," says the rabbi.

"All right, let's take it from the top," says the executioner, gamely.

"When your mother was pregnant with you—"

"Hold it," interrupts the executioner. "Are you referring to *my* mother?"

"No, I'm talking to my son."

"Well then don't look at me, look at him. And, Mark, while your father's addressing his last words to you, why don't you hold his hand?"

I make a face.

"What's the problem?" asks the executioner. "Are you two uncomfortable touching each other? Is that an issue?"

"No," we both say, simultaneously defensive.

"Well, then, c'mon. Mark, slide your chair up next to the gurney and hold your dad's hand. Now, Dad, you look at Mark and talk to *him.*"

I pull my chair up alongside the gurney next to the IV drip stand and grasp Dad's left hand, which is secured at the wrist with a supplementary nylon-webbed restraint with Velcro fastenings. Dad looks at me and begins again.

"When your mother was pregnant with you—"

"Much better!" the executioner says in a stage whisper.

"—I fell for this bank teller who used to keep her deposit slips in her cleavage. And I'd go down to the bank every day to watch her and it would just drive me fuckin' nuts. Unbeknownst to me at the time, she had this whole incredibly elaborate, idiosyncratic filing system—regular savings account withdrawal and deposit slips in her cleavage, money market deposit slips under her right bra strap, IRA and Keogh deposit slips under the left bra strap, payroll checks went in the front waistband of her panties, mortgage payments back panty waistband, Christmas club deposits gartered at the thighs, etc. All I knew is that I was completely sexually obsessed with this woman. All day, all night, it's all I'm thinking about. So I learn from a friend of a friend of a friend that this bank teller loves steak. And you know those ads in the back of *The New Yorker* for Omaha Steaks? Well, I start having four filet mignons packed in dry ice sent to her house every week accompanied by little romantic poems. Call me old-fashioned—but I still think there's no better way to say 'I want you' to a woman than sending her meat in the mail. So one day some idiot from Omaha Steaks calls and leaves a message on the answering machine about whether I'd like to include eight free 4-ounce burgers in my next delivery and your mother plays the message, finds out about the bank teller, and the next thing you know, I'm getting a call from her psychotherapist forbidding me to send any more meat to this woman because it's jeopardizing your mother's mental health, and I say, 'I'm *forbidden*? What is this, some kind of edict, are you issuing a fatwa?' and he says, 'Call it a fatwa if you wish,' and I say, 'Well, fuck you and fuck your fatwa.' Meanwhile these filet mignons are starting to set me back like sixty, seventy bucks a week. So I start moonlighting at this very exclusive, very posh beauty salon uptown. Very high-profile clientele—Lainie Kazan, Kaye Ballard, Eydie Gormé, Eddie

Arnold—y'know, you reach a point where you don't even notice anymore, it's like, 'There's Piper Laurie, pass the rugelach.' Anyway, one day this woman comes in, she's got a 4:45 P.M. appointment, her name is Meredith, and she's missing the top half of her cranium, and her entire brain is exposed. Y'know the line from that Eurythmics song that goes *I'm speaking de profundis. / This ain't no joke. / A medium-boiled egg with the upper portion of its shell and albumen removed reveals a glaucous convexity of coagulated yolk. / Oh yeah . . . It hurts . . . Oooo, c'mon . . . A glaucous convexity of coagulated yolk!* Well, that's the image. It's as if someone had taken this woman's cranium and meticulously—"

"That's Duran Duran," the operations officer interjects.

"What?" says Dad, turning to the voice that comes from behind a one-way mirror separating the control module room from the execution chamber.

"I'm pretty sure that line's from a Duran Duran song, because I remember that in the video, the guy who sucks out the yolk is Simon Le Bon."

My father furrows his brow for a moment and then nods.

"You're right," he says, "you're absolutely right. Simon Le Bon sucks out the yolk, starts choking, and then Nick Rhodes Heimlich-manuevers Le Bon, who expels the yolk which arcs through the air and settles in a corner of the sky where it begins to throb and radiate, and the video which had heretofore been sepia-toned takes on this incredibly garish, heavily impastoed Van Gogh-at-Arles coloration as they sing the refrain, *Spit the sun into the sky / I'm so hard, I think I'll die!* over and over again. It's Duran Duran. You're absolutely right."

He turns back toward me.

"Anyway . . . it's as if someone had meticulously sawed around the circumference of this woman's cranium at about eyebrow-and-ear level and just lifted the top right off. But the *really* amazing thing is that she has a full head of long brown hair growing directly out of her brain. So apparently her condition was not the result of a freak workplace accident or a sadistic experiment—which is what I'd initially assumed—but the result of a congenital defect. She was either born without enclosing cranial bones or had suffered some sort of massive fontanel drift. And, remarkably, her hair follicles are distributed in a perfectly normal pattern directly on the pia mater of her cerebral cortex. The other beauticians are too squeamish to work on her and, in fact, fled to the pedicure and waxing rooms the minute she walked through the door, so I volunteer. As soon as she's in the chair, it's obvious to me that she's feeling a bit uncomfortable, so the first thing I say is, 'Meredith, take your eyeglasses off.'

"She's like, 'Excuse me?'

" 'Take off your glasses.'

"She doffs the thick-lensed violet frames.

" 'Did anyone ever tell you how much you resemble Reba McEntire? It's uncanny.'

"She giggles, blushing. The ice is broken. I intuit immediately that Meredith is a warm, friendly person with a wonderful, understated sexiness. We start talking about what kind of a cut she wants.

" 'First of all,' she says, 'I'm sick of always having to brush these bangs off my prefrontal lobes.'

" 'The bangs have to go,' I say.

"Meredith explains that she'd like a hairstyle that doesn't look 'done.' She wants to be able to just wash her hair and finger-style it, without needing a brush, because the bristles can apparently nick cerebral arteries and cause slight hemorrhaging and mild dementia. She also wants to be able to let it dry naturally—hair dryers can overheat and sometimes even boil her cerebrospinal fluid. And electric rollers and curling irons are absolutely con-traindicated—they tend to induce convulsions.

"I start by trimming off all the extra hair that had been hang-ing down over Meredith's shoulders and bring the length up to a point where the hair can curve gently against the sides of her neck. I want a fuller, more luxurious look to her hair, and since she's got plenty of it, I control the volume with a graduated cut. Meredith's hair had parted naturally between the cerebral hemi-spheres, along the superior sagittal sinus. I think a slight asym-metry will create a more sophisticated shape and line, so I sweep her hair over from a side part at the left temporal lobe. This is a very versatile style. It can be tied back for aerobics, worn full and smooth at the office—Meredith is a commercial real estate bro-ker—and then swept up for evening. In other words, there are no limitations to what Meredith can do with this cut, which is exactly right considering her sports activities, her business, her charity benefits—she's co-chairperson of the Rockland County chapter of the American Acrania and Craniectomy Society—and her busy social life. Meredith's hair is a very dark, nondescript brown, so I suggest to her that we lighten it. She enthusiastically agrees. I start by coloring in a soft, cool blond to maximize the impact of the wet, pinkish gray tissue of her brain. Then I add a few extra highlights to play off the deep ridges and fissures that corrugate her cortex.

"Meredith is ecstatic about the make-over, but she has one lingering concern.

" 'I won't need barrettes, will I? When I wear them, they put too much pressure here,' she says, indicating the posterior peri-sylvian sector of her left hemisphere, 'and it disrupts my ability to assemble phonemes into words. That can really be a problem when I'm showing property.'

" 'No barrettes, clips, combs, hairpins, headbands—that's the beauty of this style. You wash it, let it dry, run your fingers through it—done. No fuss, no aphasia, no memory loss, no motor impairment. You're ready to rock.'

" 'It's just perfect!' she says, turning her head this way and that, as she admires herself in the mirror.

"Before she leaves, we discuss which shampoos and conditioners won't permeate the blood-brain barrier. She gives me a big kiss, a huge tip, and nearly skips out of the shop, at which point the other beauticians filter back to their stations.

"About two weeks later, I receive a note at the salon from Meredith. It says: 'The office manager was very, *very* impressed—if you know what I mean! Some people took a while to notice how different I looked, but all of them *love* it! You're *THE BEST*!'

"And so, son, the point is—any asshole with a Master of Social Work degree can put on a turban and start issuing fatwas about whom you can and whom you can't mail meat to, but it takes real balls to turn a brunette without a cranium into a blonde."

I've whipped out a pad and pen, and I'm trying to scribble this down as quickly as I can: *Any asshole with a Master of Social*

Work degree . . . can put on a turban and start issuing fatwas . . . about whom you can and whom you can't mail meat to—

And my pen runs out of ink.

"Fuck!" I squawk. "Excuse me, anybody have a pen or a pencil?"

"Here," says the prison superintendent, reaching into his jacket pocket and handing me a syringe-shaped pen, the bottom half of which is emblazoned with the words *New Jersey State Penitentiary at Princeton—Capital Punishment Administrative Segregation Unit,* its upper half a transparent, calibrated barrel filled with a viscous glittery blue liquid that undulates back and forth as you tilt it.

"Cool pen!" I exclaim.

"Thanks," he says. "I get them from the potassium chloride sales rep. It's one of those 'put your logo here' freebies."

I finish transcribing the maxim: —*but it takes real balls to turn a brunette without a cranium into a blonde.*

And as the superintendent and warden usher me into the witness room, I experience two serendipitous visual thrills.

First, as the warden extends a guiding hand, there's a slight billowing of fabric at the top of her dress that gives me a sudden glimpse of the etiolated curvature of a breast and then (I catch my breath!) a sliver of a crescent whose slight variance in coloration might indicate—I suspect, I hope!—just maybe (gulp!) the very top of an areola!

(Or perhaps not. My seventh-grader brain could be creating an areola where there is none, my adolescent libido "filling in the blanks," investing ambiguous retinal input with its own meaning. I may be processing visual stimuli with the little head instead of the big one. In fact, this could be a perfect example of an idiomatic expression that Ms. Frey, my Spanish teacher, taught us: *Mirando con el bastón en ves de los bastoncillos y los conos.* Seeing with the rod instead of the rods and cones. In other words, this phantom areola might simply be a cathected version of the Kanizsa triangle—a famous optical illusion in which the observer perceives a triangle even though the interconnecting lines forming a triangle are missing—that we just learned about in Mr. Edelman's biology class. Weird . . .)

And then, moments later, as the warden lowers herself into one of the witness room's orange extruded-plastic chairs: Visual Thrill #2. A taut, faintly stubbly swath (yum!) of pale and dewy armpit flesh!

I desperately need to preempt an erection. First of all, a hard-on here would be terribly inappropriate (just because I'm only in the seventh grade doesn't mean I lack a modicum of decency), and second, it would be impossible to conceal—remember, I'm shirtless and these Versace leather pants are tight and ride really low on the hips. It might also suggest the perverse possibility that I find the imminent execution of my father sexually arousing, which would be a gross misreading. And at the very least, it might imply that I'm callous and self-absorbed. (Totally wrong. I'm empathetic and I'm sensitive, but I belong to a peer group that's temperamentally and philosophically averse to verbalizing real feelings. [For a comprehensive discussion of this psychological paradigm, see Renata Mazur's *Fetuses with Body Hair: The Loathsome World of Pubescent Boys.*] We choose to speak a language that conveys as little information as possible. Like mites signaling each other across great distances with minuscule puffs of

pheromone, we identify ourselves to each other with monosyl-
labic, opaque shibboleths of diffidence—"huh," "cool," "fucked,"
"weird," etc. This is our special language and we're proud of it—
in this way, we're no different from the Basques or the Kurds or
any other linguacentric separatist group. But don't think that
simply because we're affectless and inarticulate, and harbor a deep
distrust of romantic bromides, that we don't have intensely passionate and turbulent inner lives.)

At any rate, obviously this is neither the time nor the place
for what Walter Pater called "burning with the hard, gem-like
flame" (my English teacher, Mr. Minter, interprets this as a kind
of *aesthetic rapture,* but my friends and I believe that Pater was
referring to a *hot bone*). So in an effort to quell arousal, I try con-
juring unpleasant thoughts. But I can't think of anything at the
moment. I guess, on balance, I'm a pretty upbeat, sanguine guy.
I'm basically a morning person. And I consider this a bona fide
psychological category, because when you wake up in the morning, the first thing that really hits you is that you're not dead, and
if you tend to greet that basic fact with any degree of enthusiasm
if not outright alacrity, then I think that's a fairly strong indica-
tor of an optimistic disposition. And man, I'm out of the chute
each morning with out-and-out zipadeedoodah alacrity! I set the
clock-radio alarm to 95.7 FM, which until recently was a classical station and is now all-Pathoco. Pathoco—which was originally called "Texas 12-Step"—is a musical subgenre that
originated in some of the country's most parochial, inbred, and
anomic white suburbs. It features a bouncy sort of Tijuana Brass
sound that completely belies its dark and often disturbing lyrics.
For instance, the #1 Pathoco single right now is a song called

"The Beasts of Yeast." Against a very festive, up-tempo mariachi background, a man sings of his wife's recent confession that every night she dreams of beating him with a baseball bat, covering his bloodied head with a plastic bag, sitting on his chest, punching his face, and screaming, "Die, David, Die!" and then once he dies, relaxing and smoking crack. In the next verse he sings about his five-year-old daughter, who euthanizes all of her stuffed animals and dolls. The father returns home from work each day to find his daughter's dolls and teddy bears on the floor of her bedroom with plastic bags over their heads secured with thick rubber bands. When he asks her why she's assisted her little friends in committing suicide, she says simply that they were "stressed out." Then in the ensuing verse—in the phlegmatic, acquiescent falsetto of one whose ability to register indignation has corroded from years of living in New Jersey—he reveals that the underlying cause of all his family's problems is severe food allergies. And in the chorus, husband, wife, and daughter, in shimmering three-part harmony, enumerate the offending substances: "Wheat gluten. Lactose. Yeast. Shellfish. Eggs. Tropical oils. Etc." The malevolence of the banal—Legionnaire's disease from a motel hot tub, toxic shock from a tampon, lung cancer from radon, leukemia from the electromagnetic radiation of high-voltage power transmission lines, MSG-induced spontaneous abortions from take-out lo mein—is a central Pathoco motif. But the music's irrepressibly ebullient beat and the shrill, deliriously mirthful horn arrangements rouse me like reveille each morning. Bathroom ablutions consist of ground azuki-bean scrub for the blackheads, followed by a quick yogic deep-gargle (you swallow about a foot of what's called "esophageal floss" and then pull it back out—I learned it from Mr. Vithaldas, he's my Ayurvedic Health teacher, that's my 7th-period elective), and then I descend on the kitchen and, if it's a school-day morning, I have an espresso laced with a shot of calvados and some thinly sliced bichon frisé on a plain bagel, and then I'm out the back door and I'm at the tetherball pole. It's difficult to adequately describe how important the sport of tetherball is to me. Yes, I love playing tetherball more than doing anything else in the world. Yes, I adore the way that the dew flies off the ball when I hammer that first serve each morning and the cord wraps in a tight spiral around the top of the pole and the ball caroms with such force that the cord uncoils with almost equal torque, and I crouch in a low, ballasted stance and let the ball sail over my back and then, my bodyweight cantilevered like a discus thrower's, wield a lethal and quasi-legal cupped palm to sling it in an opposite orbit, and back and forth, in clockwise and then counterclockwise centrifugal arcs that whine as they split the air. Yes, the spiritual sludge of late-second-millennium life literally evaporates in the thermal vectors of my frenzied footwork, my bobbing and weaving, my parries and pirouettes, and it becomes like this atavistic dance, and I feel as if I'm dancing in the center of the sky. And yes, I feel as if everything most precious within myself is awakened and I experience an ineffable kinesthetic beatitude. But the *coolest* thing is that after I've been hitting for a while, there's something about the way my pants smell when they get sweaty—I don't know if it's the kind of leather Versace uses or it's just the way any leather smells when it gets wet—but it makes me completely euphoric, and I enter a highly evolved, massively parallel quantum fugue state during which I achieve tachyphrenic processing speeds of ten trillion floating-point oper-

your point total equals or exceeds 3,000, proceed to the section beginning *All of this—the warden escorting me into the witness room, the momentary glimpse of the slope of her breast, possibly her areola . . .* If your total is under 3,000, return to the words *Felipe, his older sister Gretel, and I are watching TV Thursday night,* and begin masturbating again.

Felipe, his older sister Gretel, and I are watching TV Thursday night. *20/20* is running a profile of Silvio Barnes, the painter who was blinded after being hit on the head with a frying pan while surfing the 35-foot breakers at Waimea Bay in Hawaii and then, less than a week later, suffered a massive stroke during a full-body wax at an after-hours depilation bar in Manhattan. Thanks to the Dove unauthorized biography, we all know the story by now of how, when Silvio was only fourteen, his father— the inventor of the Miracle Collar, the push-up collar for men's dress shirts that gives the appearance of a larger, more protuberant Adam's apple—offered Silvio a yearly stipend and a studio of his own. But Silvio, perceiving his father's patronage as an instrument of control, refused, and catching the next plane and hydrofoil to Chiang Mai, a resort city in northern Thailand, took a job as a busboy at the Gesellschaft für Schwerionenforschung (Society for Heavy Ion Research), a gay dance club. Snatching a minute here and a minute there during breaks, he'd sneak off to the club's sulfurous boiler room cum atelier, where he'd eventually complete his two astonishing master-pieces:

Teenage Neofascist Skinheads Suffering From Progeria (That Rare Premature Aging Disease) Play Mah-Jongg at a Swim Club in Lake Hayden, Idaho is a 94-by-66-inch, acrylic-on-canvas work that, notwithstanding a title that leads one to expect several freakishly wizened nazi youths wanly shuffling mah-jongg tiles outside a lakefront cabana, actually depicts, in delicate flecks of color, several peonies in a vase.

Anna Nicole Smith Before and After Fire-Ant Attack is a 90-by-120-inch acrylic-on-canvas diptych. In this case, the title does literally describe the painting's content. In the left-hand panel, the former Texas checkout girl turned Guess? Jeans model is splayed lasciviously on a dirt road. The right-hand panel features the identical pose except that the lasciviously splayed Smith is stippled with hundreds of Seurat-like inflamed pustules.

Barbara Walters conducts a brief interview with Silvio, whose garbled responses are subtitled. In the closing minutes, wiping drool from his chin, she says, "Silvio, you completed only two paintings in your entire career, both of which you sold for a fraction of their current value [the paintings now hang in opium warlord Khun Sa's splendid new museum in northern Myanmar] and then squandered the money on an endless succession of skanky male prostitutes. As a result of a frying pan and a body wax, you'll never paint again. And your desperate attempt to reinvent your career as a movie director was an unmitigated critical and financial disaster."

Barnes wrote and directed a film entitled ¡*Hola Mami!* about an eccentric middle-aged optometrist who marries a sullen, zit-spangled 16-year-old who loiters around his office every day after school, chain-smoking in a fuchsia PVC bustier, a huge gaudy crucifix bobbing on her bosom. The "plot" revolves around the optometrist's use of a varietal rice chart instead of the traditional lettered eye chart. Long, uninterrupted stretches of the movie consist of the following sort of dialogue:

OPTOMETRIST: Let's start with the top row, moving from left to right.

PATIENT: All right. Arborio. Valencia. Lundberg's Christmas Rice. Black Japonica. And Wehani.

OPTOMETRIST: Perfect. Second row.

PATIENT: Red. Sri Lankan Red. Wild Pecan. Jasmine. White Basmati.

OPTOMETRIST: Perfect. Let's skip down a few rows. How about row five?

PATIENT: American White Basmati. American . . . Umm . . . American Brown Basmati, I think. Maratello. And that next one's either Black Sticky or Thai Sticky. And I'm not sure about the last one.

OPTOMETRIST: OK. How about the next row down, row six?

PATIENT: That's really tough. Converted? Sambal? Gobind Bhog? They're really fuzzy.

OPTOMETRIST: OK. Back up to the fourth row—

PATIENT: Japanese Sticky. Sticky Brown. Short-
Grain Brown. Long-Grain White. And Wild
Rice.

OPTOMETRIST: Is row six sharper now or . . . now?

PATIENT: The first way.

Following the clip from *¡Hola Mami!* they cut to
Hugh Downs and Barbara Walters back in the studio.

And Walters says with her patented withering
aplomb, "Hugh, in all our years together on the show,
we've profiled so many wonderful people whose lives have
been shattered by tragedy, but I've never before come
away with the feeling that—hey, this guy is such an overweening, self-absorbed asshole, he deserves his misfor-
tune, and, in fact, there's something so divinely *just* about
it, that it's actually funny. It's so rare that we can derive
some cathartic enjoyment from another person's suffering.
But every so often our fervent prayers are answered and an
obnoxious enfant terrible's meteoric success is abruptly
and irrevocably snuffed. Silvio Barnes—now blind, inca-
pacitated, and anathema in New York *and* Hollywood—
is an individual whose precipitous ruin all Americans can
celebrate with big, hearty, guilt-free gales of laughter."

And Hugh looks at Barbara and says, "Fascinating."

As they break for a commercial, Felipe, Gretel, and I
do an instant postmortem.

"I'm into Barbara's rancid schadenfreude," says Felipe.

"I hear you, dude," I say. "It had wings. But Downs
killed it with that perfunctory 'Fascinating.' "

"Hugh's hot!" objects Gretel.

"Yuuuk!" Felipe and I make the international sign for hemorrhagic vomiting.

"You'll appreciate Hugh Downs when you're more mature," she says, haughtily readjusting her brassiere.

"I don't think I'll ever be *that* mature," I say, huffing glue from a brown paper bag and passing it back to Felipe.

All of this—the warden escorting me into the witness room, the momentary glimpse of the slope of her breast, possibly her areola, and the flesh of her armpit as she sits down, and then the frenzied search through my memory for just the right *20/20* segment to temporarily neuter myself so that a healthy, perfectly normal, and involuntary heterosexual reflex won't be misinterpreted in such a way that I'm seen as an execrable son—all of this takes place in a span of no more than ten seconds. I wonder if, like, Bill Gates when *he* was 13, had the ability that I have at the age of 13 to anatomize minute fluctuations of consciousness that are occurring literally in femtoseconds. Anyway . . .

It's 5:25 P.M. Appeals exhausted, reprieves forsaken, last words ardently orated, the execution of Joel Leyner C.P. #39 6E-18 commences.

Inside the control module room, the executioner activates the delivery sequence by pushing a button on the control panel. A series of lights on the panel indicates the three stages of each injection: Armed (red), Start (yellow), and Complete (green).

As the lights for the initial injection sequence switch on and a piston is loosed from its cradle and falls onto the plunger of the first syringe, the delivery module introduces 15 cc of 2-percent sodium thiopental over ten seconds, which should cause unconsciousness.

I nudge the superintendent with my elbow.

"Thanks," I whisper, returning his pen.

"Keep it," he says.

"Are you kidding?"

"No. It's yours."

"Cool!" I gush.

After a minute, the red light pulses again, then the yellow, and the machine injects 15 cc of pancuronium bromide, a synthetic curare that should produce muscle paralysis and stop his breathing.

Following another one-minute interval, the lights flash and the final syringe, containing 15 cc of potassium chloride, is injected, which should induce cardiac arrest, with death following within two minutes.

Thirty seconds pass.

A minute.

In the dark witness room, we are mute and absolutely still. And in this riveted silence, the physiologic obbligato of human bodies—the sibilant nostrils, the tense clicking of temporomandibular joints, the bruits of carotid arteries, and the peristaltic rumblings of nervous bowels—becomes almost a din.

Ninety seconds elapse.

Two minutes.

The muscles in my father's neck appear to become rigid, actually lifting his head slightly off the gurney.

His eyes open wide.

"I feel shitty," he says.

The doctor, who's been monitoring the EKG, frowns at the operations officer, who turns to the warden and shakes his head grimly. Scrutinizing an EKG printout incredulously, he emerges from behind the screen and approaches my dad. He checks his pupillary reflexes with a penlight and then listens to his respiration and heart with a stethoscope.

"Physically, he appears to be absolutely fine," he says, grimacing with bewilderment.

The operations officer in turn gives a thumbs-down to the warden, who's now risen from her seat in the witness room.

"Mr. Leyner," says the doctor to my father, "I'm going to give you several statements and I want you to respond as best you can, all right?"

My father nods.

"Bacillus subtilis grown on dry, nutrient-poor agar plates tends to fan out into patterns that strongly resemble this fractal pattern seen in nonliving systems."

"What is a diffusion-limited aggregation?" responds my father.

"Music played by this Vietnamese ensemble consisting of flute, moon-lute, zither, cylindrical and coconut-shell fiddles, and wooden clackers is the most romantic and, to Western ears, melodic of all Southeast Asian theater music."

"What is cai luong?"

"This Hollywood legend kept a secret cache of Dynel-haired toy trolls."

"Who was Greta Garbo?"

"According to the American Mortuary Society, these are currently the two most widely requested gravestone epitaphs."

"Wake Me Up When We Get There and *If You Lived Here, You'd Be Home Now."*

The doctor brightens momentarily.

"I'm sorry," amends my father. "What are *Wake Me Up When We Get There* and *If You Lived Here, You'd Be Home Now?"*

The doctor sags.

"Neurologically, he's perfectly normal," he announces, punctuating his diagnosis with a dejected, frustrated fling of his *NJ State Capital Punishment Division of Medicine* loose-leaf binder, which skitters across the floor.

"Cool binder!" I marvel sotto voce, helplessly susceptible to logo merchandising.

My father is returned to his cell. The operations officer confers with the warden, who informs me that the doctor would like to see me in his office.

I slip two hastily scrawled notes into her left hand.

The lights have come back on in the witness room and programmed music resumes over the ambient audio system—Kathleen Battle and Courtney Love's haunting performance of Mozart's aria "Mia speranza adorata" from the *Ebola Benefit—Live from Branson, Missouri* CD (Deutsche Grammophon), which segues into "Sarin Sayonara" from the Aum Supreme Truth Monks' *Les Chants d'Apocalypse* CD (Interscope), which is followed—as I enter the elevator—by the Montana Militia Choir (accompanied by

Yanni and the Ray Coniff singers) singing—I swear to god!—
"The Beasts of Yeast."

Read along with me, as I peruse this *People* magazine article
in the waiting room of the prison doctor:

> When Viktor N. Mikhailov, Russia's Minister of
> Atomic Energy, invited Hazel R. O'Leary, the U.S. Secre-
> tary of Energy, to a dinner party arranged to facilitate a
> discussion of Russia's plutonium stocks, he probably
> expected Mrs. O'Leary and her retinue to arrive with the
> first editions and bottles of rare vintage champagne that
> are the traditional accoutrements of diplomatic courtesy.
>
> What he certainly didn't expect was for Mrs. O'Leary
> to arrive, Fender Stratocaster slung across her back, along
> with bassist Ivan Selin, Chairman of the Nuclear Regula-
> tory Commission, guitarist John Holum, Director of the
> U.S. Arms Control and Disarmament Agency, and drum-
> mer J. Brian Atwood, Administrator of the U.S. Agency
> for International Development. Instead of propounding
> her views over cocktails or across the dinner table—as
> would be the norm at such a gathering—Mrs. O'Leary
> and her bandmates delivered a blistering set of original
> songs, thematically linked, each exploring a different
> facet of her overarching position that Russia must render
> its surplus weapons plutonium unusable.
>
> Mrs. O'Leary, soignée and austere in a black Jil Sander
> dress, opened with a smoldering rocker about the global

security risks of stolen fissile material that seemed to gradually implode with intensity as it slowed to the tempo of a New Orleans funeral march, achieving the exaggerated slow-motion sexual swagger of the Grim Reaper bumping and grinding down Bourbon Street. Next, Mrs. O'Leary almost shattered the huge Czarist-era crystal chandelier with an opening riff that tore from her amp like shrapnel from an anti-personnel bomb. She repeated the riff—an irresistible and diabolically intricate seven-note figure—over and over again, plying each shard with the obsessive scrutiny of a monkey grooming its mate, it becoming more squalid, more lewd, more intoxicating with each iteration, until finally the band launched into the song, a hammering sermon about how Russia must mix its plutonium in molten glass and bury it deep underground.

In the midst of the song, which, like an asylum inmate gouging at his own scabs, exacerbated itself into a raging cacophony, Mikhailov; Viktor M. Murogov, director of the Institute of Physics and Power Engineering at Obninsk; Yuri Vishevsky, the head of Gosatomnadzor or GAN, the Russian equivalent of the Nuclear Regulatory Commission; and Aleksei V. Yablokov, an adviser to President Boris Yeltsin, and their spouses formed a throbbing mosh pit in the center of the living room.

Following the set, when asked what had made her appear with the band, Mrs. O'Leary, drenched in sweat, paused to catch her breath and then replied, "I'd asked Viktor [Mikhailov] if I could bring my guitar . . . and he

said sure. And one thing led to another . . . and, well . . ."
She gestured toward the throng of guests still pumping
their fists in the air.

After dinner, a bizarre incident occurred that has had
the diplomatic community and entertainment industry
abuzz with wild rumor and rampant speculation.

Sergei Smernyakov, a well-known nightclub hypno-
tist invited to the soirée by Mikhailov to provide post-
prandial entertainment, hypnotized guests Dorothy
Bodin, Deputy Secretary of the Department of Energy;
Cynthia Bowers-Lipken, a weapons expert at the Natural
Resources Defense Council; and LaShaquilla Nuland, wife
of Adm. C. F. Bud Nuland, Vice Chairman of the Joint
Chiefs of Staff. Each woman was given the posthypnotic
suggestion that at the tone of a spoon striking a wineglass
she would become a frenzied Dionysian orgiast with an
uncontrollable compulsion to instantly gratify her every
carnal desire.

Brought out of their trances, the women, each one a
paragon of professional accomplishment, dignity, and
decorum, blushed at the suggestion, and laughingly
assured their companions that—with all due respect to
Mr. Kavochilov's mesmeric prowess—they could certainly never be induced to behave in such an outrageously
uncharacteristic manner.

But sure enough, when Yeltsin aide Yablokov tapped
a tiny silver jam spoon against his wine goblet, Ms.
Bodin, Ms. Bowers-Lipken, and Mrs. Nuland immediately disrobed, rending the garments from their bodies as

if they were aflame, and then, like deranged children, spreading caviar and blintz filling over each other's naked flesh. Then, after a brief huddle, they overpowered a chosen male guest, shackled his legs, cuffed his hands behind his back, and took turns sitting on his face as they swigged caraway and jimsonweed-infused vodka from cut-crystal decanters.

Having finally sated themselves and tired, the women released the man, who staggered back to his hotel covered in their juices, followed by a howling cavalcade of rutting dogs, cats, raccoons, and possums whose demented caterwauling awakened sleeping Muscovites throughout the city.

Although invited guests refuse to comment on the identity of the male victim, *People* has learned that it was none other than celebrated television personality and Tony Award–winning actor

continued on p. 115

"Mark Leyner?"

"Huh?" I say distractedly, my attention monopolized by the foregoing magazine article.

"Mark, the doctor will see you now."

"Right now?" I whine, my fingers riffling furiously through a multipage Lincoln Town Car insert in a frustrated effort to reach the jump on page 115 and learn the name of the celebrity "victim."

"Right now," answers the nurse with a peremptory lilt.

"Fuck," I mutter, and toss the magazine atop a pile.

Have you ever read an article in *People* that was so perfectly suited to your interests that it seemed as if the writer had intended it exclusively for you, so that you could—in the way that mentally disturbed individuals glean divine messages from advertising jingles or laundering instruction labels—perhaps derive some subliminal or encrypted communication or some secret gnostic insight? That's how I feel about this particular article.

I can't tell you how many afternoons I've frittered away contemplating what it would be like to be held captive and abused by various groups of fanatical and/or unbalanced and/or unwashed women. For a while, it's *all* I talked about, which I realize became rather tedious for my parents. I remember one night at the dinner table, I was going on and on about what it might be like to get kidnapped and tormented by a group of rogue policewomen, when my dad interrupted me and said, "I didn't think I'd ever hear myself saying this, but—could we talk about Napoleonic War muskets [my previous fixation] for a while?"

Actually my parents were pretty cool about it, though. In fact, they got me a subscription to one of these young-adult book series called *Around the World With Rusty Hoover.* In each book, this kid Rusty Hoover—who's about my age—invariably finds himself mistaken for someone else and then gets abducted by gorgeous women who torture him. Like in *Rusty Hoover Goes to Peru,* Rusty's on vacation with his parents, and he's misidentified as a Peruvian Treasury officer, captured and brutally interrogated for weeks in a sweltering Lima apartment by giggling cadres at a Shining Path pajama party. In *Rusty Hoover Goes to Portugal,* Rusty's on vacation in the Algarve with his parents, where he's erroneously targeted as an unethical shipbuilding magnate by an underground cell of shrouded fishermen's widows who turn out to be particularly sadistic and horny. There's *Rusty Hoover Goes to Law School,* where Rusty accompanies his parents to visit his older sister Tara at law school, and he's confused for some pervert who's been sending pornographic E-mail to fellow students in his Patents class, and he's forced to sign a confession in his own prostatic fluid, subjected to pseudoscientific experimentation, and flogged by Professor De Brunhoff—a loose composite of Catharine MacKinnon and Lisa Sliwa—and her frothing acolytes. And then—one of my favorites—*Rusty Hoover Goes to Indiana,* in which, en route to Yellowstone Park, the family car's cruise control malfunctions on Route 70 near Terre Haute, where Rusty's mistaken for a locker-room Peeping Tom by a women's fast-pitch softball team that has just completed a double-header in 100-degree heat and that—in the words of the jacket copy—"teaches Rusty a lesson in pine tar and voyeurism he'll never forget."

But until I read the article in *People* magazine, this sort of thing had only existed for me in fiction and in my own febrile fantasies. And now I see that it's actually happened to some guy who was lucky enough to be in Moscow at just the right dinner party. But who is he?

Isn't it one of life's—well, maybe *tragedies* is too strong a word—one of life's most vexing conundrums, that just at the exact moment that you really get into a magazine article in a doctor's waiting room, the nurse calls your name?

The doctor's office features standard-issue M.D. furnishings and bric-a-brac with three notable exceptions: on his desk, a photograph of a dismayed woman (whom I presume is his wife) in a gauzy lavender negligee drowning a four-inch Madagascar "hissing" cockroach with spray from a White Diamonds cologne atomizer; on the wall alongside an array of diplomas and certificates, a huge LeRoy Neiman painting of Socrates drinking his cup of hemlock; and above the credenza, a framed needlepoint of Cleopatra's valediction from Shakespeare's *Antony and Cleopatra:* "The stroke of death is as a lover's pinch, / Which hurts, and is desired"—the cursive embroidery bordered by intertwined asps.

"I'm very sorry about your father, Mark."

The doctor, downcast and shaken, rises from his chair and walks out from behind his desk. "I'm terribly, terribly sorry," he says, embracing me.

Perhaps I have deferred or suppressed my emotions—numbed myself. Also—and I realize that I may have been naive or unrealistically optimistic—it simply hadn't ever occurred to me that my dad wouldn't respond to the lethal drugs. But now the emotions come surging forth. My eyes begin to fill. I sob, I heave, I weep unrestrainedly.

"Why did this have to happen?" I wail, clutching him.

"Mark, I wish there was a simple answer," he says, with a reciprocal squeeze.

I unclasp his arms and step away from him.

"But everyone said it would work," I contend with aggrieved composure.

"For the overwhelming majority of inmates, sodium thiopental, pancuronium bromide, and potassium chloride is the terminal regimen of choice and proves to be completely efficacious. Unfortunately, it was not as deleterious to your father as we would have hoped."

"Doctor, isn't there anything more you can do?"

"I'm afraid not."

"What about trying other lethal drugs?"

"The *only* drug protocol that the Food and Drug Administration has approved for executions is sodium thiopental, pancuronium bromide, and potassium chloride." He bristles. "There are literally scores of promising new lethal drugs in development, but each one is hopelessly mired in FDA bureaucracy. Glaxo Wellcome has a compound called Mortilax, which combines the industrial solvent carbon disulfide and a neurotoxic insecticide, pyrethrum, with death-cap fungus, but it's bogged down in phase-one animal studies. Johnson & Johnson's Panicidin—whose active ingredients include several nitrated derivatives of phenol, zinc phosphide (a hepatotoxic rat poison), dioxin, and tetrodotoxin (a poison extracted from the livers of Japanese blowfish)—was sailing through phase-two human efficacy trials when the FDA declared a moratorium on further testing because the drug was apparently causing moderate new hair growth in men with male-pattern baldness. And Pfizer has a very exciting new product in the pipeline called Necrotropin, which is a year into a four-year phase-three clinical trial. Necrotropin is composed of tetraethylpyrophosphate (an insecticide that blocks the enzyme cholinesterase, resulting in a fatal buildup of acetylcholine), caustic potash (for corrosive destruction of internal organs), santonin (an alkaloid from wormseed that causes cardiovascular collapse), strychnine (for tetanic spasms leading to asphyxia), methyl isocyanate (the chemical that killed 3,000 people in Bhopal), and a concentrate of Gaboon viper venom (which is both hemotoxic and neurotoxic, causing diffused hemorrhages *and* respiratory paralysis). Pfizer is planning to offer it as an injectable, a transdermal patch, and a pleasant-tasting chewable tablet.

"So, potentially—and in spite of the appalling ineptitude of the FDA—the future is very bright. I emphasize the word *potentially*—one of the things that causes me so much anguish about the destruction of the rain forest is the possibility that we're irrevocably losing indigenous plant toxins and venoms that could be used in the development of new and more powerful lethal drugs. But look, even if the FDA approved one of these experimental agents, there's no guarantee that it would prove any more effective on your father than the drugs we administered today. I suspect that your father's habitual abuse of angel dust and his hypersensitivity to gamma radiation have somehow conferred an immunity to toxins. Although I have no idea what the precise biochemical mechanisms are here, my hypothesis is that chronic anaphylactic reactions to gamma rays occurring concomitantly with sustained exposure to phencyclidine has actually altered the genetic matrix in each of your father's cells, rendering him resistant to the lethal drugs presently available to us."

"Well, why can't any of these companies develop a drug that will kill gamma-ray-sensitive angel-dust users?" I ask.

"It's more an issue of economics than scientific or technological capability. How many people in the United States with severe gamma ray sensitivity who habitually abuse phencyclidine do you think commit capital crimes each year?"

"Probably not that many . . . I don't know . . . maybe 50,000 a year?"

"Try 1,500. Compare that to the 600,000 new cases of congenital generalized hypertrichosis each year. [Individuals with this disorder, thought to be transmitted on the X chromosome, have an upper body and face covered with hair and often end up in sideshows as human werewolves.] Or the 1.2 million annual cases of Lipid-Induced Inuit Hyperthermia. [Sufferers of this malady, which primarily affects the Eskimo people of Arctic Canada, maintain exceptionally high body temperatures—about 107°F or above—as a result of heavy consumption of blubber and tallow. Geologists have long been concerned that an LIH epidemic could raise ambient temperatures sufficiently to weaken and finally destroy the ice underpinnings of the West Arctic Ice Sheet. The entire sheet would then slide rapidly into the sea, causing an abrupt and catastrophic rise in global sea levels, and flooding low-lying countries like the Netherlands and Bangladesh.] But even these are considered third-tier markets. In terms of the bottom-line mindset of the pharmaceutical industry, 1,500 cases is a negligible patient base. It's just not economically feasible for a company to expend the necessary R&D resources on a drug that's designed to kill only 1,500 people a year. So we'd be talking about an orphan lethal drug. And who do you think awards orphan-drug status? The FDA."

"It sounds hopeless," I say.

"It's not hopeless if we set a national agenda. If we as a country commit ourselves and our resources to developing a drug that can kill gamma-ray-sensitive angel-dust abusers, we can do it—and we can do it by the year 2000. But it has to be a national priority with the full support of the American people. Do you know much about North Korea?"

"Not really. I'd like to, though. In fact, I was going to take *Pariah States* as my 7th-period elective for next semester, but I decided to take *English Punk 1975–1978* instead."

"Well, you want to talk about setting agendas and making national commitments, these guys could teach us all a thing or two. Their leader, Kim Jong Il, is apparently always developing these little growths on his face and he's an extremely vain guy, so the government spends about $1.8 billion constructing this fabulous thermonuclear dermatological facility the likes of which have never been seen anywhere. The device works by firing a dazzling light from 192 lasers down a labyrinth of mirrors, focusing a titanic bolt of energy—a thousand times the output of all the power stations in the United States—onto a single tiny pellet of supercold hydrogen fuel placed on Kim Jong Il's mole, wart, or wen and creating a miniature thermonuclear blast lasting one-billionth of a second, which completely vaporizes the lesion. That's what a country can do if it puts its mind to it. . . ."

Frustration with the failed execution, the inaccessibility of more-potent lethal drugs, and the vagaries of the federal bureaucracy; envy for the ruthless fecundity of totalitarian technocrats; and utter physical and emotional fatigue seem to cumulatively crest, as the doctor's voice trails off and, with a sort of spent serenity, he gazes out the window.

The window affords a view of an emerald green lawn upon which sits a filigreed wrought-iron gazebo completely swathed in concertina wire. In 1996, singer Michael Jackson presented then-governor Christine Todd Whitman with the original gazebo used in *The Sound of Music* as a gift to the State of New Jersey—the only proviso being that the gazebo be used for the delectation of the state's penal population. Rotated every two years among New Jersey's several maximum security institutions, the gazebo—in which Liselle and Rolf serenaded each other with "I Am Sixteen Going on Seventeen"—is used both for conjugal visits and punitive solitary confinement.

During this lull, I become aware of a softly pulsing obbligato—the *ch-ch-ch* of innumerable inmates engaging in unlubricated sodomy, which, like the *ch-ch-ch* of stridulating male cicadas, can be heard on summer evenings in villages and towns miles from the prison.

Emerging from his reverie, the doctor turns back to me.

"Do you play any sports? You look like you're in pretty good shape," he says.

"Tetherball," I reply, miming an overhead smash.

"Y'know, when I was your age, the jocks wore pearls . . . that was *the big thing* back then . . . freshwater pearls. You'd be in the locker room after football practice, and there'd be these big hairy naked guys wearing single strands of pearls, snapping towels at each other . . ."

"No way!" I snort, not bothering to hide my contempt for the fleeting fads of bygone generations.

"It's funny when you look back . . . the things you thought were so cool, so tough . . . Freshwater pearls . . ." he trails off, returning his gaze out toward the gazebo.

Our conversation continues desultorily, the doctor intermittently blurting a question or offering some random reminiscence, and then fading off again into mute introspection, the gaps filled with the ubiquitous *ch-ch-ch*.

Despite the fact that, beyond a gustatory preference for brains and marrow, we have almost nothing in common, I find myself bonding somewhat with the doctor. Having long accepted the stereotype of the physician as the stolid professional who views the fates of his patients with cold, clinical detachment, I was all the more moved by this doctor's genuine empathy. He responded with such grief, and with such a sense of personal responsibility, that it was almost as if it were his own father he'd failed to kill.

Perhaps also contributing to my feelings of affinity for the doctor is the fact that a V-shaped area from the waist to the crotch of my leather pants had become sodden with tears, causing a distinctive odor to waft upward. And whereas the pungent aroma of sweaty leather makes me feel omniscient, the bittersweet fragrance of tear-soaked leather engenders in me a sense of interconnectedness with all sentient beings.

"Has lethal medicine always been your specialty?" I ask, infused with *agape*.

"I was a third-year medical student when I made up my mind," he replies. "I was assigned to the pediatric-execution wing of a large state prison up in Connecticut—it was the first of my clinical rotations in what was then called Malevolent Medicine. From that point on, I was hooked. For me, the field of pediatric executions has always been the most gratifying. There's absolutely nothing in the world that compares to the look on the faces of a mother and a father after they've been told that the execution of their sociopathic, incorrigibly homicidal child has been a success. There's an instant realization—you can see it in their eyes—that the courtroom vigils, the legal bills, the civil suits, the endless hours of family therapy are all over, that they and the deceased demon seed's siblings can now go on and live a normal happy life. It's an expression that never ceases to touch you deeply, no matter how many times you see it."

The telephone rings.

The doctor reoccupies the high-backed chair behind his desk, picks up the receiver, and swivels around so that his back is to me and his conversation—save for an initial "I think that would be wise under the circumstances"—is inaudible.

I pluck a lollipop from the fishbowl on his desk, wander over to the window, and gaze bemusedly at the gazebo.

Ch-ch-ch. Ch-ch-ch. Ch-ch-ch.

Shortly the doctor swivels back into view and hangs up the phone.

"The warden's going to make an announcement in her office in a few minutes," he says.

He stands, circumambulates his desk, and embraces me again.

"If it provides any solace, I want you to know that, medically, I've done everything at my disposal to kill your father."

"I understand," I quaver, nodding solemnly. "And thank you."

I pivot and race out of his office, heading straight for the pile of magazines in the waiting room. I retrieve the *People* I'd been reading and flip frantically to page 115 so I can finally learn the identity of the television personality and Tony Award–winning actor who was ravaged by the three hypnotized wives at a Moscow dinner party. But when I reach 115, I find—to my absolute horror—that someone has cut a rectangular section out of the page including the all-important final paragraphs of the story that had so captured my imagination. And it's all the more frustrating to discover that the excision of my article was inadvertent. The culprit had cut out a coupon on the reverse page—116—for two Bradford Exchange limited-edition collector's plates commemorating, respectively, the 1977 professional debut of transsexual tennis player René Richards and the 1993 beating of Reginald Denny during the Los Angeles riots.

"Inmates aren't allowed to have scissors, are they?" I ask the nurse.

"No," she says.

"Well, how did someone cut a coupon out of this magazine?" I ask, wiggling my fingers through the hole in the page.

"They use shanks—y'know, homemade knives."

I shudder.

The image of hardened convicts daintily clipping coupons with their shanks gives me goose bumps.

The warden's office is a serried, murmuring Who's Who of penal officialdom: the warden, of course, seated at her desk, signing papers proffered assembly-line-fashion by a feline male secretary with close-cropped orange hair; and milling about and filling the room with gossip and banter are the superintendent; the operations officer; the executioner; the doctor; two of the prosecuting attorneys from the ice-cream scooper murder case; my dad's lawyer; my dad, who, despite a slightly bilious tinge to his complexion, is chewing his gum mirthfully and talking golf with the rabbi; and a state-appointed stenographer, her fingers a kinetic blur as she endeavors to somehow transcribe the babble of simultaneous small talk.

Given the self-importance and solipsism endemic to seventh

graders, I'm assuming that the warden's impending announcement is about me. After the execution attempt and just before I
met with the doctor, I'd scribbled and surreptitiously conveyed to
the warden two notes that read, respectively, "You wanna get
high?" and "Be my sweaty bosomy lover?"

Why she would choose to make such a public response to my
homey blandishments, though, I have no idea.

The lithe arm swings over her desk with one final form. The
warden signs with a culminating flourish and rises. A dainty
throat-clearing and a tentative, collegial "Folks . . ." goes
unheeded. And then a great gurgling hawking up of phlegm and
a stentorian imperious "Gentlemen!" effects an instant
decrescendo of chitchat, the rabbi's punch line "So Moses flings
the Pharaoh's ball into the Sinai and says, 'Here, use my sand
wedge . . .' " trailing off in the corner of the room, the stenographer's fingers momentarily still.

"Gentlemen," the warden says, "I have an announcement to
make concerning Joel Leyner C.P. #39 6E-18, and pursuant to
Volume 2C, Part Five, Article 11-3 of the *New Jersey Department
of Corrections Digest of Procedural Regulations and Guidelines,* a state-
appointed stenographer will herewith transcribe all remarks ger-
mane to the disposition of Mr. Leyner's sentence.

"The State Legislature has vested in the Governor, the Attorney General, and the warden of this institution the following
authority, as specified in Section 42J of the Penal Code: 'In the
event of an abortive execution by lethal injection in which the
condemned inmate survives, any and all further attempts to execute that inmate by lethal injection within that institution and
under the medical supervision of said institution's physician(s) are

prohibited. Subject to unanimous consent of the Governor, the Attorney General, and the institution's warden, said inmate shall be, with all due speed and by public decree, resentenced to State Discretionary Execution, and thereupon immediately released. Although the State is not hereby required to enforce the death sentence, it may, at its discretion, execute said inmate immediately upon his or her release into the community or at any time thereafter. Said inmate (hereafter referred to as "the releasee") is subject to discretionary execution immediately upon vacating said institution's premises and at any time thereafter. In the event of an abortive Discretionary Execution in which the releasee survives, the State may, but is not required to, make an additional attempt or unlimited attempts on the life of the releasee. The Discretionary Execution of the releasee shall be carried out—if at all—whenever, wherever, and however the State of New Jersey deems appropriate, subject only to the inalienable caprices of the State of New Jersey.'

"It is so ordered and adjudged that Joel Leyner be sentenced to State Discretionary Execution and promptly discharged from this institution, this sentence to remain in force until Mr. Leyner's decease."

"En inglés, por favor," I chafe, gnawing my lollipop stick.

"Basically, Mark, your dad's free to go, but the State reserves the right to kill him the minute he walks out the front gate," says the warden. "Plus, the State has complete latitude in terms of execution protocols and rules of engagement. In the next ten minutes your dad could be pithed with an English pub dart in the car on the way home from here. On the other hand, he might never be killed—he could live out his life unperturbed and die of natural causes in his slobbering dotage. Or the State could wait until he's 99 years, 11 months, and 30 days old and then, on his 100th birthday, replace his dentures with molded plastique so that morning, as Willard Scott is telling America what a goodlooking man he is, god bless him—BA-BOOM! Now, if you'll excuse me for just a moment, there's some material I'd like you to have before you leave, Mr. Leyner," she says, exiting her office.

"And this is called what, again?" my father asks the superintendent.

"NJSDE—New Jersey State Discretionary Execution."

"I think I read about this in *Elle*," Dad says. "It's sort of like an optional fatwa."

"The feature we like to stress to releasees is the indeterminacy," continues the superintendent. "You're living your life, rowing merrily along, and suddenly one morning you wake up and there's a dwarf ninja crouched on your chest who deftly severs your carotid arteries with two honed throwing stars. Or you're on a flight to Orlando, Florida, giggling to yourself as you read the *Confessions* of Saint Augustine, and meanwhile, 35,000 feet below, a New Jersey state trooper steps out of his car, kneels alongside the shoulder of I-95, aims a shoulder-held antiaircraft missile launcher, and blows your 727 into friggin' curds and whey."

"They'd do that?" I ask excitedly. "They'd sacrifice all those people just to kill my dad?"

"NJSDE gives us a lot of leeway. We're no longer encumbered by the federal government, by the FDA, the FAA, the Justice Department . . . it really unties the hands of the state. I think it's an extremely innovative piece of statutory legislation. And you have to give the Governor the bulk of the credit. She takes a lot of flak for the narcolepsy and the lathery horse posters, but she was committed to this and very savvy about the politics."

"How do you feel about it?" my father asks, turning to the rabbi.

"It's a very postmodern sentencing structure—random and capricious, the free-floating dread, each ensuing day as gaping abyss, the signifier hovering over the signified like the sword of Damocles. To have appropriated a pop-noir aesthetic and recontextualized it within the realm of jurisprudence is breathtakingly audacious. I think you're going to find it a very disturbing, but a very fascinating and transformative way to live, Joel."

Personally, I don't find it all *that* innovative, audacious, disturbing, fascinating, or transformative. It just seems like normal life to me—not knowing from day to day if you'll be pithed with a pub dart or sliced into sushi by some hypopituitary freak in black pajamas, or if your false teeth will blow up in your head. That's just late-second-millennium life. I mean, isn't everyone basically sentenced to New Jersey State Discretionary Execution from, like, the moment he's born?

Although, OK—I have to admit—a statutory algorithm designed to amplify the anarchic cruelties of human existence and arbitrarily inflict its violence upon innocent bystanders, exponentially expanding the nexus of fatal contingencies, is pretty intense. And also, I assume that any ninja who works for NJSDE is involved in the state civil service bureaucracy—and there's something really appealing to me about the image of ninjas waiting in lines for hours at state offices for application forms and photo IDs. And I absolutely adore the notion of elite units of New Jersey State Troopers, magnificently loathsome in their Stetsons and jackboots, sworn by blood oath to enforce the stringent dicta of NJSDE, wending the corniches of the French Riviera or the Spanish Costa del Sol in their emblazoned cruisers, in inexorable pursuit of some targeted releasee, some hapless New Jersey expatriate shambling along the boardwalk, camera and wine sack slung across his belly, oblivious to the cataclysmic, surreal violence in which he'll be momentarily engulfed.

But do I say any of this when the rabbi, in turn, asks me what *I* think of NJSDE? No, of course not. Instead I mutter some facile, meaningless catchphrase.

Why do I nullify my own intelligence with this willful, stereotypical inarticulateness? Why do I immure my thoughts in this crypt of sullen diffidence?

Do I perhaps derive some sadomasochistic pleasure in the mortification of my own intellect, akin to those who cut and burn their own bodies? After all, isn't the act of making oneself mute a mute-ilation?

Am I ultimately knowable?

Is it ludicrous and stilted for a 13-year-old to describe himself, even facetiously, as "an individual of daunting complexity"?

Why is it, then, that when the rabbi, in turn, asks me what *I* think of NJSDE, I glibly reply: "It's cool, like a video"?

The warden returns.

"This should help answer any questions you might have, Mr. Leyner," she says, handing my father a booklet, which I peruse over his shoulder.

The glossy brochure is entitled *You and Your Discretionary Execution.*

Q. *What is New Jersey State Discretionary Execution?*

A. NJSDE was developed by Alejandro Roberto Montés Calderón, a cashiered Guatemalan Army colonel who fled Guatemala after his counterinsurgency unit was accused of "crimes against humanity" by Americas Watch and Amnesty International. Mr. Calderón resettled in the United States, where he became a gym teacher at Emerson High School in Union City, New Jersey. The Governor, who had Mr. Calderón for gym in both her junior and senior years, appointed him to chair the Select Committee on Capital Punishment and Tort Reform.

NJSDE is a pioneering sentencing program designed to give the State of New Jersey maximum—one might even say *giddy*—latitude in dealing with condemned inmates, like yourself, who have survived unsuccessful institutional executions.

Q. *Am I responsible for the cost of my unsuccessful institutional execution?*

A. You are responsible only for the cost of the lethal drugs. Most health insurance plans and HMOs cover lethal prescription drugs, paying for them directly or through reimbursements to the insured individual. Check your policy and consult with your broker or benefits administrator.

Q. *How does the State determine whether I will live or die?*

A. Your status is reevaluated on a daily basis. At precisely 9:00 P.M. each night, at the New Jersey State Discretionary Execution Control Center in Trenton, data processors insert every

NJSDE releasee's social security number into an intricate equation whose variables include the current pollen count at Newark International Airport and the total daily receipts collected at toll-booths along the Garden State Parkway as of 7:45 P.M. If, factored through this algebraic operation, your SS number yields a prime number, any five-digit sequence from pi, or the Governor's PIN code for her MAC card, you are subject to Discretionary Execution over that ensuing 24-hour period.

Q. *Is NJSDE painful?*

A. Yes! The State avails itself of a potpourri of execution methods including bare hands and teeth, sharpened stick, flint ax, bisection by lumberyard circular saw, car bomb, drive-by shooting, rocket-propelled grenade, Tomahawk cruise missile, etc., any of which can cause significant discomfort. The *degree* of pain you experience may vary in accordance with the efficacy of the execution attempt and with your body's ability to produce natural opiates, called endorphins, at moments of extreme stress. If you choose to augment your endorphins by prophylactically self-anesthetizing through heavy alcohol consumption and you develop cirrhosis, bear in mind that some hospitals in New Jersey will not perform liver transplants on patients who face possible execution within 48 hours of surgery.

Q. *How does the State make certain it's executing the right person?*

A. Prior to any execution attempt, your identity will be surreptitiously confirmed using sophisticated DNA-fingerprinting autoradiograph techniques developed by the LAPD Forensic Crime Laboratory.

Q. *What will happen to me after I'm killed?*

A. You will experience a sense of well-being. You (i.e., your soul) will separate from your body. You will travel through a dark tunnel. Emerging from this darkness, you will encounter a field of white radiant light. And you will enter this light. You will conduct a review of your life. You may encounter a "presence." You will probably meet deceased loved ones. At some juncture, you may hear what you think is your body calling out, beseeching you. *Do not return to your body!* This bark or whooping sound is made by a spasm in the muscles of the voice box caused by increased acidity in the blood of the corpse.

Your body will undergo rigor mortis (rigidity), livor mortis (discoloration due to settling of blood), and algor mortis (cooling). Tissue will break down through enzymatic action, and putrefaction will ensue through the decomposition of proteins by bacteria. Your body will be colonized by necrophage insects, including blowfly larvae and saprophagous beetles, and within three to six months, caseic fermentation should occur.

Q. *This is a change of subject, but— Why, after he'd been so successful as a starting pitcher and in fact had recently thrown a no-hitter against the Boston Red Sox, was Dave Righetti pulled from the starting rotation and put in the Yankee bullpen? Was this just*

the result of one of Steinbrenner's autocratic tantrums, or was there
some sound baseball reasoning behind the decision?

A. The months following Righetti's July Fourth no-hitter
against the Boston Red Sox were among the most tumultuous
in Yankee history. Players had the locker room repainted,
replacing the traditional Yankee pinstripe motif with gyrat-
ing chained dancers and huge flying griffins bearing futuris-
tic bare-breasted Valkyries with laser guns. Each game was
preceded by a ritual team circle jerk. Post-game revels raged
into the early morning. It was not unusual to find Meg Tilly,
Teri Hatcher, Amanda Plummer, Vanessa Williams, Jaye
Davidson, Kate Capshaw, Janet Reno, Daphne Zuniga,
Helena Bonham Carter, and the like sprawled languidly
across the locker-room floor as players sipped sweat from their
navels with teeny coke spoons. Sports fans will not soon forget the image of a simpering Don Mattingly injecting Ritalin
into his neck for the benefit of press photographers. Steinbrenner's capricious mean streak was exacerbated by the
cheese-free diet he'd been put on by his cardiologist. One
minute, he seemed too spaced out to recognize anyone; the
next, he was clubbing or pistol-whipping whoever was handy.
Predictably, players and coaches oscillated between rhapsody
and despair, their heady self-confidence undermined by an
involuntary nihilism. Righetti, the crotch of his uniform distended by the heavy cock rings he now insisted on wearing
when he pitched, circumambulated the mound between
pitches muttering what a *New York Post* headline described as
"Hermetic Incantations and Insane Glossolalia!" Righetti was
ultimately placed on the disabled list and committed by

Steinbrenner to the psychiatric hospital in Rodez, France, where the visionary dramatic theorist and poet Antonin Artaud had undergone sixty convulsive shock treatments. Pledging that his star pitcher would receive "the finest care money can buy," Steinbrenner stipulated that Righetti be given *sixty-one* convulsive shock treatments—one for each of the home runs Roger Maris hit in 1961. Three weeks later, Righetti rejoined the team in Kansas City. That night, in the eleventh inning, Yankee utility infielder Hector Peña hit a mammoth 600-foot shot to dead center field. Following a protest by Royals manager Dick Howser that Peña was using an illegally doctored bat, umpires confiscated his Louisville Slugger, sawed it open, and discovered two pounds of stolen Russian plutonium. The Yankees were forced to forfeit the game and effectively dropped out of pennant contention. That off-season, in an effort to restore morale, Steinbrenner took the team on a tour of Japan, Southeast Asia, and the Indian subcontinent. Although several Yankees tore anterior cruciate ligaments slipping on the raspberry-colored snail-egg pods that litter ballparks in the Mekong lowlands of southwest Laos, and during a game in the Mujahedeen Dome in Kabul, Afghanistan, rookie prospect Andre Knoblauch lost his legs when he stepped on a land mine chasing a line-drive hit into the gap in left-center, the trip was a great success. Steinbrenner was particularly impressed with the custom practiced by Japanese players of wearing glass vials of potassium cyanide on cords around their necks. And in an exhibition game against the Yomiuri Giants, a Yomiuri player, caught in a run-down between second and third base, did

increasing the degree and rapidity with which NJSDE releasees are stigmatized by, and ostracized from, their communities. The fact that being anywhere near you puts someone at risk of being killed or paralyzed by a stray 9-mm round, gruesomely disfigured by an errant machete, or blinded by a wayward crossbow arrow makes it unlikely that—in the gym, for instance—that person will choose the StairMaster next to yours, never mind join you in tucking away some sea leg fra diavolo and Chianti at the local trattoria, and less likely still that he or she will have sex with you later that evening. As an NJSDE releasee, you'll be amazed not only at the corrosive anxiety of living with an indeterminate death sentence, but at how quickly you'll be shunned as a pariah wherever you go. That's why *The American Spectator* awarded NJSDE five bastinados—its highest rating—in a recent evaluation of state-funded internal security apparatus, calling it "A breath of fresh air . . . The most whimsical deterrent program in years!"

Q. *Given the potential for "collateral damage," can I be killed while praying in a crowded church, synagogue, or mosque?*
A. Yes, you can!

Q. *Can I be killed while visiting a friend's premature infant in a neonatal intensive care unit?*
A. Sure!

Q. *Can I be Discretionarily Executed while giving someone CPR?*
A. I don't see why not!

Q. *My girlfriend and I have a bet. She insists that it's illegal for an NJSDE releasee to be executed in a casino on an Indian reservation. I say that's nonsense—an NJSDE releasee can be executed absolutely anywhere. If she's right, I take her out for sushi. If I'm right, she treats at the steakhouse of my choice.*

A. Try Peter Luger's, 178 Broadway at Bedford Avenue in Brooklyn. Order the double porterhouse and a bottle of 1975 Lafite Rothschild.

Q. *If I'm convicted of another crime and sent back to prison, can I be Discretionarily Executed while serving that sentence?*

A. Absolutely, but it probably won't be necessary. Because you expose fellow convicts and guards to the risk of incidental death or injury, you will be one *extremely* unpopular inmate. NJSDE releasees who reenter the correctional system are rock-bottom on the institutional totem pole, ranked below informers and pedophiles. So don't count on your new cellmate greeting you that first day with a lei and ukulele—the chances of your surviving 24 hours are nil.

Q. *As an NJSDE releasee, will I find it difficult to secure employment?*

A. Unfortunately, you may. Most businesses are reluctant to hire NJSDE releasees, despite the fact that they often make stellar employees. You'll have better luck with those companies, nonprofit organizations, and public-sector agencies that are less squeamish about workplace violence, such as 7-Elevens, Planned Parenthood clinics, and the U.S. Postal Service.

Q. *Will I be issued special license plates?*

A. Yes. NJSDE vehicular license plates feature the "NJSDE" pre-fix, a specially designed logo (three guillotined heads chatting amiably in a basket, superimposed over the State of New Jer-sey), followed by a random or vanity five-digit sequence. State law requires that all parking areas provide specially desig-nated spaces for NJSDE cars. Given the possibility of car-bomb execution attempts, though, these spaces are not always conveniently situated. For example, the Short Hills Mall in Short Hills, New Jersey, generously allots six NJSDE park-ing spaces, but they are located in North Battleford, Saskatchewan.

Q. *What savings or premiums does my NJSDE card entitle me to with restaurants, hotels, sports and leisure facilities, and airlines?*

A. Because there may be an NJSDE attempt on your life at any moment, you put the lives of those around you in constant jeopardy. Consequently, many fine restaurants, hotels, and airlines offer NJSDE releasees substantial cash premiums to take their business elsewhere. Simply present your NJSDE card to the maitre d', or at the front desk or ticketing counter. Following a spate of Discretionary Executions, airlines typi-cally engage in NJSDE No-Fly Premium "wars," so consult with your travel agent about which carrier is offering releasees the most money to fly with its competitors.

Q. *Are there support groups for people who've been sentenced to Discre-tionary Execution?*

A. Yes. Local NJSDE Support Groups meet throughout the state. The day-to-day burden of living with an NJSDE sentence can be psychologically debilitating, and many releasees find the NJSDE Support Group enormously helpful. The fellowship of others who are experiencing the same dread and paranoia, and the guidance of specially trained counselors, can ease your feelings of isolation and significantly enhance the quality of your life.

Q. *Can I be Discretionarily Executed while attending a New Jersey State Discretionary Execution Support Group meeting?*

A. Absolutely! In fact, the chances of being killed while attending an NJSDE Support Group meeting are extraordinarily high. Not only are you subject to an NJSDE attempt on your own life, but you are at increased risk of being collaterally killed in an attempt on any one of your fellow NJSDE Support Group members!

Q. *If I avoid execution and survive into my senescence, but then develop a fatal disease or disorder, will I—at that point—be removed from the NJSDE "active list" and allowed to die a natural death?*

A. No. Your status as an NJSDE releasee is irrevocable and remains in effect until you are declared legally brain dead. Unless certification of brain death is received by the NJSDE Control Center, your social security number remains active in the NJSDE system, and if that number yields any of the triggering values, you are subject to Discretionary Execution over that ensuing 24-hour period, regardless of your age or infirmity.

Several years ago, an octogenarian NJSDE releasee who'd suffered a serious thromboembolic stroke was sent to the hospital for an MRI scan in order to determine the degree of neurological damage. As he was rolled into the tunnel-like magnetic machine, an NJSDE commando hidden inside, splayed stealthily against the scanner's cylindrical walls, garroted the releasee to death, as bewildered physicians squinted at their monitors in the control room.

In a recent incident, an elderly NJSDE releasee was about to undergo a lithotripsy—a procedure for fragmenting bladder stones, in which the patient is immersed shoulder-deep in a special tub and high-frequency ultrasound shock waves transmitted by a machine called a lithotripter are focused on the stones and shatter them. As he was lowered into the lithotripsy tub, several clandestinely submerged NJSDE frogmen fired a salvo from their spearguns, killing the shriveled releasee instantly.

NJSDE operatives dispatched to execute ailing releasees in New Jersey hospitals frequently disguise themselves as grossly negligent physicians, thereby enabling them to move freely about operating rooms and intensive-care units.

Be advised, though, that if you die as a result of premeditated medical malpractice at the hands of an NJSDE assassin disguised as a grossly negligent physician, your loved ones are *not* entitled to compensatory and punitive damages. But if they can show that, during a Discretionary Execution attempt by NJSDE assassins disguised as grossly negligent physicians, the primary cause of death was actually the inadvertent result of a bona fide grossly negligent physician's own gross negligence, then they *are* entitled to compensatory and punitive damages.

The most celebrated lawsuit resulting from an NJSDE releasee's death due to concomitant deliberate and inadvertent gross negligence involved the renowned signage copywriter Leonard Gutman.

Although most signage copywriters are unheralded, their work is among the most widely apprehended language-product in the world. The lay public is aware that copywriters are critical in the creation of brochures, direct mail, print ads, radio spots, television commercials, etc. And some advertising copywriters have even achieved celebrity status in this country, commanding salaries commensurate with Hollywood screenwriters and best-selling novelists. Most people, though, tend to disparage—or ignore altogether—the role of highly skilled copywriters in the creation of the text-driven signs that we see everywhere around us.

Len Gutman was not only considered technically virtuosic in his craft, he was deemed a visionary genius. In the course of his career, he garnered every significant award bestowed by his colleagues, and was ultimately designated a "Living National Treasure" by the American Signage and Display Association (ASDA). His work is so ubiquitous and prototypical that it smacks of the primordial, as if it's somehow existed *always,* independent of human artifice.

Use Other Door—one of the very first signs that Gutman wrote as a young man—became an immediate classic. Gutman went on to write a stunning series of signs that fundamentally redefined our sense of public language, including: *Out of Service, Visitors Must Sign In,* and *Push to Start.* Then— in what is considered Gutman's *annus mirabilis*—an astonishing burst of creative activity in which masterpiece followed masterpiece in astonishing succession: *Do Not Enclose or Obstruct Access to Meter, Turn Knob to Right Only, Right Lane Must Turn Right,* and the sublime *Employees Must Wash Hands Before Returning to Work.* (That same year, Gutman also co-wrote *We Deliver, Totally Nude,* and *Void Where Prohibited.*)

There's an austere beauty to much of his work, pared down to its irreducible essence. In a famous television interview with Gutman late in his life, a critic is standing with him in front of a restaurant's lavatories, admiring what is indisputably Gutman's most popular, and arguably his finest, sign: *Men.*

They then move over to the distaff door.

"You didn't write *Women?*" asks the critic.

"No, I wish I had," Gutman smiles wistfully.

In contrast, there's an almost rococo exuberance to some of his work—*The Plinth Is Not Edible,* for example, a sign Gutman wrote for an exhibition of halvah statuary at the Walker Art Center in Minneapolis.

Gutman was writing what would be his final and unfinished sign, *Excuse Our Appearance, We're——,* when he suffered a severe coronary and was rushed by ambulance to a nearby hospital.

Unbeknownst to the EMS paramedics and hospital staff who ministered to him that afternoon, unbeknownst to his wife and children, unbeknownst to his dearest friends and his peers in the signage and display industry, Len Gutman was an NJSDE releasee.

As a result of a youthful indiscretion, Gutman had lived

each day of his adult life with the specter of impending Discretionary Execution. Remarkably, though, graced by the vagaries of the NJSDE condemnation process, there was not to be a single attempt on his life until he was 78 years old.

That autumn evening at 9:00 P.M., at the Control Center in Trenton, Gutman's social security number was factored into the NJSDE computer as it had been every day for the past 60 years, only this particular night—according to unsealed NJSDE records—it yielded the numerical sequence 94375—the four billionth to four billion and fourth decimal digits of pi—exposing Gutman to Discretionary Execution for the ensuing 24 hours. Ironically, on the afternoon of the following day—and as yet unrelated to any NJSDE activity— he suffered the aforementioned heart attack, and was wheeled into the emergency room in a state of cardiac arrest.

Gutman's heart was in ventricular fibrillation. The cardiologist on call at the time, New Jersey native Dr. Richard Cuozzo, administered a precordial thump in an effort to mechanically stimulate Gutman's heart and convert it to a normal rhythm. A precordial thump is a firm blow to the lower half of the sternum, delivered with a closed fist, from a distance of about 15 inches above the chest. Cuozzo gave Gutman two additional precordial thumps, all to no apparent effect. He then initiated external cardiac massage, in an effort to drive blood out into the pulmonary artery and aorta. With one hand placed over the other, Cuozzo positioned the heel of the bottom hand on the lower third of Gutman's sternum and sharply depressed it, holding it down for a moment and then releasing. He performed some 60 massages per minute for approximately two minutes—again, to no apparent effect.

It was at this point that two NJSDE operatives—disguised as grossly negligent physicians assisting Dr. Cuozzo—placed external defibrillator paddles on Gutman's chest and administered two shocks in rapid succession. The maximum charge for defibrillating a human heart is 300 to 350 joules. The disguised NJSDE agents used approximately 5,000 joules of electricity, delivering to Gutman a charge sufficient to jump-start a Winnebago. Then, leaving nothing to chance, they administered an intravenous injection of lidocaine, an anesthetic used as a ventricular antiarrhythmic, giving Gutman 20 grams, a lethal quantity some ten times the recommended dose.

Gutman, of course, died.

Early that evening, a hospital spokesman announced that Len Gutman had arrived at the emergency room suffering a heart attack and had expired as a result of deliberate and premeditated measures taken by NJSDE agents disguised as grossly negligent physicians, acting without the foreknowledge or complicity of Dr. Cuozzo or anyone else on staff. The media had no reason to question the veracity of the hospital's account, and the story, along with Leonard Gutman, was seemingly put to rest.

Gutman's wife and son, though, were not quite so credulous. Retaining the services of prominent medical malpractice attorney Irvin Wachtell, they initiated a private investigation, resulting in a disinterment and a new autopsy, and two months later they filed a $25 million wrongful death suit against the hospital and Dr. Richard Cuozzo, claiming that it was Cuozzo's genuine gross negligence and not the feigned gross negligence of the NJSDE agents that resulted in Gutman's death. Specifically, they charged that Cuozzo had used "egregiously excessive force," causing "CPR-induced thoracic wall trauma and fatal injury to abdominal and thoracic organs."

At the trial, a nuanced and often sympathetic portrait emerged of Dr. Richard Cuozzo.

"Richie's a surf-and-turf kind of guy," testified Cuozzo's best friend, Victor Polumbo, a hospital maintenance man. "Not your typical cardiologist, y'know what I'm saying. He never talks down to you like the other doctors. He's a good guy. A Rangers fan."

A podiatrist, who'd been a fraternity brother of Cuozzo's at medical school in Guadalajara, testified about his extraordinary ability to drink and parallel-park. "I been out with Richie where we'd be doin' shots and beers all night, and I got a Lincoln Town Car, and Richie, he could put that car in a space where you get out and look and you go, there's like no fuckin' way he just did that."

"He's never too tired to spot for somebody," testified a gym buddy.

"He's fun, y'know what I mean?" said OR nurse Sheri Hildebrand. "The other doctors, they're so serious all the time. Richie, he can always make you laugh. Even when he loses a patient, he can immediately say something funny, and, y'know, you just forget about it."

Called to the stand by the Gutmans' attorney, Cuozzo was asked to demonstrate—on a CPR dummy laid out on a table in front of the jury—the force of the precordial thumps he administered to Len Gutman that fateful afternoon. Cuozzo made a fist and thumped the dummy, breaking the table in two. The CPR dummy was then laid across several cinder blocks. Cuozzo delivered another precordial thump, this time splitting the cinder block under the dummy's sternum. At the request of plaintiff's counsel, Cuozzo then demonstrated how he'd administered external cardiac massage to the deceased. This time the CPR dummy was placed on a four-inch-thick marble tabletop with thick reinforced-steel legs. Cuozzo began his forceful depressions of the dummy's chest. By the twentieth massage, the steel legs began to buckle, and marble dust was sprinkling from a spreading fissure in the tabletop. In less than a minute, the legs snapped completely.

Indeed, Gutman's autopsy disclosed extensive hemorrhage investing the pectoralis regions, intercostal musculature, and parasternal muscles. The sternum had two fractures with extensive localized hemorrhage. The left first through seventh ribs were fractured with severe accompanying soft-tissue hemorrhage. The right first through ninth ribs were fractured with similar soft tissue and muscular hemorrhage.

The autopsy further disclosed liver lacerations, splenic and pancreatic injury, cardiac rupture, pneumothorax, aortic laceration, and systemic fat embolism—each of which could be distinctly certified as a cause of death and of all of which were directly attributable to Cuozzo's ungainly attempts at cardiopulmonary resuscitation.

In the unequivocal opinion of the plaintiff's expert witnesses, Len Gutman was already dead when the NJSDE agents gave him the 5,000 joules of electricity and 20 grams of lidocaine.

The jury deliberated for less than fifteen minutes and awarded the Gutman family $40 million in damages.

Although Dr. Richard Cuozzo experienced a dramatic surge in his malpractice premiums, he was given an honorary fourth-degree black belt by the Passaic County Tae Kwon Do School in recognition of his accomplishments in the emergency room and during the trial.

And in a final irony, as he accepted his honorary black belt—the first ever bestowed by the Passaic County Tae Kwon Do School on a nonpractitioner—Cuozzo stood under one of Leonard Gutman's earliest signs, which, though immediately recognizable as fledgling Gutman, betokens the compression and allusiveness that would so distinguish his mature oeuvre:

Students Must Remove Shoes
Before Entering Dojo

So here we are—you, my father, and I—having arrived simultaneously at the word *Dojo*.

Now you can perhaps feel the kinetic sensation of reading apace with us. Share the sensation of neurolinguistic motion with me and my dad. The hair in the breeze! I don't know what you'd call it exactly . . . Is there a strictly cerebral kinesthesia . . . a lexical kinesthesia? A proprioception associated with reading-speed?

Every male Leyner from the very beginning (I'm talking about the original botched eugenics experiments in Galicia and Estonia in the mid-nineteenth century) reads at exactly the same speed—620 words per minute. A moderate clip. (Female Leyners read at about 750 words a minute.) I don't care what you give my father and me to read—a three-syllable Leonard Gutman sign or the 2,815-page Fermilab Fixed-Target Proton Accelerator service manual—we'll reach the final word with perfect coterminous symmetry.

Dojo.

And then we look up with what appears to be this impassive bored expectancy but is really a moment of cognitive processing during which our facial muscles go slack.

"Any questions?" asks the warden.

"Nuh-uh," Dad and I say in unison.

"Very comprehensive," says my father, slipping the brochure into the inside breast pocket of an orange blazer with a three-guillotined-heads-chatting-amiably-in-a-basket NJSDE escutcheon sewn onto the breast pocket.

The superintendent then asks if we'd like to purchase a video of the execution. (Videos of all executions, successful or abortive, are made available—at a fee, of course—to the families of the condemned inmate and his or her victims.)

This occasions a lightning-fast colloquy between my father and I that, in its susurrant urgency, will remind you of—depending on your taste in nonfiction TV—either the ad hoc huddles convened by teammates on game shows or the microphone-muffled, privileged powwows between witnesses and their lawyers at Congressional hearings:

"I don't really want it," I say, cupping a hand to my mouth and whispering into his ear.

"Get one, for Christ's sake," says my father, eyeing the superintendent, but addressing me under his breath, through a clench-toothed ventriloquist's grin. "I wish I had a goddamn video of *my* father's execution."

"I don't have any money on me."

"I'll pay for it."

"But it's so stupid," I complain, spitting on his ear-lobe.

"I WILL PAY FOR IT!" he insists, grin frozen, lips motionless.

"But, Daaaaaady . . ." I whine, regressing in the face of his peremptory largesse.

"Superintendent, we'll take a video," Dad announces.

Now the superintendent wants to know whether we'd like a soundtrack. (The video is $24.95 without the soundtrack—for an extra $10 they'll dub in any song you want.)

"What exactly is *in* the video?" my father asks.

"It's the entire lethal-injection sequence up to and including when you say 'I feel shitty.' You can choose any song you'd like—we have a CD library with over 10,000 titles."

Now my father's pondering this. He's taken a seat and he's poring over this catalog of CD titles. And I'm beginning to feel really pressed time-wise. In order to collect the Vincent and Lenore DiGiacomo / Oshimitsu Polymers America Award, I need a screenplay written by tomorrow. I know, I know—I shouldn't have waited until the last minute . . . Anyway, I need to get to the library *today* before it closes. I never expected this thing to take so long. I thought I'd be in and out of here.

And also I'm getting in a bad mood because . . . well, for two reasons: First of all, I have a feeling that my father is going to ask me to share a cab with him—which I absolutely won't do. I mean, you're aware of the highly complex social structure of 13-year-old boys with its intricate, hierarchical, and unyielding code of decorum in which various forms of behavior and activities are proscribed by taboos, so you know how mortifying it is for someone my age to be seen with a parent in public by his peers, the ignominy of which is made even more unbearable by anything that calls attention to the fact, and nothing calls attention to itself more conspicuously than a fiery execution attempt—so you can understand my feelings of dread about the possibility of sharing a taxi with a father who might be brutally assassinated by NJSDE operatives while we're stopped at a traffic light. God, I'd absolutely die with embarrassment! And, second, I'm starting to feel really weird about the warden not having responded to or acknowledged in any way the two clandestine notes I slipped her: "You wanna get high?" and "Be my sweaty bosomy lover?" Maybe—I'm thinking—if you do something so fulsomely inappropriate—like slipping her these billets-doux—maybe the reproach is this massive silence, this nullifying indifference that expunges the act right out of existence, making you question whether you'd ever committed it in the first place. So I start to wonder if I'd ever given her the notes—I rummage around for them in the mealy pockets of my leather trousers, but find only a phenobarbital, an ossified yellow Starburst, and my folded-up fake movie review (more about which later)—or if I'd ever really written them at all.

"What about 'Night of the Living Baseheads'—Public Enemy?" Dad asks, running a finger down a page from the CD catalog.

"Too old," says the superintendent. "What about something from . . . like Snoop or Wu Tang Clan?"

Dad moistens his finger and flips a couple of pages ahead.

"They got Raekwon . . . *Only Built 4 Cuban Linx.* What about something off that?"

"That shit's too aggressive, man. Too strident," says the executioner. "Think about it, Joel—you're just stretched out there on the gurney. It's very . . . supine."

Dad nods.

"Y'know what might be really good?" he asks. "But you gotta think about it for a minute. 'My Jamaican Guy.' Grace Jones."

Grimaces of disapproval.

"You're strapped to a gurney with lethal drugs dripping into your vein and we hear 'My Jamaican Guy' . . . I don't get it," says the doctor.

"Yeah, you're right . . . maybe if I was Jamaican . . ." Dad says, perusing along.

Then the rabbi pipes up.

"See if they have the Smiths' CD, *The Queen Is Dead,*" he says. "The song 'I Know It's Over.' 'Oh Mother / I can feel / the soil falling over my head . . .' That presentiment of being buried could be really intense."

"Please, not Morrissey," grumbles the doctor, rolling his eyes. "You have this great abortive-execution video and you're gonna ruin it with Morrissey?"

"I think Morrissey's perfect for an abortive execution," the rabbi replies defensively.

"You know what would be *really* intense?" says the operations officer. "The White Zombie song 'Soul-Crusher.' 'Burning like fat in the fire / The smell of red, red groovie screamed mega-flow / A stalking ground without prey / A flash of superstition whimpering like a crippled animal / Dogs of the soul-crusher / Pulling closer like the blue steel jaws of hell.' "

"That's a cool song," the superintendent agrees.

"You like Fugazi?" the operations officer asks my father.

"I don't really know any specific songs," says my Dad.

"Fugazi! Yes!" raves the superintendent, pumping his fist in the air.

"You ever see them live?" asks the operations officer.

"No, man, I wish I had."

"You gotta see them in Bethesda. That's like the ultimate place to see Fugazi."

"Fugazi . . . Fugazi . . . Fugazi . . . OK, here we go," says Dad, sliding his finger across the page from Performer to CD Title. "They have *Red Medicine.*"

"Perfect!" the operations officer says. "That's got 'By You'— 'Generation fuck you / to define and redefine / you'd make them all the same / but molds they break away / safely inside / looking outside / go keep on picking at it / it's just going to get bigger . . .' It's got 'Target'—'It's cold outside and my hands are dry / skin is cracked / and I realize that I hate the sound of guitars / a thousand grudging young millionaires / forcing silence / sucking sound . . .' "

My father shakes his head.

"It's too bleak . . . Too apocalyptic. I survived the execution attempt, right?"

The warden's male secretary floats a concept.

"Echo and the Bunnymen. 'Over You.' 'Feeling good again / always hoped I would / never believed that I ever could.' "

"You know what song might really work?" Dad says. " 'Don't Go Breaking My Heart.' Elton John and Kiki Dee."

The rabbi shuts his eyes, his head bobbing to the imagined music.

"That might work," he says.

"Or maybe a standard . . ." says Dad. " 'The Best Is Yet to Come.' Sinatra. Y'know, real brassy optimism . . ."

"What about something from *Phantom*? Like Michael Crawford singing 'Music of the Night,' " suggests the warden's secretary. "That could be very dramatic. Because, frankly, I think you could use something with a little schmaltz, 'cause seven minutes of a motionless body on a steel cot is not particularly compelling."

Dad looks up from the catalog.

"This is gonna sound weird," he says, "but I think it could be really good. 'I'm Hans Christian Andersen.' Danny Kaye, from the movie."

"You're lying there with a lethal drug IV in your arm and the soundtrack is 'I'm Hans Christian Andersen'? That doesn't make any fucking sense to me," says the superintendent.

"That's the point," asserts my father. "We see me—Joel Leyner—on a gurney. But we hear 'I'm Hans Christian

Andersen / Andersen—that's me.' See, it's like: How are we iden-
tified? And how do we denominate ourselves? What's *me/Leyner*?
What's the meaning of that classification? Names are arbitrary
designations used by the state apparatus to facilitate surveillance
and control. That could be Hans Christian Andersen on that gurney. You know what I'm saying? See, you'll be watching Joel
Leyner and hearing Danny Kaye claim that he's Hans Christian
Andersen. You'd get this dissonant dialectic going between image
and sound. . . ."

"I think people would just think it's a goof," the superintendent says.

"Well, what about 'Inchworm'—from the same movie.
Y'know, 'Inchworm / inchworm / measuring the marigolds . . .'
Like measuring out the last moments of my life."

"I just wouldn't use a Danny Kaye song. That's my personal
feeling, man. I just don't think he's right for this."

"I have an idea, but it's in a completely different direction,"
says the warden. "We see a man lying on a gurney, *strapped* to a
gurney, right? That, to me, connotes surrender—a kind of erotic
surrender. Y'know, you can do whatever you want to me and take
however long you want to take doing it. Because I'm ceding control to you. So I thought maybe something like Luther Vandross . . . y'know the song 'The Glow of Love.' 'There is no better
way to be / Hold me, caress me / I'm yours forever and a day / We
are a sweet bouquet / Seasons for happiness are here / Can you feel
it? / The reason we're filled with cheer is / We're in rapture / In
the glow of love.' "

"Is he restricted to one song, or can you lay in parts from different songs?" asks the executioner.

The superintendent shrugs.

"I don't see why we couldn't use sections from several songs, if that's what Mr. Leyner would like."

"OK, maybe we go like this," the executioner says excitedly. "We key the music to the control-panel lights for the drugs' delivery sequence. Red light, yellow light, sodium thiopental injection—boom—Elton John and Kiki Dee, 'Don't Go Breaking My Heart.' Green light—fade music. OK. Red light, yellow light, pancuronium bromide injection—boom—Luther Vandross, 'The Glow of Love.' Green light—fade music. OK. Red light, yellow light, potassium chloride injection—boom—Michael Crawford, 'Music of the Night' from *Phantom of the Opera.* Green light—fade music. Joel looks up and says, 'I feel shitty.' Fade to black."

"You like Arnold Schoenberg's *Suite for Piano,* opus 25?" the rabbi asks my father.

"How's it go?"

The rabbi hums the entire fourteen-minute composition.

"Nuh-uh," Dad says.

I stick my two pinkies into my mouth and produce an excruciating, hideously high-pitched whistle.

"Hey! People! C'mon, I gotta get out of here already!"

"We have a soundtrack to finish, son," says my father, without looking up from the catalog.

I turn to the superintendent.

"Can you remix an existing song? Patch in some samples, add some tracks?"

"Y'know the remote-fired stationary tear-gas network control console booth above the maximum-security eating hall?" says the superintendent. "Well, I have a little studio in there—Korg DSS-1 Digital Sampling Synthesizer, Kawai R-100 Digital Drum Machine, Roland MC-500 MIDI Sequencer. What are you thinking?"

"Well . . . this is like completely off the top of my head, but . . . After the drugs, my dad looks up and says 'I feel shitty,' right? Why don't we take the Bernstein/Sondheim tune from *West Side Story*—'I Feel Pretty'—overdub the word *shitty*—make 'I Feel Shitty.' And I'd slow it down to a dirge. Do a sort of Trent Reznor mix. 'I feel shitty / oh so shitty / I feel shitty and witty and bright / and I pity / any girl who isn't me tonight.' "

"That's it!" hails the rabbi. "It's lovely."

Dad closes the catalog. "I can live with that."

"It's excellent, man," says the executioner, giving me five.

"And I'd add a wheeze rhythm track," I say. "Get a slow, really labored wheeze. Do you have any, like, asthmatic or black-lung wheeze samples?"

"I'll check," the superintendent says, rising to his feet.

With a ripple of cracking knee joints, everyone stands.

C'est fini. Finally.

It's bye-bye time.

My father embraces me. He rocks me gently from side to side. And then, enclasped, we begin to revolve in a counterclockwise rotation, a dirty dance of sorts.

The room is hushed. The stenographer cranes her neck to better apprehend our murmured farewell, made even less audible by the Doppler effect of our axial motion.

"I don't know when I'm going to see you again."

"I know that, Dad."

"There's no going back, now."

"I know."

"No more fairy tales, ace. No restoration of the status quo ante. You know what I'm saying? You have to be the man now."

"I know that, Dad."

"And you have to start wearing a shirt."

"Awwwwwww, Dad," I whine. And then, testily, under my breath: "I wear a shirt when you lose the false eyelashes and titty-torture clamps, you punk-ass dusthead."

Our faces slip in and out of crepuscular shadow as we slowly spin.

"It's going to be tough on your mother. And you have to take care of that woman now. I'm an NJSDE releasee, and I can't do it. You understand? In a few minutes I'm going to call and tell her that I may never see her again. And she'll probably be wearing her black Thierry Mugler suit. And from that moment on she might sit home like Miss Havisham in that black Thierry Mugler suit— and she might wear that same fucking suit every single day for the rest of her life. And you have to be prepared to deal with that."

I'm beginning to feel light-headed and slightly nauseated from the continuous counterclockwise gyre.

"Look at me, boy."

"What's the matter?"

"I have something I need to ask you," he says gravely. "And I want you to take your time and think it over seriously before you give me your answer."

"I will, Dad."

We stop moving.

"Son . . . what's the maxim that more eloquently than any other articulates a Leyner's self-image, his worldview, his pride and ambition as a man, as a pagan moralist and as an American— the call to arms, the *cri de coeur,* the phrase-that-pays that can inspire and galvanize him for the rest of his life? I need to hear you say it, son."

I peer fervently into my father's eyes and squeeze him hard, as hard as I've ever squeezed another human being. And I recite those words, those stirring, unforgettable words, in defense of which—in the ensuing months—so many brave Bougainvillean boys will lose their minds:

"Any asshole with a Master of Social Work degree can put on a turban and start issuing fatwas about whom you can and whom you can't mail meat to," I intone, "but it takes real balls to turn a brunette without a cranium into a blonde."

The room bursts into applause and I can see several people daubing tears from their eyes.

There's now—as if conveyed via the sort of subliminal, instantaneously communicated signal that causes an entire herd on the savanna to suddenly change direction—an implicit sense of adjournment, and everyone gathers his or her personal effects and begins to filter out of the warden's office.

"You're going to the library from here to work on that screen-play, right?" my father asks.

"Yeah . . ." I answer, anticipating the inevitable corollary.

"So . . . you want to share a cab?"

I stare down at the floor, shifting my weight uneasily from foot to foot.

"I can't, Dad . . . no way."

I cringe, awaiting his response. And when none is forthcoming, I look back up.

He's gone!

I scan the room and he's nowhere to be seen.

"Hey, where'd my dad go?"

"He left," says the superintendent, who's just returned from his studio in the tear-gas control console booth. "I just passed him in the hall."

That's it. He's gone, I say to myself, shaking my head. My father has now begun the grim, tormented, and macabre life of an NJSDE releasee, a life that may very well come to a violent and agonizing end within the next five minutes, within the next hour, or in a month, or a year, or—who knows?—flourish without untoward incident for another fifty years and *then* the blast of shrapnel or the Colombian necktie.

"Oh, by the way, I searched the patch files," says the superintendent, "and we have a bronchitis wheeze sample."

"Bronchitis . . . that sounds cool," I say. "Just make sure the tempo is right—very, very slow, larghissimo, funereal. Like 'I feel shitty / wheeze . . . wheeze / oh so shitty / wheeze . . . wheeze . . .' "

"Gotcha," he says, extending his hand. "Mark, take it easy and good luck on the screenplay."

"Thank you very much."

We shake and he exits.

Ditto the operations officer.

"All the luck in the world on that screenplay."

"Thanks, I appreciate it."

The doctor.

"I'm keeping my fingers crossed for you on that Vincent and Lenore DiGiacomo / Oshimitsu Polymers America thing."

"Thanks so much."

And the executioner: "How much was that—$200,000 a year? *Madonna!* Whack that script out of the ballpark, chief."

"I'm gonna try. Thanks a lot. And thanks for everything today."

And then the rabbi.

He gestures elaborately at the mythical multiplex marquee in the sky. *"Eventually, Even Mighty Mouse Is Vivisected by the Dour Bitch in a White Lab Coat,"* he says, flashing a pair of avid thumbs-up.

"Thank you. *Vaya con Dios,* Rabbi."

Now only the warden, the warden's male secretary, the stenographer, and I remain in the office.

"Absolutely no calls and shut the door on your way out, please," says the warden.

For a second I assume she's talking to me.

"Absolutely no calls," parrots the secretary, winking at me as he closes the door behind him.

When I turn and look back at the warden, she's perched atop her desk, smirking cryptically, one eyebrow arched high, little diamond chips like crushed ice gleaming across the straps of her stilettos. And she's got my two little notes in her hand: "You wanna get high?" and "Be my sweaty bosomy lover?" And she's waving them in the air like a pair of theater tickets. Like front-

row orchestra, opening night, Aeschylus' *Prometheus Bound* at the
Greater Dionysia in Athens in friggin' 468 A.D. I mean, like a
pair of real hot ducats.

Gulp.

Boing.

Three quick procedural items before we move on to substantive issues—namely, my impending drug- and alcohol-addled liaison with the warden. (What symmetry, right—the exile of my father and my initiation into manhood!)

First, to paraphrase Oxford zoologist Richard Dawkins, during the minute that it takes you to read this sentence, "thousands of animals are being eaten alive, many others are running for their lives, whimpering with fear, others are being slowly devoured from within by rasping parasites . . . It must be so. In a universe of electrons and selfish genes, blind physical forces and genetic replication, some people are going to get hurt, other people are going to get lucky, and you won't find any rhyme or reason in it, nor any justice." Now if you take another minute and reread that sentence, even more animals will be eaten alive and devoured by parasites. In fact, it's almost as if reading that particular sentence actually *causes* the animals to be eaten alive and devoured by parasites. Is this possible? Well, yes, according to CERN physicist John Stewart Bell's theorem of nonlocal interaction. Anyway, my point is—doesn't it all make what we're doing right now seem pretty ludicrous? I mean, there's all that predation and whimpering and devouring going on out there, and you and I are just sitting here, writing and reading. It's not the writing per se that bothers me, it's the venue, the sedentarinous, the insularity. If only there were a more public, a more athletic, more agonistic way of doing it. What do you think I'd rather be doing right now: sitting in this book-lined atelier, stroking my chin, lost in this solitary reverie *or* striding into a domed stadium with a bag full of laptops, wearing a shirt emblazoned with logos—Apple, Microsoft Word, Xerox, Roget's Thesaurus, Chivas Regal, Marlboro, Zoloft—and going head-to-head against the world's top-ranked professional prose stylists, as 75,000 raucous, beer-swilling fans cheer our sentences as they instantly appear on the huge Diamond Vision screens?

So why do I do it then? Why do I sit here like this?

Because if writing this book—which, according to several people who are knowledgeable about literature, is the first tetherball novel *ever*—can help just one other kid who's gone through a similar experience, i.e., having a dad who survived an attempted execution by lethal injection and is resentenced to NJSDE, and losing your virginity to a 36-year-old warden, then it will all have been worth it.

Second, some of you may find the following depiction of my sexual encounter with the warden to be too explicit or even pornographic. Before reading this section, click the Scramble icon if any of the following activities or anatomical areas are objectionable to you: (1) human genitals in a state of sexual stimulation or arousal; (2) actual or simulated acts of human masturbation, sexual intercourse, or sodomy; (3) fondling or other erotic touching of human genitals, pubic region, buttock, anus, or female breast; (4) less than completely and opaquely concealed (a) human genitals, pubic region, (b) human buttock, anus, or (c) female breast below a point immediately above the top of the areola; or (5) human male genitals in a discernibly turgid state, even if completely and opaquely concealed. By clicking the Scramble icon, your mind will supplant any of the above depictions with images of Buddhist monks paginating toilet tissue. This exclusive bowdlerizing feature is available only in *The Tetherballs of Bougainville.* And remember, at any point you can reread the Dawkins sentence and kill more animals. Whatever you want. It's way interactive.

And finally, as you'll soon see, in the midst of the tryst, I peek at my Tag Heuer and realize there's no way I'm going to get to the Maplewood Public Library before it closes and that I'll probably not be able to come up with a screenplay in order to win the Vincent and Lenore DiGiacomo / Oshimitsu Polymers America Award. Did I ever really expect to ensconce myself in a library carrel and produce an original screenplay in one afternoon? Actually, no. I'd always anticipated making a cursory attempt at researching "story ideas," looking for books to "adapt," like, y'know, *Spin's Alternative Record Guide: The Movie,* and then, quickly tiring of that endeavor, simply plagiarizing an existing screenplay—something prestigious like Michelangelo Antonioni's *Red Desert* or Jean-Luc Godard's *La Chinoise.* Sure, in a half-hearted attempt at "originality," I'd have tried to make some cosmetic alteration, like changing the young Parisian Maoists in *La Chinoise* to followers of Vellupillai Prabhakaran, the leader of the Liberation Tigers of Tamil Eelam, or to fanatical devotees of leveraged-buyout titan Henry Kravis or maybe fanatical devotees of Amy Tan or Rabbi Schneerson or Ukrainian figure skater Oksana Baiul or whatever, and then finding even this an intellectual conundrum beyond my patience and attention span, just

copying Godard's screenplay word for word, and then, after two
pages, annoyed by the prospect of having to retype the whole
script, finally just photocopying it and then doing a fast cut-and-
paste job on the title page so it read *La Chinoise by Mark Leyner,*
because I figured with the clout of an ICM agent, I'd *still* be able
to win the award.

But I realize, given the time, that it's going to be impossible
to do even that—you'll be reading all this in a couple of pages—
and the warden, grabbing a handful of hair and lifting my head
from her crotch, says, "I've got an idea, why don't you make a
screenplay out of this?"

And I look at her, or try to look at her, try to focus, squinting
through this gooey scrim of secretions that covers my eyes. And
I'm like: "This?"

And she says, "Yeah, this," indicating, with a panoramic ges-
ture, the whole drug- and alcohol-addled liaison we're presently
engaged in. And she says, "Do a screenplay that appears to be a
faux autobiographical documentary, but that's actually—here's
the irony—completely factual. *Faux* irony."

My head is spinning. I'd gone from never having even seen a
real live vagina one minute to being literally immersed in one the
next, which is like having gone from wiggling your toes in a little backyard kiddie pool to scuba diving in the Marianas Trench
without any intervening training, and on top of it all, now I'm
trying to figure out "*faux* irony," which apparently is like multi-
plying negative numbers, which—I think—we did in Mr.
Hawes's math class. But then a little lightbulb goes on.

"It's like plagiarizing life, sort of. Right?" I ask. "It's, like, no
work."

"Basically," she concurs. "As soon as you get home from here, just write down everything that happened and just put it in screenplay form. In fact, it wouldn't hurt if you started thinking in terms of camera angles from here on," she says, pushing my head back down.

Not only do I find transposing my experiences into camera angles simultaneous to actually having those experiences to be an extraordinarily soothing exercise in self-consciousness, but I realize that it's a correlative to that near-death state during which your spirit hovers over your body and observes the frenzied efforts at resuscitation with this sort of dégagé bemusement, all of which further corroborates my theory of the afterlife that I first proposed in Ms. Kazanjian's Comparative Thanotology and Eschatology class. As a final project, I built this papier-mâché diorama—well, my friend Felipe actually constructed it; it was my idea, but I seem to have this problem with deadlines—*we* built this papier-mâché diorama basically illustrating that in our mortal, corporeal existence we're all sort of like actors and actresses—marionettes endowed with rudimentary attributes like sycophancy and sanctimony, but lacking the capacity for generative thought. But then at the moment we die—unless, of course, we've been grossly iniquitous, in which case we plummet on this gondola flume-ride, as Billy Idol sings Venetian boat songs, to some infernal grotto where we become infomercial studio audience members, rapturously applauding nose-hair clippers and sonic plaque removers for eternity—but otherwise we become screenwriters, which is why your life flashes before your eyes in the form of a storyboard. At some point thereafter, you begin your ascension of the empyreal hierarchy—you direct, you produce, you head a studio, you achieve moguldom, and ultimately you implode and, depending on how dense you are, you become either a white dwarf or a black hole. And Ms. Kazanjian said—and she said it in front of the whole class—that of all the seventh-grade final projects linking postmortem ontogeny, *Entertainment Weekly,* and stellar evolution, mine was one of the best she'd ever seen.

So on the way home from the prison, I stop at Nobody Beats The Wiz and buy this screenplay-formatting software program called SkriptMentor. All in all, I'd recommend SkriptMentor to aspiring screenwriters. In addition to formatting features like slug lines, scene numbers, dialogue breaks, etc., SkriptMentor also offers "idea generator and story guidance" options that include over 50,000 plot and subplot possibilities, 20,000 character combinations, and some 5,000 conflict situations. But I do have some serious reservations. I find several of the tutorial features rather intrusive and cumbersome.

For instance, whenever there's a sex scene in your script, a dialog box is displayed on-screen reading: *Penis size?* You're given several standard options: Harvey Keitel, Jeff Stryker, and Porfirio Rubirosa. There's a 5-inch default setting. You're also able to customize the penis size of your characters in much the same way as you adjust tabs and margins in word-processing programs, by manually dragging a size box. Some users may appreciate features that enable you to cut and paste penises from one character to another, or the Find and Replace command that allows you to change penis sizes throughout your script with a single keystroke, but I find it annoying that every time I have a male character engage in or even discuss sex, this penis-size dialogue box plops into the middle of my screen and I have to scroll through the entire Tool Palette just to choose the default setting and continue with my scene.

I find the Ass Menu equally aggravating. With the introduction of every new male character, however subsidiary, a dialogue box is displayed reading *Ass?* and offering a menu with several options: Hirsute, Hairless, Dimpled, Smooth, Blemished, etc. Clicking any of these options opens a submenu. For instance, there are six levels of Hirsute, from Blonde Down to Coarse Simian. Within Blemished, you can choose Birthmarks, Moles, Keloid Scars, Needle Tracks, Pimples, Folliculitis, Boils, and then you can customize buttock-boil placement with a click, drag-and-drop feature, etc. Again, although some of you may find these features creatively stimulating, I think it would behoove the makers of SkriptMentor to allow users to more easily circumvent these options. Having to scroll through an Ass Menu whenever a FedEx deliveryman appears at the door can really bog you down, and that's the last thing you need, especially when you have this looming deadline.

And perhaps most distracting of all is that every two pages or five minutes, a dialog box appears on-screen reading: *Requisite Springsteen Dirge?*

You click *No.*

Five minutes later: *Requisite Springsteen Dirge?*

Again you click *No.*

Five minutes later: *Requisite Springsteen Dirge?*

No!

It's really irritating. Perhaps this is a valuable feature for those aspiring screenwriters who may have written a script and inadvertently omitted the requisite Springsteen dirge, but at least they could provide some sort of bypass option. Wouldn't it be better, when you initially set the format parameters of your screenplay, if you could just choose *No Springsteen Dirge,* double-click, and move on?

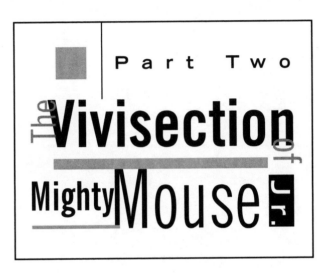

A Screenplay
by
Mark Leyner

(7th Grade, Maplewood Junior High School)

---

*Submitted in competition
for the Vincent and Lenore DiGiacomo /
Oshimitsu Polymers America Award*

FADE IN:

EXT. SPACE, 520 MILES ABOVE EARTH'S SURFACE

We HEAR faint CH-CH-CH.

KH-12 PHOTORECONNAISSANCE SPACECRAFT'S POV

SLOWLY ZOOM in from KH-12 satellite (at 98-degree sun-synchronous inclination) to prison

Earth. Western Hemisphere. North America. United States. East Coast. New Jersey. Princeton. New Jersey State Penitentiary.

As CAMERA ZOOMS in from space, CH-CH-CH becomes LOUDER and LOUDER.

EXT. NEW JERSEY STATE PENITENTIARY IN PRINCETON

A SERIES OF ANGLES

Concertina Wire. Guard towers. Exercise yards. Etc.

GAZEBO (originally used in *The Sound of Music*) that Michael Jackson presented to then-governor Christine Todd Whitman for use in state's maximum-security institutions for conjugal visits and punitive solitary confinement.

CH-CH-CH is now literally deafening.

(The loudest sounds that can be tolerated by the human ear are about 120 dB. For CH-CH-CH at GAZEBO SHOT, use Dolby Spectral Recording at 150–175 dB.)

TITLE FILLS SCREEN:

The Vivisection of Mighty Mouse, Jr.

We hear PERSIAN SANTOUR (72-STRING HAMMERED DULCIMER) AND TAR (SIX-STRING LUTE WITH SKIN BELLY) WITH TECHNO RHYTHM TRACK AND SAM-

PLED CHORUS FROM JESUS AND MARY CHAIN'S "JUST LIKE HONEY"

Hold, then:

DISSOLVE TO:

INT. WARDEN'S OFFICE

WARDEN gets down from her desk, crumples two notes into little balls, shuffles them behind her back, and then extends two fists.

> W A R D E N
>
> Pick one.

MARK'S POV

His eyes dart anxiously from fist to fist—from right fist to left fist, to right, to left, back and forth, back and forth, and back and forth. This oscillating pan continues for seven minutes, becoming steadily faster until camera movement is a pendular blur.

Display boilerplate MOTION PICTURE ASSOCIATION OF AMERICA WARNING at bottom of screen:

> Prolonged exposure to this cinematic effect
> may induce petit-mal seizures in some viewers.

Finally, MARK taps the Warden's left fist.

WARDEN opens fist and smooths crumpled note.

CLOSE SHOT of note:

> You wanna get high?

> M A R K
>
> *(coyly)*
>
> You . . . wanna?

WARDEN

Do you have any drugs?

MARK

(patting pockets of leather trousers)

I have one linty phenobarbital, which we could split. Or if you have any, uh, air freshener or Pam, we could, like, huff the butane . . .

WARDEN

(De haut en bas, but generous. Keep in mind that this is a woman from a dreary rust-belt town in the northwestern corner of Pennsylvania, who, as the child of emotionally withholding working-class parents, grew up with no sense of entitlement, but, motivated by a passion for discipline and punishment and impelled by sheer Polish-Catholic chutzpah, clawed her way up the New Jersey Department of Corrections hierarchy to become the first female warden of a men's maximum-security facility in the state's history. At this precise moment in the movie, she transcends the stereotype of the "compulsively glamorous yet tormented warden" and achieves a hard-won noblesse. It's worth doing hundreds of takes to achieve the finely nuanced delivery that this line requires.)

Hmmm . . . I think we can do a little better than that.

SLOW-MOTION TRACKING SHOT
as warden puts arm around Mark's shoulder and walks him to a locked room adjacent to her office.

We hear DONNA SUMMER'S "MACARTHUR PARK" (dance mix).

(The distance between the warden's office and the adjacent locked room is less than five feet, but the Giorgio Moroder dance mix of Summer's "MacArthur Park" is some eight and a half minutes long, so this TRACKING SHOT of the WAR-

DEN and MARK should be slowed down as much as possible to accommodate the FULL LENGTH of the SONG.

In addition to super slow motion, intercut long shots, detail shots, retracking dolly shots, high angles, wide angles, reverse angles, freeze frames, canted frames—whatever is necessary to stretch this five-second walk into an eight-and-a-half-minute shot coextensive with the sound track.)

CLOSE SHOT of sign on door:

Contraband Control Room

WARDEN opens door by entering code on mounted numeric keypad.

INT. CONTRABAND CONTROL ROOM

VARIOUS ANGLES showing cornucopia of confiscated material.

Impounded items are categorized according to methods of concealment and extraction:

- Body Cavity/Rectal
- Body Cavity/Oral
- Body Cavity/Other
- Swallowed/Excreted
- Swallowed/Stomach-Pump
- Miscellaneous

The extensive variety of goods rivals an in-flight duty-free catalog: glassine envelopes of heroin, cocaine, methcathinone and PCP; condoms and balloons filled with heroin and cocaine; amytals, Doridens, Fentanyls, Rohypnols, Stelazines, Trancopals; assorted blunts and spliffs; sundry crack vials and pipes; peyote buttons; N_2O cartridges; a plastic honey bear dispenser filled with chloral hydrate syrup; a 75-ml Anaïs Anaïs eau de toilette atomizer filled with liquid cocaine; liquefied LSD painted on the backs of postage stamps; liquefied Ecstasy painted onto the adhesive strip of a business reply envelope in an issue of *George* magazine; a Richard Simmons Deal-a-Meal card saturated with DMT; an 8"H x 10"W x 5"D Braun Pop-Up Hot Dog Cooker; a polished brass shower head with a 10-inch extension arm; a Black & Decker Xenon SnakeLight; etc.

Displayed in a special vitrine are those objects smuggled in for the pure aesthetic and conceptual pleasures of subterfuge. These items have no practical illicit value, and, beyond the allure of their exquisite craftsmanship, function metaphysically, as talismans of dissemblance: a Toblerone Honey & Almond Nougat chocolate bar in a Godiva Hazelnut and Cherry wrapper; a 200-ml Elizabeth Arden Visible Difference Refining Moisture Creme container filled with Christian Dior Svelte Cellulite Control Complex; and perhaps the most elegant and rigorous formal exercise in dissimulation—a 16-ounce bottle of Diet 7UP, emptied, filled with Diet Sprite, and meticulously resealed, including delicately resoldering the tiny metal flanges that clinch the screw-cap to the breakaway drop ring.

M A R K   (voice-over)

As I browse through this astonishing array of contraband, I can't help but marvel at the ingenuity of the inmates. In the Body Cavity/Rectal section, for instance—I can imagine someone smuggling in a wrapped shank, a box-cutter, or a honed nail swathed in plastic wrap, lubricated with Vaseline, and inserted in the rectum. But four 5-piece place settings of Bastille stainless-steel flatware? And a 7-piece Henckels Cutlery set (boning knife, paring knife, chef's knife, serrated bread knife, utility knife, and shears) in an 11-inch high, slotted beechwood block? Unbelievable! And in the Body Cavity/Oral section—I can see how, during a visit, a girlfriend could convey, through a kiss, a condom partially filled with heroin. But a 959-piece 3D Alsatian Village Puzzle? How? Piece by piece, one kiss per visit per week? Imagine the incarcerated hobbyist's Zen-like equanimity required to abide such glacial progress! And what if, on the other hand, the puzzle had been con-

veyed all at once? All 959 pieces. In one single passionate and protracted kiss! Wouldn't a supervising guard
have found it even slightly suspicious that as the
grotesquely distended cheeks of the girlfriend subsided,
the inmate's grotesquely swelled?

CLOSE SHOT OF ASSEMBLED 3-D ALSATIAN VILLAGE
PUZZLE, GLAZED IN SALIVA.

We hear ADAGIO INTRODUCTION TO FINALE OF
MOZART'S STRING QUARTET IN G MINOR and see

VARIOUS ANGLES of the scale-model village, its gables and
chimneys gleaming, as if sheathed in the ice and rime frost of an
Alsatian winter.

DISSOLVE TO:

INT. WARDEN'S OFFICE

MEDIUM SHOT OF WARDEN AND MARK DRINKING
"GRAVY" FROM PLASTIC SUNNY-D BOTTLE

(Gravy—also known as Red Sauce, Grave Juice, G, General G,
Gravity, Gravitas, Gravlax, Sh'ma, Sh'ma Yisroel, Rupture, Her-
nia, Enema, Portnoy, Mom, No Mom, I Can't Talk Now Mom,
Lodi, Wanamassa, Bogota, Leonia, Leona, Ivana, Kato, Seneca,
Pirandello, Brecht, Borscht, Won-Ton, Duck Sauce, Bug Juice,
Booger Juice, Oyster Stew, White Clam, Pus, Pee, Elle, Allure,
Glamour, Harper's Bazaar, Harper's, Atlantic, Pacific, Cortez,
Stout Cortez, John, Jackie, Lady Bird, Pat, Checkers, Chess,
Go, Come, Cream, Milk, Half & Half, Comme Ci Comme Ça,
Après Moi Le Déluge, Louis Louis, and Knob—is a psychedelic
beverage pharmacologically analogous to ayahuasca, the pan-
Amazonian hallucinogenic potion made from the alkaloid-rich
bark of the *Banisteriopsis caapi* vine and various admixture plants
including *Psychotria carthaginensis, P. viridis, Tetrapterys methystica,*
and *Banisteriopsis rusbyana,* the leaves and stems of which contain
large amounts of DMT.
    A black, viscous liquid with the surface iridescence of motor
oil, Gravy is made from scrapings of the outer bark of the *Banis-*

teriopsis lutum vine, which is indigenous to the northeastern United States and thrives especially in areas downstream of pulp and paper mills that are contaminated with effluent containing high concentrations of polychlorinated biphenyls (PCBs). Gravy also consists of a crucial admixture plant, *Phalaris dromos,* a reed grass species that grows near stadiums and indoor sports arenas, particularly in the dioxin-saturated marshy areas of Queens, Long Island, and New Jersey. The leaves and stalks of this lavender marsh grass contain several psychoactive tryptamines including the very short-acting 5-methoxy-DMT.)

CLOSE SHOT OF MARK, seated, motionless, silently experiencing the hallucinogenic effects of the Gravy.

Aside from an initial 90-second sequence at the onset of the drugs' effect, during which his eyeballs twitch rapidly beneath closed lids, and he's then stricken with transient Bell's palsy with paralysis of the facial nerve causing weakness of the muscles in the left side of his face and an inability to close the left eye, superseded by a paroxysm of facial tics—involuntary grimaces, pouts, cracking of the temporomandibular joints, gaping rictus, etc.—accompanied by a spasm of the sternomastoid muscle that forcibly wrenches his head up over the right shoulder, followed by a simultaneous episode of exophthalmos—a protrusion of the eyeballs from their sockets—and heterotropic nystagmus—rapid involuntary movements of the eyes first from side to side, then up and down, and then one eye moving from side to side as the other moves up and down, and then one eye spinning clockwise as the other spins counterclockwise, and culminating in violent undulations of the cheeks akin to those experienced by subjects in G-force experiments, MARK's face is impassive throughout.

(CASTING NOTE: If the actor playing the role of MARK is incapable of achieving some of the foregoing ophthalmic effects, a stuntman may be required for this particular shot.)

Although, in the middle of the following voice-over, the camera pans to a brief close shot of the warden, who is similarly seden-

tary, mute, eyes either shut or gazing into the middle distance
as she experiences her own hallucinations, we are otherwise
locked into a head-shot of Mark for the five-minute duration of
the Gravy's peak effect.

MARK   (voice-over)

I know, from having seen Claude Lévi-Strauss and Alicia
Silverstone on *The Charlie Rose Show,* that certain drugs,
particularly the botanically derived hallucinogens used
by shamanistic tribal societies in South America, induce
a remarkably wide incidence of consistent and specific
images—geometrical patterns, jaguars, tigers, anacon-
das, naked sorceresses, the color blue, phantasmagorical
cities, etc. In that regard, I'd be curious to know if my
Gravy experience is similar to those that other people
might have had; i.e., I wonder if these are the archetypal
Gravy motifs encountered by everyone who does the
drug:
    First, I become fixated on the word *mohair.*
    Then, every surface in the room is overlaid with
checkerboards of neon orange, lime green, and hot pink,
and patterns like shattered stained-glass windows of
plum and magenta.
    I begin to hear a high-pitched carrier tone, I'd say
about 600 Hz. And soon I hear a clicking sound, like
call-waiting. I realize that someone or something is trying to contact me and that I must "free the line," in
other words, sever and jettison my habituated consciousness in order to make myself available to more advanced
modes of knowledge.
    Stucco patterns detach themselves from the ceiling,
hover in the air, and reconfigure themselves into a vault-
ing dome of dazzling microelectronic circuitry. The floor
melts into a percolating ooze of filamentous blue-green
algae. The walls are animated Paleolithic cave murals,
alive with yellow ochre and hematite bison and ibexes. I

discern a faint melismatic voice, like a call to prayer from a distant minaret, but originating seemingly from within the huge Meridian DSP-6000 speaker suspended from ceiling brackets at the far end of the room.

Suddenly I sense that I am in the presence of a host. A palpable, yet transcendent entity—ubiquitous, omniscient, and eternal.

The entity smiles at me and says: "Yes, don't you see now how we are absolutely *not* all part of the same whole. Your ultimate spiritual value is based on your body-fat percentage, how much money you make, and how well you do on tests."

I smile to myself. I suppose this realization may be startling to some people, but it happens to be the basis of my own personal cosmology, so I am pleased. I'm perfectly at peace. Somewhere inside, intuitively, I knew the world was always like this—that the soul of every sentient life-form is locked into a rigid and immutable hierarchy based primarily on physical appearance, scholastic aptitude, and salary—but I lacked the divine insight to actually prove it. Blissfully, the Gravy has provided me with the incontrovertible corroboration I've been seeking for so long.

The entity departs.

I now have the following succession of stunning personal revelations:

- A moment comes in the life of every man or woman when he or she must decide whether to be an average middle-class American who adheres to moderate political views and believes in some form of "higher power," or a drunken, pork-eating, whoremongering infidel.

- The coolest videos to watch when you're high are: *Caligula, Necrophagous Insects of the Borneo Rain Forest,* and *The Red Army Kegel Exercise Video.*

- Although the 900-number hotline psychic was correct in gleaning that I was put on earth to provide an anodyne to sorrow with comedy rooted in the indignities of corporeality, and that I will have no friends or loved ones—just servants, subordinates, and sexual partners—she was mistaken in her prediction that I will die in a San Diego hospital of kidney failure following aneurysm surgery. I will die violently in prison.

- The world record for hyperthermophyllic bacteria—presently held by *Pyrolobus fumarius,* which live near hot deep-sea vents at temperatures of up to 113° Celsius (235°F)—is, like all records, *made to be broken.*

- My idea for a television series about a wandering, samurai-errant-like tetherball player, who travels through the Berkshires and Adirondacks from summer camp to summer camp, solving campers' problems by defeating bullies and malefactors at tetherball, may be fundamentally flawed.

    I originally thought of pitching it as a sort of *Kung Fu*–like concept, except that instead of a mastery of the martial arts, the hero possesses a mastery of the arcane skills and profound philosophy of tetherball. I'd worked up a pilot episode in which our itinerant protagonist arrives at this particular summer camp and finds a morbidly shy, agoraphobic boy who's being mercilessly tormented by a sadistic bunkmate who takes special delight in ridiculing the unfortunate boy about his chronic bed-wetting. The bully is a brawny, swaggering, privileged loudmouth who thinks he's God's gift because his father owns a chain of Chi-Chi's–like Mexican restaurants across the country. Although the bed wetter has several insufferable qualities, including a purse-lipped piety that's particularly repellent in a 9-year-old, he exhibits admirable determination and courage in pursuing his two great

passions: art nouveau windows and Hummel collect-
ing. After a futile attempt at persuading the trouble-
maker to desist in persecuting the enuretic Hummel
maven, the hero—cryptically known only as "Teth-
Ba"—challenges him to a tetherball match in front of
the entire camp. And, of course, in a pyrotechnic display that's both brutal and balletic, he vanquishes
him—in slow motion, his sweat misting iridescently
in the midsummer sun. The campers, who at first
watch in stunned silence, explode in rapturous jubila-
tion. And the following morning, as reveille sounds,
the afflicted child—for the first time in his life—
wakes up triumphantly in a dry bed. And—in a
delightfully arch stroke of poetic justice—the humili-
ated bully awakens in a clammy pool of his own
urine.

Teth-Ba turns down an invitation to stay the
weekend for a mixer with nearby Camp Bon Temps
Macoutes, a Duvalierist summer camp for overweight
girls, whose chubby, wild-eyed camperettes are said to
be among the most licentious in the entire Lake Little
Lake region, and he unassumingly sets off for parts
unknown.

The problem with the concept—which I can now
see clearly for the first time, thanks to my drug-
induced mental acuity—is that I may not be able to
come up with enough crises that are resolvable via
tetherball to sustain a series through an entire season.

Perhaps I should reconceptualize the pilot as a
stand-alone, full-length, made-for-TV feature . . .

The ellipses of that final epiphany swell to the size
of three bowling balls, which float before my eyes and
burst in sequence, like a visual countdown—three,
two, one.

And I am now launched on an incredible out-of-
body journey.

I am not exactly sure how to interpret the meaning of this journey. Perhaps the symbolism of the "difficult passage" represents an attempt to transcend opposites, to abolish the polarity typical of the human condition in order to attain to ultimate reality, to restore the "communicability" that existed primordially between this world and heaven. I'm not sure. But I'd be curious to know if other people who've taken Gravy have experienced a similar sort of transmigration. Here's a brief summary:

I am suddenly flying through the air, moving at great speeds, tens of thousands of feet above the ground. It's terrifying. I pass a flushed, sinewy woman furiously pedaling a LifeCycle as she reads Dr. Charisse Goldberger's runaway bestseller *Why Big, Semiliterate, Uncircumcised Men Make the Best Lovers (And How We've Known It All Along),* while listening on her Walkman to an audio-book, *Wake Me Up When the Zionist Entity Is Liquidated: Sheik Abdel Hassan Easton Ellis's Courageous Battle With Chronic Fatigue Syndrome.* And I'm thinking to myself, that name's gotta be a joke—Sheik Abdel Hassan Easton Ellis. And then, without warning, I begin plummeting to earth. I shut my eyes and brace myself for fatal impact. But when I open my eyes, I'm not only walking safely on the ground, I'm in a Kenneth Cole shoe commercial with various diplomats like Strobe Talbot and Warren Christopher. The premise of the commercial is that we're trying to negotiate the release of Michael Eisner and Joe Roth, who've been taken hostage by Amish fanatics who are trying to stop Disney from producing a Paul Verhoeven–Joe Eszterhas erotic thriller about "bundling." We're attempting to traverse a field covered with what appear to be cow pies, but are actually land mines. In our Kenneth Cole shoes (and, for some reason, bright yellow rubber minidresses slit open in the back like hospital gowns), we dance jauntily around the explosive cow pies à la Gene Kelly, but one by one each of us is blown up, until I'm the only one left. I pirouette several times and then try to vault over a clutch of mines, but there's an explosion that projects me into the air.

I'm flying again. And again, I approach the woman on the LifeCycle, this time as I hurtle in the opposite direction.

"Don't I look awesome in my boyfriend's 'Greek Week' T-shirt?" she asks.

And then she doffs the shirt and casts off her sports bra.

Deploying various aeronautical techniques, including using my arms as rotors and churning them about perpendicular axes, and forcibly exhaling from my mouth for retrothrust, I'm able to decelerate from a velocity of about Mach 2 to a complete standstill.

I'm hovering now, and watching her breasts undulate in rhythm with her strenuous pedaling.

We are enveloped in a thick cumulus cloud.

And when we emerge, she is holding my stiff penis in her hand. I've lost the power of flight, and I am dangling by my erection from her grip, some 36,000 feet above the ground. It's not painful, as one might expect, but there's definitely a significant amount of strain. But it's a very pleasurable strain. And I know that if she lets go of me, I'll fall out of the sky. But I feel very peaceful. Very dreamy. There we are, suspended in the perfectly empty azure void, which is absolutely quiet except for the sound of her pedaling and the occasional electronic chirp (she's doing a "hill program" on her LifeCycle, and whenever she completes a "hill," the display panel emits a short little beep).

And I want to ejaculate, but I know that if I do, I'll become flaccid and shrink, and there won't be enough for her to hold on to, and I'll fall. And I'm also concerned that if I fall, I'll hit innocent people on the ground and perhaps kill them.

But then I have another powerful revelation—one that perhaps every male in every species has in his life,

and one that might very well mark the passage from
boy- to manhood. I realize that at this moment, ejacu-
lating takes precedence over absolutely everything else
in the world, including the death of innocent people.
I realize that this overwhelming, heedless desire to
ejaculate right now so dwarfs any other consideration,
including my own death and the death or grievous
injury of others, that I'm incapable of resisting it and
unwilling to even try. And I succumb. It's literally a
letting go. A release. A surrender. A fall. A fall from
grace.

And I begin to plunge again.

This descent is the stuff of nightmares—the terror
excruciating, maddening. The acceleration of the free-
fall seems to produce an internal decompression; I
have the sensation of a vacuum in my hollow organs,
cavities, and sinuses. Adrenaline spews across my nervous system, a gelid effervescence of animal panic.

I shut my eyes and cover them with both my
hands.

And then, after what seems like hours and hours
of falling, I finally open them . . .

I'm in the warden's office.

I'm seated on the couch.

And now I experience a steady return to baseline
consciousness. The neon checkerboard patterns and
microelectronic overlays, the Paleolithic imagery and
blue-green ooze all revert back into familiar aspects of
the room. And the keening carrier tone fades to silence.

WARDEN

Pretty intense, huh?

MARK   (voice-over)

I checked my watch. From the time we returned from
the Contraband Control Room and drank the Gravy to
now, *only thirty seconds had passed!*

Part of me wanted so much to profusely expatiate upon this bewildering, implosive contraction of time; to concoct some erudite correspondence—to propose, for instance, that it was like not only seeing your entire life flash before your eyes in an instant, but like experiencing the entirety of *Homo sapiens* phylogeny, as narrated by some jabbering Dominican A.M. drive-time merengue DJ, in the time it takes for an air bag to inflate in a 90-mile-an-hour head-on collision (and you're in, like, one of those little Suzuki Sidekicks and the other vehicle is, like, a fucking Amtrak locomotive); part of me desperately wanted to somehow articulate to her my sense of awe and wonder that, from a warm broth of prebiotic molecules splashed up on Precambrian rocks and baked in the sun some 4 billion years ago, three pounds of deeply fissured neural tissue could evolve—the human brain—capable of apprehending—as evidenced by my own dumbfounding epiphanies (e.g., the karmic and eschatological merits of body-fat composition and LSAT scores, etc.)—not only the most recondite principles of the physical universe, but the origins, structure, procedures and modalities of consciousness itself.

But all I said was . . .

CLOSE-SHOT of MARK

MARK

It was weird . . . like a video.

WARDEN

Are you OK?

MARK

I feel kinda . . . kinda like I'm still . . . falling.

WARDEN

Post-lapsarian Stress Disorder, n'est-ce pas?

SUBTITLE: Post-lapsarian Stress Disorder, isn't it?

MARK

Uh . . . peut-être.

SUBTITLE: Uh . . . maybe.

WARDEN

Venge-toi, punis-moi d'un odieux amour.
Digne fils du héros qui t'a donné le jour,
délivre l'univers d'un monstre qui t'irrite.

SUBTITLE: You were blown into the sky by an exploding cow pie, a mythological gym siren gave you a hand job, and then you experienced a terrifying plunge to earth, yes?

MARK

Madame, pardonnez. J'avoue, en rougissant,
Que j'accusais à tort un discours innocent.
Ma honte ne peut plus soutenir vontre vue.

SUBTITLE: Yeah . . . pretty much. Whatever.

WARDEN gets corkscrew and two wineglasses from cabinet, and sits back down on couch. She arranges an assortment of pills—Fentanyls, Roxanols, and Demerols—on an antique Persian brass tea-glass coaster, opens a bottle of wine, and lights a hollowed-out Phillies blunt filled with marijuana.

She takes a long hit and passes the blunt to MARK.

WARDEN

Glass of wine? It'll help cushion the fall.

MARK

(Exhaling thick plume of smoke)

Uh . . . sure. What is it?

WARDEN

It's a white Burgundy—a '73 Meursault-Charmes from the Domaine Roulot.

She pours, and then raises her glass in the air.

WARDEN

To Vincent and Lenore DiGiacomo.

MARK

To Vincent and Lenore DiGiacomo—without whose
wise, generous, and indefatigable support, the screen-
writing aspirations of seventh, eighth, and ninth graders
at Maplewood Junior High School might well go unful-
filled. We thank you from the bottoms of our hearts and
will never forget your unswerving commitment to this
venerable art form.

They click glasses and sip.

MARK grimaces and spews wine back into his glass.

MARK

(indignant)

It's hot! Shouldn't a white Burgundy be served chilled?

WARDEN

Oh, it's still warm? I'm sorry about that. We just pulled
it from a convict less than an hour ago, and I never had
a chance to get it in the fridge.

MARK takes bottle and reads affixed Contraband Control label.

INSERT SHOT of label:

Contraband Control Number: 56113
Confiscation: 5/21/96, 1630 hours
Inmate 77-64-0835
Body Cavity/Rectal

WARDEN

You want to send it back?

He tries another sip, rolls it in his mouth, and shrugs.

MARK

Nuh-uh. I guess it's good.
*(pointing to the two huge Meridian DSP-8000
speakers—each 52" by 21" by 27"—suspended
in opposite corners across the room)*
How much does each of those weigh?

WARDEN

About 300 pounds.

MARK

No fuckin' way!! What's keeping them up? It looks like
they're just floating there.

WARDEN gets up from couch, rummages through desk drawer,
and returns to couch, having retrieved Oshimitsu Polymers
America Corp. product brochure.

WARDEN

(reading from brochure)

"Materials engineers have hypothesized that a single
strand of orb-weaving spider silk, as thick as clothesline,
could actually stop the Concord supersonic transport in
flight!

"Oshimitsu Polymers America Corporation—a subsidiary of Shimazaki Chemical Company—has created a
synthetic spider silk that has greater tensile strength
than steel and is capable of supporting audio speakers of
any weight.

"Using sophisticated computer simulation techniques and recombinant DNA technology, Oshimitsu
scientists have been able to utilize the unparalleled ingenuity of the biosynthetic process by controlling polymer
sequence and chain length to produce analogs of the natural silk proteins.

"Synthetic Spider-Silk Speaker-Suspension Line® is
one of the many innovative synthetic fiber products that

have made Oshimitsu Polymers America internationally recognized as the preeminent pioneer in advanced materials development.

"Because of their light weight, strength, and ductility, Oshimitsu synthetic biopolymer fibers may also have applications in military and commercial satellites and aircraft, earthquake-resistant suspension-bridge cables, and huge synthetic fiber-mesh space-nets designed to snare and divert errant asteroids and protect the earth from catastrophic and potentially species-threatening collisions.

"Oshimitsu Polymers America—committed to facilitating our increasingly complex synthetic fiber needs into the 21st century."

M A R K

That is *so* cool! How can I get more information about Oshimitsu Synthetic Spider-Silk Speaker-Suspension Line® and learn how other Oshimitsu synthetic biopolymer products can help enhance my home theater?

OVER-THE-SHOULDER SHOT of Warden circling phone number in catalog.

ZOOM in until phone number fills screen:

1-800-POLYMER

W A R D E N

Just call 1-800-POLYMER. An Oshimitsu Polymers America customer service representative is waiting to answer any questions you might have about how Oshimitsu's innovative line of biopolymer products can make your home theater the very best that it can be.

COMPUTER-ANIMATED OSHIMITSU LOGO SEQUENCE (8 seconds):

- We hear hyperkinetic BONGO RHYTHM.
- Phone number detaches itself and rises from catalog page, which dissolves, leaving numerals on empty cool-blue background (0.75 sec.).
- Numerals break into rods and spheres, which then arrange themselves into polymer chain (1.50 sec.).
- Polymer chain metamorphoses into fibers, and then fibers into spider's web (2.25 sec.).
- Web becomes asteroid net, which snares massive meteor hurtling toward earth and slings it harmlessly into deep space (3.00 sec.).
- Asteroid net contracts, elongates, and divides into suspension-bridge cables spanning serpentine river (3.75 sec.).
- Suspension-bridge cables metamorphose into speaker suspension lines supporting huge loudspeaker over teeming indoor arena (4.50 sec.).
- Speaker and suspension line remain foregrounded as indoor arena dissolves into sumptuous penthouse apartment with skyline view and amorous couple on sofa (5.25 sec.).
- Penthouse apartment, speaker and couple dissolve back into cool-blue background (5.75 sec.).
- Speaker suspension line breaks into rods and spheres (6.25 sec.).
- Rods and spheres reconfigure into Oshimitsu Polymers America LOGO. Bongo solo crescendos and abruptly ends—and we hear astringent KOTO ARPEGGIO. Audio track and animation are synchronized so that koto arpeggio sounds at precise instant that logo coalesces (7.00 sec.).
- HOLD LOGO for full second and dissolve (8.00 sec.).

WARDEN takes quick hit from blunt and proffers it and tea coaster with pill assortment to MARK.

MARK sticks blunt in mouth and, squinting through smoke, chooses two Demerols, and washes them down with a mouthful of tepid Meursault-Charmes.

WARDEN selects a single Fentanyl, tilts her head back, whacks the 2-mg tablet toward the back of her throat, and gulps it down dry.

WARDEN

What kind of sound system do *you* have?

MARK

In my room?

WARDEN

(nonchalantly wanton, pupils dilated, absently singeing armpit stubble with lit end of blunt)

Yeah.

MARK

(momentarily lost in pagan reveries)

Huh?

WARDEN

(also having lost her train of thought)

What do you think of Guiliani banning the Calvin Klein fist-fucking billboards?

MARK

(avoiding politics)

Did you ever look at De Kooning's Alzheimer paintings on glue?

WARDEN

Now I remember what I was asking you . . . What kind of sound system do you have? In your room.

MARK

I have a Sherwood RV7050R receiver, a Yamaha CDC-655 CD player, and a pair of Bose speakers.

WARDEN

Which Bose?

MARK

The Acoustimass 5 Series.

WARDEN

Excellent speakers.

MARK

They're OK . . . I got them as a gift for acing my Intro-duction to Recursive Function Theory final. They're nothing compared to those things, though . . . *(marveling at the suspended Meridians).* Those are motherfuckin' monsters!

CAMERA DOLLIES toward and then CRANES out through window.

VARIOUS ANGLES of honking Canada geese banking in crimson-streaked crepuscular sky over prison.

WARDEN   (off-screen)

What are you running from your receiver to your speakers?

MARK   (off-screen)

XLO ER-12. Braided construction.

WARDEN   (off-screen)

Tinned ends?

MARK   (off-screen)

Spade banana pin.

W A R D E N   (off-screen)

Excellent. What do you clean your CDs with?

M A R K   (off-screen)

Acoustic Research Fiber-Optic Lapping Slurry. And if they're really scuzzy, I have a Marantz KR-II CD Gamma Irradia-tion Deck.

W A R D E N   (off-screen)

What do you use to dust your components?

M A R K   (off-screen)

For the CD player, I use Phase Technology Electrostatic Gauze, and for the receiver, a Hitachi BPA-500 Isopropyl-Impregnated Cheesecloth.

W A R D E N   (off-screen)

How about for your hands?

M A R K   (off-screen)

Klipsch Chlorhexidine Gluconate Audiophile Scrub.

W A R D E N   (off-screen)

What do you dry them with?

M A R K   (off-screen)

I'd always used the Polk Audio NS7 Post-Lavage Moisture Management System, but lately I like the Cambridge Soundworks Egyptian Cotton Pile Matrix X-130 Ablution Residue Stanching Shammy.

W A R D E N   (off-screen)

The S Series?

M A R K   (off-screen)

The SE.

WARDEN   (off-screen)

That's a nice towel.

PULL-BACK SHOT—using fiberoptic endoscope—beginning in WARDEN'S STOMACH, moving slowly up esophagus, and emerging from mouth, and then widening into shot of WARDEN and MARK, seated on couch, drinking Meursault-Charmes and smoking blunt.

(If the actress playing the role of the WARDEN finds the experience of having the endoscope passed in through her mouth and down into her stomach too much of an ordeal, an injection of diazepam is recommended to relax her.

(If, despite the diazepam injection, the actress still finds the scope excessively uncomfortable, a stuntwoman may be necessary to accomplish this shot.

(Be very careful when selecting the stuntwoman that the inside of her stomach and esophageal lining resemble the stomach cavity and esophagus of the actress.

(Recently, in the film *My Angel's Bitter Kiss,* a stuntwoman was used for a pull-back shot that was to have originated in Michelle Pfeiffer's duodenum. When the movie was shown to test audiences, it was so obvious that this was *not* the duodenum of Michelle Pfeiffer that—despite the intended poignancy of the scene—the theater erupted into derisive laughter. The entire sequence had to be hastily reshot at great additional expense.

(If, in the course of the pull-back shot, any polyps are found, they might as well be removed, since you're in there anyway. Snip or vaporize polyps using the diathermy snare or laser attached to the endoscope head—this is assuming, of course, that the actress or stuntwoman has signed the appropriate SAG release forms.)

WARDEN

So, what's your room like?

MARK

Pale colors, a good amount of bare floor, and a light and airy treatment at the windows.

When I turned 13, my mom and I decided to completely redo the room because the whole prepubescent Power Ranger/Michael Jordan thing had gotten so stale. And when we sat down and started talking about what we wanted to do, I initially envisioned a cross between the hunting lodge of Prince Augustus of Hanover in Upper Austria and a Level 4 Biohazard Decontamination Chamber. I wanted that mix of virile Bavarian coziness—that kind of very traditional sylvan gemütlichkeit—and a more hyperreal, more cyber-tea-ceremony, more sort of post-plague digital-necropolis feel. But it's become *so* much more eclectic than that. I am *not* a proponent of the monolithic style. I think it's just so wrong to try to force one's naturally mercurial aesthetic temperament into a single procrustean stylistic formula. . . .

But, gosh, if I had to characterize the room . . .

I'd say that it's a living space that, in its restraint, clarity, and openness, is timeless. I'd describe its distinguishing features as superb proportion, wonderful scale, elegant simplicity, and marvelous objects. I'd call it a simple, uncluttered space designed with equal measures of panache and pragmatism for a 13-year-old boy to do the basic things that a 13-year-old boy does—talk on the phone, surf the net, get high, watch TV, listen to music, and masturbate.

I've done the walls in Benjamin Moore Super White and on one I've hung lengths of sheer muslin from a row of small hooks a few inches below the ceiling. But a white room *must* be anchored by something dark, or it just floats away. So that's what motivated my large pieces. I've got a cherry veneer queen sleigh bed with a waffle-weave duvet cover, I've got a Shaker-style enter-

tainment armoire, and I've updated two Directoire arm-
chairs with ecru-and-black leaf-print cotton slipcovers.
Those are the pieces that give the room what I call
ballast.

Then, of course, I have a stainless steel rack of
leather motorcross trousers.

And I have a steel-and-glass vitrine for my objets
d'art.

WARDEN

What kind of objets d'art do you have?

MARK

I have some pretty cool stuff that my dad brought me. I
have a scrimshaw engraving tool from Nantucket. I have
a Ming Dynasty jade angel-dust urn, a Kangxi-period
porcelain angel-dust ladle, and a 17th-century English
sterling-silver and hobnail cut-glass angel-dust flacon. I
have a foot-long lozenge-shaped piece of vitrified
Ukrainian radioactive military waste. And I have a
defused Italian Valmara-69 antipersonnel fragmentation
mine and a Russian PFM-1 "butterfly" mine, which I
was going to write a story about once, but never got
around to—which is kind of typical of me. . . .

WARDEN

A story about a mine?

MARK

Uh-huh. In Mrs. Zimmer's English class we read a story
by Nathaniel Hawthorne called "The Artist of the Beautiful," which takes place in New England in, like, the
1830s, and it's about this guy Owen Warland who's this
wimpy genius who's supposed to be a watchmaker but
spends all his time working on this beautiful, intricate
mechanical butterfly, and he's in love with a woman by
the name of Annie Hovenden who's not really in love
with him because I think she figures he's too wimpy and

quixotic and he'll never amount to much career-wise, and she ends up marrying this stupid albeit totally buff blacksmith named Robert Danforth and they have a kid, and at the end of the story the kid accidentally crushes the mechanical butterfly.

Do you get what it means?

WARDEN

I'm not quite sure.

MARK

It's basically about how artists are too delicate to exist in a world where the ability to earn a living and having a good body are considered, like, the most important things. So, y'know what butterfly mines are?

WARDEN

Nope.

MARK

They're antipersonnel mines, but they're released from helicopters and they have little wings that enable them to glide to the ground. The Soviets dropped a ton of them on Afghanistan. They explode when cumulative pressure is applied to the wings.

So I had this idea to do a remake of "The Artist of the Beautiful" where, instead of just making this exquisite mechanical butterfly, Owen Warland makes one of these PFM-1 butterfly mines, and at the end when the kid starts playing with it, his father takes it away from him and, not being the brightest guy in the world, he starts pulling on its wings and it explodes and blows his hands off, and Annie, who's nothing if not pragmatic, realizes that Danforth's blacksmithing days are over and she finally acknowledges that maybe Owen has a future after all—apparently as a munitions expert—and leaves her maimed husband for the Artist of the Beautiful, and they live, like, happily ever after.

See, at least in my version the reader would get some satisfaction. But since I never got around to actually writing it . . .

WARDEN

Do you read a lot?

MARK

Primarily books and magazines about art.

When I first started masturbating, I'd look at the photographs in some of my mother's books, most frequently one called *Our Bodies, Our Selves.*

WARDEN

Were you too young to appreciate the irony of having appropriated a classic feminist reference for use as a male adolescent stroke book?

MARK

Heavens yes, I was much too young! You have to remember, this was almost two years ago.

Anyway, one day my father had a talk with me and he said since you've reached the age where you're going to be spending so much time in your room masturbating, you should have books with color plate reproductions of nudes painted by the world's greatest artists, instead of having to drool over these clinical photographs designed to teach women to love their own labia. And he was right. You can say what you want about my father's indiscretions, but he was a very caring, enlightened parent.

WARDEN

So what were your favorite paintings?

MARK

For jerking off? At first I liked Velázquez's *Venus and Cupid,* Alexandre Cabanel's *The Birth of Venus,* Rubens's

The Judgment of Paris, Ingres's *Grande Odalisque,* Manet's *Olympia . . .*

VARIOUS ANGLES of MARK gesticulating animatedly, as he expatiates on various masterpieces ranging from the High Renaissance and Baroque eras to the pointillist and post-impressionist movements, sometimes assuming the languid poses of the nude subjects of the paintings, sometimes vividly pantomiming a painter in the throes of his work in order to better illustrate some bravura effect—a passage, perhaps, of virtuosic impasto or frankly voluptuous chiaroscuro.

Over this, we HEAR

> MARK   (voice-over)
>
> I'm not sure what it was that made me feel so comfortable discussing subjects such as art and masturbation with her. Certainly the drugs and the wine had relaxed me, made me less reserved, given me an enhanced feeling of self-assurance . . . but also I felt that I was getting to know her so much better now as a person. At first she was just The Imperiously Voluptuous Warden. And she was obviously, like, preternaturally brilliant—I mean, she was one of the most successful women in the entire New Jersey state penal system. So it was like being in the presence of a movie star in the sense that she initially seemed so intimidating and inaccessible. And I certainly never ever thought for a second that she'd respond positively to my notes. And when she did, I was absolutely terrified. But then she seemed so genuinely interested in my sound system and in my room . . . and I began to find it easier and easier to talk openly with her about almost anything.

NEW ANGLE of MARK

> MARK
>
> . . . but then my taste started evolving beyond mimetic art, beyond the figurative and representational, beyond

naturalistic renditions of nude women, actually beyond
any biomorphic imagery at all. And I arrived at this rev-
elatory and—to me—profound appreciation of pure
abstraction. The very notion of an abstract painting done
by a woman became a huge turn-on. And that's when I
started using paintings by Helen Frankenthaler, Joan
Mitchell, Agnes Martin, Elizabeth Murray, Jennifer
Bartlett, early Jo Baer, Rebecca Purdum . . .

WARDEN

It seems to me an unusually sophisticated autoerotic
deployment of art for someone your age—eschewing
woman-as-subject-matter for woman-as-generative-
agent.

MARK

I think it was just an inevitable consequence of intellectual and psychosexual maturation. I was twelve, I was
becoming very active onanistically, and I was reading all
the classic criticism of Clement Greenberg and then
people like Michael Fried, E. C. Goossen, Sandler,
Alloway, Perreault, Barbara Rose, Lucy Lippard, and my
entire notion of what constituted erotic visual content
changed radically.

WARDEN

Are there certain paintings that you find particularly
provocative?

MARK

Absolutely! There's a Jo Baer painting, *Untitled (Double
Bar Diptych—Green and Red),* which is two panels with
vertical black bars parallel to each side, a thin red or
green line limning the inner edge, and recapitulating
the shape, of each bar . . . There's an Agnes Martin,
Untitled #9, which is a composition of contrasting hori-
zontal brick-red and sky-blue bands separated by much

narrower bands of flat white . . . A fleeting glimpse of either painting gives me a frightful hard-on.

WARDEN

I find it simply amazing . . . that you actually masturbate looking at abstract paintings.

MARK

Abstract paintings *by women.* Once I got an erection looking at a painting, and then I realized that it was a Frank Stella, and for a while I thought I might be homosexual. But it never happened again.

WARDEN

Do you have paintings up on your walls—I mean like reproductions, prints, posters?

MARK

Nuh-uh. I have one wall reserved for posters, but it's all Bougainvillean tetherball players.
    Do you follow Bougainvillean tetherball at all?

ANGLE ON WARDEN FROM MARK'S POV

WARDEN

No.

CUT TO INSERT SHOT of MARK'S REFLECTION in silver PILL TRAY

MARK

Do you know anything about International Grand-Prix Tetherball or the Melanesian tetherball circuit?

WARDEN

No.

CUT TO metallic blue HOUSEFLY alighting on MARK'S WINEGLASS and CIRCUMAMBULATING RIM

MARK   (off-screen)

Have you ever watched a professional tetherball match
on television?

COMPOUND-EYE SHOT of WARDEN from FLY'S POV

WARDEN

No.

COMPOUND-EYE PAN to MARK as FLY FOLLOWS
CONVERSATION

MARK

Have you ever listened to a professional tetherball match
on the radio?

COMPOUND-EYE PAN to WARDEN

WARDEN

No.

COMPOUND-EYE PAN back to MARK

MARK

Have you ever played tetherball?

EXTREME COMPOUND-EYE CLOSE-UP OF WARDEN
as she takes mental inventory of all the games and sports she's
ever played: Candyland, hopscotch, the home-version *Wheel of
Fortune,* mumblety-peg, video boccie; *Doom, Mortal Kombat,* and
Gianni Isotope; the pommel horse, calf-roping, spelunking, and
skeet shooting; being carpooled to Thai kick-boxing lessons on
Tuesday afternoons, and increasingly esoteric martial arts like
Filipino PVC Vent-Pipe Fighting and Okinawan "Mason-Style"
Jukendo, a lethal form of self-defense in which bricks, mortar,
and a trowel are used to subdue and sometimes entomb your
assailant; there were the five-hour bus rides to Washington
Heights each Thursday night for Dominican cockfighting
classes; the short-lived infatuation with falconry; that semester
abroad in the Transvaal, hunting springbok with chloroform-

infused handkerchiefs; the salmon-roe eating contests; the silly
nursing-school sorority contrast-media drinking games, guzzling shot after shot of barium sulfate; and then, of course, the
bearbaiting, the Russian roulette, the elevator surfing . . . but
never tetherball.

WARDEN

No.

CLOSE SHOT of MARK FILLIPPING FLY INTO HIS WINE

CUT TO FLY'S POV
as it thrashes and sinks in wine.

We see its life flash before its compound eyes—a rapid chrono-
logical montage of highlights—feeding on rotting hamburger
meat in a cafeteria Dumpster with several hundred other wrig-
gling white larvae, barely eluding the bifurcated tongue of a
skink at some miasmic fen in Manahawkin, buzzing around various mounds of garbage and excrement, laying several hundred
eggs in the putrefying viscera of some unidentifiable roadkill,
more mounds of manure and miscellaneous heaps of rancid offal,
and finally, flying toward the window of the warden's office after
the olfactory receptors on its antennae detect wafting sugar molecules from the evaporating white Burgundy . . .

And then FADE TO BLACK.

FADE IN on MEDIUM SHOT of MARK and WARDEN

MARK

Well, you know what it is, right? There's a ball suspended by a string—or a *tether*—from an upright pole,
and the object for each player is to wrap the tether
around the pole by striking the ball in the opposite
direction from his opponent. See?

Now, in the United States, there's no real organized
tetherball. You find tetherball poles occasionally in
schoolyards and playgrounds and at summer camps, but
there aren't any, like, pee-wee or little leagues, or high

school or college teams, or anything like that. It was only at the last Olympics that we even sent a squad, and, of course, we totally sucked. And professional tetherball doesn't exist at all in this country.

But in Bougainville— Do you know where Bougainville is?

WARDEN

Nope.

MARK

It's part of Papua New Guinea, but it's one of the Solomon Islands—it's actually the largest of the Solomon Islands.

In that whole part of the South Pacific—what's called Melanesia, which also includes Vanuatu, New Caledonia, Fiji—tetherball is *the* game. But *especially* in Bougainville. I mean, tetherball in Bougainville is like soccer in Italy. It's like football in Texas.

And that's what every kid from Bougainville wants to be when he grows up—a tetherball star.

And so, basically, Bougainvillean players completely dominate international tetherball. Just to give you an idea of how ascendant they are in this sport, of this year's eight Grand Prix tournaments, Bougainvilleans won seven, and in the past three Summer Olympic Games since tetherball was made a medal sport, Bougainvillean competitors have captured *all* 18 medals—the men's and women's gold, silver, and bronze in each Olympics. Then there's the Ma Ling Master's Tournament—Ma Ling is a Japanese canned-goods company that is very big in the Solomon Islands, your canned mackerel, canned luncheon meat, canned chicken feet, corned beef, goose meat in gravy, lichees in syrup— it's the final tournament of the tour and it's only open to players who've won a Grand Prix title, and it's invariably got three or four Bougainvillean semifinalists and a

Bougainvillean champion. And then you've got this whole, more informal Melanesian winter circuit, which provides an even richer substrate of totally excellent tetherball.

WARDEN

Who are the big stars over there?

MARK

Oh man, let's see . . . There's Fagi Pinjinga, there's Mapopoza Tonezepo . . . there's Lyndon Kakambona, Wuwa-Bulolo Puliyasi, Wamp Kominika, Onguglo To'uluwa, Ezikiel Takaku, Wia Kemakeza, Ataban Tokurapai . . . And then of course there's Offramp Tavanipupu—you've probably heard of *him,* he's, like, the biggest tetherball star in the world, and he's also a really big pop star in the Solomon Islands, he's kind of the Leonard Cohen of Melanesia, I mean in addition to his tetherball—I guess you'd say he's like the Mike Tyson/Leonard Cohen of Melanesia.

WARDEN

He actually sounds familiar. What is it—Avram Topopovuni?

MARK

Offramp Tavanipupu. I'm sure you've run across articles about him in magazines. About how when he was a kid, he almost died from carbon monoxide poisoning huffing fumes from barbecue propane tanks, and how he was later diagnosed with having a monoamine oxidase A deficiency—what's called a MAOA-deficiency—which made him abnormally belligerent . . .

WARDEN

What made him abnormally belligerent, the deficiency or the diagnosis?

MARK

Huh?

WARDEN

Never mind.

MARK

. . . so he was always in and out of reform schools and jails. But he developed into this incredibly ferocious player. He's probably the hardest pure hitter ever in tetherball—y'know, if you're talking just raw pounds-per-square-inch force. And then the year after he won his first Ma Ling Masters, he was in a Koru's Department Store, which is like the Bougainvillean equivalent of Sears, and he was buying a pair of maracas and the salesperson suggested that he purchase a service contract for the maracas, and Offramp very courteously declined—he's normally a very soft-spoken, urbane person—but the clerk got increasingly aggressive about this service contract, and finally Offramp just lost it and bludgeoned him to death with the ceremonial war club he always carries around with him. So he had to leave the country and he missed two full seasons. And then when he came back, he was appearing on *The Patimo Nambuka Show* (which is like the *Good Morning America* of Bougainville), and an anaconda swallowed his mom in the green room.

WARDEN

It all sounds vaguely familiar.

MARK

The guy's like an international superstar. He dated Lolita Davidovich and PJ Harvey. He dated Fusako Shigenobu, the female head of the now-inactive Middle East faction of the Japanese Red Army. He dated Peruvian president Alberto Fujimori's daughters Keiko and

Sachi. And, during a period of heavy Ecstasy use, he was rumored to have been simultaneously engaged to wayward tennis phenom Jennifer Capriati *and* Yasmin Buschbacher, coxswain for Liechtenstein's Olympic women's quadruple sculls crew.

So then, after going out with all these glamorous starlets and celebs, he marries a member of the *bhangis,* an untouchable caste of sewer scavengers in India. The bhangis are considered the absolute lowest of the low in the caste hierarchy—they're so ostracized that even the tanners and animal cremators won't go near them.

It's such *classic Offramp*—for him to have fallen in love with someone like that. He's such a romantic, such an iconoclast. I mean, here's Bougainville's paramount tetherball player and pop star—unquestionably the country's most eligible bachelor—and this is a girl ghettoized in some fetid slum colony, never went to school, completely illiterate, who's spent her entire life helping her family eke out a living cleaning pit toilets by hand.

He meets her sightseeing during qualifying rounds for the Bhopal Open, falls in love, and asks her to marry him on the spot.

WARDEN

He sounds like a real egalitarian.

MARK

Totally. She carried a bucket of excrement on her head at the wedding!

WARDEN

That's so cool.

MARK

He wouldn't have it any other way.

NEW ANGLE on MARK and WARDEN

WARDEN

So do you have posters of him up in your room?

MARK

I have a small Wuwa-Bulolo Puliyasi poster, a small
Ezikiel Takaku, and two big Offramp Tavanipupus.
They're *really* cool. In one, he's sitting on this frayed
blue plastic beach chair holding his war club, and he's
just got on a pair of these dingy, like, jockey briefs, and
he's wearing eyeliner, eye shadow, and lipstick with this
ratty teased hair that's like black cotton candy, and he's
got a bone in his nose, and it was shot using this low-
pressure sodium lamp so the betel-juice stains on his
teeth and all the ornamental scars on his face really
stand out—he's got a radiant sun carved into one cheek
and a tetherball on the other—he kind of looks like a
cross between Robert Smith from The Cure and Quee-
queg from *Moby Dick*. And then in the other one, he's
walking along a dock in Kieta playing the guitar and
he's wearing this pair of pinstriped suit pants cut off just
below the knees and he's got his shell anklets and a lei
of frangipani blossoms and his war club in this sort of
rattan scabbard. I think that poster was a promotion for
his album *Bikpela Numbawan*.

The man's music is excellent. His lyrics have been
subjected to more exegetical effort than the work of any
other Bougainvillean songwriter. I have all his albums.
I have *Bikpela Numbawan* . . . Do you understand any
Pidgin?

WARDEN

Nope.

MARK

Bikpela Numbawan—that means like "Big Fella, Number One" or "Big Man, Number One." There's *Dispela
Pisin Savvy Tok Bullseet,* which means "This Bird Knows

How to Talk Bullshit." There's *Mi Laik Kai-Kai Dim-Dim,* which is "I Like to Eat White Persons."

The singer-songwriter's current album, *Haus Pekpek Toktok Numbawan,* a two-CD set released in the U.K. as *Spent Fuel Rod in a Cooling Pond,* in which lyrics of depression, abject self-pity, misanthropy, and suicide are interwoven with wistful, elegiac, almost diaristic sketches of dreamy trysts and doomed affairs and augmented by Tavanipupu's dissonant acoustic strumming and maudlin synth string arrangements, entered the Melanesian charts at #1 nine months ago and has remained in the top 40 ever since.

Lyrics like "When people ask you what I do, you're like, 'I guess he just hits tetherballs' / And y'know, it's funny, I'd always preferred very earnest and ingenuous girls to louche, scabrously nihilistic girls / but you changed all that / The way you just loll on the sofa like a narcoleptic Doberman when my parents come over to visit / and then later the way you snarl when you're being fucked / Frenzied bodies, paralyzed minds / I can't believe I never told you that the nape of your neck is redolent of the sweltering pavement / And now when people ask me what I do, I'm like, 'I guess I just hit tetherballs,' " and "Remember that time at the Odeon when you unclasped your gold chain & crucifix, doused it in your drink and slid it, wet and cold, down the back of my pants / and I cried out 'I adore you!' and you put your hand over my mouth and said 'Not so loud, there are gossip columnists from *New York* magazine here' / and you traced the cicatrized tetherball on my cheek with your long black shellacked fingernail / and I whispered 'I adore you . . . I adore you!' succumbing completely to a dream I knew would invariably dissipate in the exigencies of our respective marriages / Oh, but I adore that dream / that dream, dream, dream, that forlorn dream" have become sing-alongs for the tens of thousands of Offramp Tavanipupu fans who pack concert halls and stadiums throughout the South Pacific.

ANGLE ON WARDEN
as she suddenly gets up and peruses several shelves of
racked CDs.

W A R D E N

I think I know where I've heard of Offramp Tavanipupu.
I belong to one of those CD clubs . . . and y'know how if
you don't order something they just automatically send
you their selection of the month? Well, I think recently
they sent me one of this guy's albums and I just stuck it
in here, without ever even listening to it . . . Yup—here
we go.

INSERT SHOT of *HAUS PEKPEK TOKTOK NUMBAWAN*
CD in Warden's hand.

W A R D E N

Should I put it on?

M A R K

Definitely.

The WARDEN's sound system features an 8-CD carousel. She
loads the two CDs of Offramp Tavanipupu's *Haus Pekpek Toktok
Numbawan.*

In addition, she loads the *Mr. Holland's Opus* soundtrack
album; the *Batman Forever* soundtrack album; the soundtrack
album for *Chernobyl,* Knut Holberg's chilling, critically
acclaimed documentary about the worst nuclear reactor disaster
in history, which features songs performed by Whitney Hous-
ton, Mary J. Bilge, Toni Braxton, TLC, Brandy, and Tony! Toni!
Toné; *Flogging Tenors,* recorded live at the Hermanos Rodriguez
Autodromo in Mexico City to commemorate the twenty-fifth
anniversary of the assassination of Nancy Spungen, tenor virtu-
osi Jose Carreras, Placido Domingo, and Luciano Pavarotti pay
tribute to early English punk by reinterpreting such classics as
the Sex Pistols' "No Feelings," "Pretty Vacant," and "Anarchy in
the UK," The Damned's "Stab Your Back," the Buzzcocks'

"Orgasm Addict" and "Why Can't I Touch It?" The Clash's "White Riot," and The Adverts' "Bored Teenagers" and "One Chord Wonders"; *Karaoke Collaboration,* ten lush instrumental tracks that enable you to perform the anthems and popular songs of Vichy France, the Croatian Ustachi, and wartime Lithuania—a must-have for nostalgic anti-Semites who love to sing; and finally, Ministry maestro Al Jourgensen and the Los Angeles Philharmonic Orchestra conducted by Zubin Mehta debut Jourgensen's foray into the classical idiom with his brooding symphonic composition, *The Meek Shall Inherit Shit.*

These eight CDs play continuously for the remainder of the movie.

WARDEN returns to couch and caresses MARK's cheek with the back of her hand. She reclines, kicks off her pumps, and lays a bare foot across his thigh.

VARIOUS ANGLES
as WARDEN and MARK listen to music.

WARDEN undulates concisely to the bass grooves and disjunctive beats.

MARK, eyes shut, grasps the neck of the wine bottle as if it were a microphone. His face contorts into a succession of histrionic grimaces, as he lip-synchs the prolix lyrics of Offramp Tavanipupu.

WARDEN flicks MARK's nipples with big toe.

MARK simpers dreamily.
He takes her toe in his mouth and sucks hard until

We HEAR sharp crack of joint connecting phalanx and metatarsal bone.

W A R D E N

(flexing toe)

You really do spend a lot of time in your room, alone . . . don't you?

MARK

Yeah. I even eat in there most of the time. My dad's away a lot and Mom doesn't cook that much. So I've got my own microwave . . . I eat a lot of, like, ramen noodles, instant grits, instant couscous, y'know . . . instant spätzle.

WARDEN

Say that again.

MARK

What?

WARDEN

Say *instant spätzle.*

MARK

Instant spätzle.

WARDEN

Your mouth looks *so* adorable when you say that. Say it again.

MARK

Instant spätzle.

WARDEN kisses MARK.

WARDEN

Again.

As he repeats the words, the WARDEN traces his lips with her tongue.

WARDEN

Again . . . c'mon.

M A R K

(muffled by WARDEN's mouth)

Instant spätzle
 . . . instant spätzle
 . . . instant spätzle.

WARDEN bites and sucks MARK's neck, giving him two huge heliotrope hickeys. She softly scrapes his earlobes between her teeth, kisses his mouth again voraciously, and, with hurried random pecks, works her way down his neck to his chest and nipples as she lightly rakes his back with her fingernails. She kneels, clasps his ass in her hands, and licks the rim of his navel in languorous circles and then begins to slowly unzip his trousers.

M A R K   (voice-over)

I can't tell you how much more exciting this was for me than masturbating to minimalist grids and neo-expressionist palimpsests. And it's definitely not my intention to disparage the work of any specific painters—but this was just *so* great.

And I thought it was really fantastic that the Warden was so out-there and so totally cool with what she wanted and was like: "Say it. Say it again."

But unfortunately here's where I started overanalyzing everything again. I realize I try to evince this swaggering, salacious, Iggy Pop kind of thing with the shirtless-sweaty-torso-low-slung-leather-pants look and whatnot, but I'm really a very pensive person who hyper-rationates absolutely everything. And this was a perfect case in point—instead of just switching on automatic pilot, instead of just relaxing and intuitively surfing the peaks, troughs, and vortices of the moment, I start thinking to myself: if she likes it so much when I say *instant spätzle,* I wonder if she'd like it even *more* if I said other German dishes. In fact, she'll probably get bored and disenchanted if I just keep repeating *instant spätzle* over and over again. So I began saying things like *Sauerbraten* and *Wienerschnitzel* and *Rollmöpse* and *Zwiebelkuchen.*

And then it occurred to me that maybe the word *instant* was significant in some way . . . The variables here were mind-boggling, and I felt increasingly like one of those chess computers designed to crunch a billion combinations in a split second.

ANOTHER ANGLE of WARDEN, still slowly unzipping MARK's pants.

> M A R K   (voice-over)

So I thought, OK, maybe *instant* is important. Maybe the idea of speed, convenience, ease of preparation somehow invests the phrase with libidinal charge. So I start going: *Instant Pichelsteiner Fleisch . . . ready-to-serve Sülzkoteletten . . . quick Gefüllter Fasan . . . one-step Blut Schwartemagen . . . shake-and-bake Käseschnitzel . . .* uh . . . *microwave Apfelpfannkuchen.*

And then I become concerned that maybe this is all too coy, and that maybe I'm coming off too adolescent, giving off too much of the whole search-for-identity-need-to-rebel-but-at-the-same-time-need-to-conform-looking-for-cues-from-one's-peers-fragile-developing-self-image thing and maybe now I should try to present myself as more mature, more worldly, and maybe slightly more decadent and lewd, so I decide to talk dirty to her, because I'd read that some women are really turned on by that. So now I'm like: *Fuckin' boil-in-a-bag Bratwurst mit sauer Sahnensosse . . . cocksucking stovetop Getrüffelte Gänseleber-wurst . . . titty-fuck brown-'n'-serve Konigsberger Klopse . . .*

And she stopped unzipping my pants and looked up at me.

WARDEN

(putting a finger to her lips)

Shhhhhhh.

MARK

(oblivious, on a roll)

Friggin' cunty frozen hungry-man Kalbshaxe mit Gewürzgurkensosse.

WARDEN

(sternly)

Seriously, you're really going to have to stop.

WARDEN gets up and produces a leather ball-gag and hand-cuffs from the top drawer of her desk.

She returns to couch and, cutting him off in mid-scatological-easy-to-prepare-German-entree, pushes ball-gag into MARK's open mouth, cinches straps tightly around his head, and cuffs his hands behind his back.

She then finally finishes unzipping his clammy leather pants and yanks them off.

Gently fondling his balls with one hand, she takes his erection and pumps it in the other.

WARDEN

Have you given any thought to what you'd say if you actually won the Vincent and Lenore DiGiacomo / Oshimitsu Polymers America Award—y'know, at the presentation ceremony?

MARK

(with ball-gag in mouth)

Aggghhhhh. Agggggghhhhhhhhhhhhhh. Agghhh. Aggghhh. Agggggghhhhhhhh. Agghhh. Agggggghhh.

SUBTITLE: *There's like no way I can win. I haven't written any-thing—and it's due tomorrow.*

W A R D E N

Well, what if somehow you did? Hypothetically, what would you say?

M A R K

Agggghhhhhhh . . . Aggghhh aggghh agggggghhhh: "Aggghhhhhh. Aggghhhhhhhhhh. Aggghhhhhh. Aggggghhhhhh. Aggghhhhh. Aggghh. Agggghhhh. Agggggghhhhhh. Aggggghhhhhh. Aggghhhhhhh. Aggghh. Agggghhhh. Agggggghhhhhh. Aggghhhhhh. Aggghhhhhhh. Aggghh. Aggggghhhh. Agggggghhhhhh. Agggggghhhhhh. Aggghhhhhhh. Aggghh. Agggghhhh. Aggggggghhhhhh. Aggghhhhhh. Aggghhhhhh. Aggghh. Agghhhh. Aggggggghhhhhh. Aggggghhhhhh. Aggghhhhhh. Aggggghhhh. Aggggggghhhh. Aggggggghhhhhh. Aggggghhhhhh. Aggghhhhhhh. Aggghh. Agggghhhh. Agggggghhhhhh. Aggghhh. Aggggghhhhhh. Aggghhhhhhh. Aggghh. Agggghhhh. Aggggggghhhhhh. Aggghhhhhh. Aggghhhhhh. Aggghh. Agggghhhh. Agggggghhhhhh. Agggggghhhhhh. Aggghhhhhhh. Agggghhhhhh. Aggghh. Agggghhhh. Aggghhhhhh. Agggggghhhhhh. Aggggghhhhhh. Aggghhhhhh. Aggghh. Agghhhh. Aggggggghhhhhh. Aggggghhhhhh. Aggghhhhhh. Aggghh. Agggghhhh. Aggggggghhhhhh. Aggggghhhhhh. Aggghhhhh. Aggghh. Agggghhhh. Aggggggghhhhhh. Aggggghhhhhh. Aggghhhhhhh. Aggghh. Agggghhhh. Agggggghhhhhh. Aggghhhhhh. Aggghhhhhhh. Agggggghhhhhh. Aggggghhhhhh. Aggghhhhhh. Aggghh. Agghhhh. Aggggggghhhhhh. Aggggghhhhhh. Aggghhhhhh. Agggggghhhh. Agggggggghhhh. Aggggggghhhhhh. Aggggghhhhhh. Aggghhhhhh. Aggghh. Agggghhhh. Agggggghhhhhh. Aggghhh."

SUBTITLE: *I don't know . . . Probably something like: "I want to thank Vincent and Lenore DiGiacomo, without whose remarkable vision and intrepid, unflagging support none of this would be possible. I'd like to express my deepest gratitude to the folks at Oshimitsu Polymers America for making this a reality. I'd like to thank everyone at ICM, particularly Binky and Sloan—even when I showed absolutely no interest in or the slightest talent for writing and hadn't as yet produced anything except for a review of an imaginary movie— you guys stuck by me and represented me with more energy and commitment and savvy than I could ever have dreamed of. I'd like to thank all the other screenwriters at Maplewood Junior High School for providing such a vibrant milieu in which to work, and I'd like to say that any of you could and should have won this. I'd like to especially say hello to my main man Felipe—yo, Felipe, ma huang rules! I'd like to thank God for having had the insight in the first place to give humans the awesome intellectual capacity to write screenplays. And finally I'd like to thank my Mom, without whose morbid phobias and apocalyptic fatalism I couldn't have become half the screenwriter I am today. And, Dad . . . the Damoclean sword of New Jersey State Discretionary Execution is hanging over your head wherever you are, but I know you're watching tonight. You always said it takes real balls to turn a brunette without a cranium into a blonde, and well . . . I hope you're proud of me. You'll always be my bikpela numbawan."*

WARDEN wipes tears from eyes.

She looks up at him with an expression of profound sadness and infinite wisdom, and flicks the tip of his dick with her tongue.

MARK ejaculates immediately.

NOTE:

The "Aggghhhh" soliloquy beginning on page 159 and continuing onto page 160 is one of the most musical speeches in the entire screenplay, and much of its power derives from that musicality—its permutations and variations on a theme.

Like music, it produces a dual effect, that is, both instantaneous and cumulative, as the echoes of the earlier variations reverberate in the mind as one hears the latter.

Here, whoever plays the role of MARK faces what is widely considered a supreme test of an actor's range.

The challenge is first and foremost to memorize the speech, with its many philosophical and often cryptic shadings. Perhaps even more daunting is the need to scrupulously observe the subtle shifts in pronunciation and time value as indicated by the meticulously nuanced spellings—"Aggghhh" as opposed to "Agggggghhhhh," for instance.

A metrical tour de force, the speech requires an actor to reconcile two simultaneous but dissynchronous rhythms—the syncopated syntactical cadences that are inherent in an award-acceptance speech and the steady rhythmic effects of the WARDEN's hand on MARK's penis.

It's critically important to remember that gagged speech is fundamentally different from dental-patient locution, although the two share some phonetic characteristics. And gagged speech during sexual stimulation is considered by linguists to be a completely distinct language, which some contend may actually predate the Indo-Iranian and Balto-Slavic branches.

Nowhere are the insuperable difficulties of the translator more conspicuous than in the "Agggghhhh" soliloquy. Notwithstanding the inevitable sacrifice of certain musical and poetic effects, the subtitled translation strives to reproduce with all possible fidelity both the words and their rhetorical form. Although the delicacy and poignance of MARK's concluding "Aggghh. Agggghhhh. Aggggggghhhhhh. Aggghhh" is irreparably altered and coarsened in translation, one hopes that, at the very least, the subtitled "You'll always be my bikpela numbawan" evokes and sustains the thought and feeling within.

MEDIUM SHOT of WARDEN unfastening ball-gag.

CLOSE-UP of MARK, bursting to speak.

MARK

(the very instant the gag is removed)

That was phenomenal! That was, like, the absolute best sex I've ever had.

WARDEN

You're a honey.

OFFICE briefly fills with pink mist.

There's a fleeting sense now that this is all taking place in a Cocteau Twins video.

It's like the afterschool afternoon you always dreamed of.

In slow motion, WARDEN unlocks his handcuffs.
MARK takes a swig of cough syrup from a bottle he finds on the credenza.
She lights a cigarette and hands it to him.

MARK takes a drag and glances at his watch.

MARK

(realizing that it's not going to be feasible for him to get to the Maplewood Public Library before it closes)

Shit . . . Do you have any, like, food?

WARDEN opens small chrome Miele refrigerator atop credenza and peers in.

WARDEN

I have a strawberry Ensure, I have a hazelnut Sustacal . . . and somewhere in here I thought I had a chocolate Slimfast. . . .

MARK

I'll have a hazelnut Sustacal and vodka.

In slow motion, WARDEN fills two highball glasses halfway
with ice and Stoly, shakes then pops a can of hazelnut Sustacal,
shakes and pops a strawberry Ensure, pours simultaneously—a
can in each hand—not quite filling the glasses, and then tops
off each drink with more vodka, and stirs with *New Jersey State
Penitentiary at Princeton—Capital Punishment Administrative Segregation Unit* swizzle sticks.

As she serves him his drink, she reaches down and gives his dick
an affectionate squeeze.

He ejaculates again, this time on the sixteenth-century Kashan
silk carpet.

MARK

Sorry. Is that an expensive rug? Will that come out?

WARDEN

Don't worry about it.

MARK

Can I ask you a stupid question . . . Have you ever done
this before?

WARDEN

(laughing)

I'm thirty-six years old.

MARK

No, I mean like—I know you've had sex before—I mean
have you ever had sex with someone whose father survived an abortive execution and was then sentenced to
NJSDE?

WARDEN

(lighting a cigarette for herself)

Yeah, I have.

MARK

In a prison where you were the warden?

WARDEN

Uh-huh.

MARK

In this office?

WARDEN

Yes, in this office. Does that bother you?

MARK

(hurt, but masking it behind phony truculence)

I don't give a fuck what you do, as long you do it after hours, on your own time, and not on taxpayer time. The taxpayers of the state of New Jersey pay your salary—don't you ever forget that! And the taxpayers of this state don't pay you to suck cock. Just punch out first, bitch.

WARDEN

You're angry.

MARK

I'm not angry.

MARK chugs entire hazelnut Sustacal and vodka, smashes glass against wall, and then takes a shard of broken glass and carves into his forearm the words "Satan," "I Love Satan," "Jews for Satan," "Satan Rocks My World," "Hey Satan, You're So Fine, You're So Fine You Blow My Mind, Hey Satan!" "Destroying Everything That's Good and Beautiful Is, Like, Funny"; "Committing Suicide on Your Birthday in Your Parents' Bed Is Excellent," "I Support a Woman's Right to Breed Babies for the Sole Purpose of Ritually Sacrificing and Eating Them," and "Buy *Only* Procter & Gamble Products."

WARDEN

Mark, you're obviously very angry and very alienated.

MARK

I am *not* angry, and I am *not* alienated.

MARK takes pair of Rollerblades, tied together at the laces, from credenza and swings them wildly at the WARDEN's head.

WARDEN ducks, kicks MARK in the solar plexus, grabs Roller Blades, and—wielding them like nunchakus—twirls them in blurred arcs over her head and behind her back before delivering, in rapid succession, two precise and devastating blows to MARK's forehead.

Repeat sequence, this time:
REVERSE ANGLE—in slow motion—
WARDEN ducks—kicks MARK in solar plexus—grabs Roller Blades—twirls them like nunchakus ambidextrously in blurred arcs over her head and behind her back—then delivers two concussive blows to MARK's forehead.

EXTREME CLOSE-UP of MARK as—in *super* slow motion—we again see the Roller Blades impact his head, driving it first to the right and then to the left of the frame.

MARK

(before he loses consciousness)

Your in-line kung fu . . . is very powerful.

FADE TO BLACK

INT. WARDEN'S OFFICE

RACK FOCUS to MARK slumped on couch.
WARDEN is bringing him to with smelling salts.

WE HEAR dark, hip-hop ambient-techno mix of "A Whole New World (Aladdin's Theme)."

And then, WE HEAR the following original lyrics written and performed by the WARDEN to the melody of "I Will Always Love You" from *The Bodyguard.*

W A R D E N

*(gazing into Mark's eyes,
and singing)*

Look, I really don't understand
Why you're getting so upset about all this.
It's been my experience that whenever you
Introduce drugs and alcohol into the workplace,
You end up in sexual situations with people whom
(in all likelihood)
you ordinarily wouldn't have had sex with . . .
It's just human nature.

(Chorus)
And I will always love you.
Etc.

This is like any other office—
You're with the same group of people
Day in and day out,
You're dealing with them in this very artificial,
So-called "professional" context,
Interacting in these habitual, stultifyingly banal
Situations, and eventually you just start wondering
Who these people really are and what they look like
When they have orgasms.

(Chorus)
And I will always love you.
Etc.

Because that's when I think a person is
Most real, most genuine—at the moment of orgasm.
It doesn't matter if it's some gorgeous, flaxen-haired,
Blue-eyed, dimpled, buff, monstrously hung UPS man
Standing in my foyer sucking on a mint,

Or my Panamanian midget gynecologist with the
Black peach-fuzz mustache, gold caps, toothpick, and
Velour pants—my sleazy little "Doggie Hauser" [sic]—
Or Bob Vila, Bernard Goetz, Jeffrey Katzenberg,
Henry Waxman, Ralph Reed, Arantxa Sanchez
Vicario . . . I try to envision what they look like
When they come.

FLASH CUT TO
Computer-extrapolation sequence of Waxman climaxing—from
the scurrilous PBS "rockumentary" *Sex Lives of the Anti-Tobacco
Zealots.*

OVER-THE-SHOULDER SHOT of WARDEN

W A R D E N

(continuing)

(Chorus)
And I will always love you.
Etc.

You see, orgasm is all about surrender—
You surrender all the pretense,
All the dissimulating,
All the vanity.
That's the trouble with this country.
We're a nation of poseurs.
I say: Off with the masks.
The orgasmic face is the unmasked self, the true self.

(Chorus)
And I will always love you.
Etc.

Imagine, for example, an orgasmic Mount Rushmore.
Wouldn't that be so much more inspiring?
Washington, Jefferson, Lincoln, and Roosevelt
Carved in granite *coming.*
Looking out from the Black Hills with these
Contorted rictuses of ecstasy on their faces,

Instead of the stolid, constipated expressions they have.
That would be a great monument.
A monument that actually said something about this
    country.

WARDEN stands, and extends her arms, entreating MARK to
dance.

MARK demurs, tapping his temples and rolling his eyes, as if
to say: thanks to the drugs and blows to the head, my equilib-
rium is, like, completely fucked.

WARDEN smiles at him tenderly, takes his hands in hers, and
gently pulls him to his feet.

The WARDEN stands in back of MARK, her right hand raised
above MARK's head with the index finger pointed downward.
MARK grasps her finger with his right hand. The WARDEN's
left hand is held forward to the left side of MARK with his left
hand resting on it. MARK does a sous-sus to the fifth position
on pointe, takes his right foot to retiré and executes a développé
croisé devant. From this position he pushes from the WAR-
DEN's left hand, executes a fouetté rond de jambe en tournant,
and continues turning with a series of pirouettes, still holding
the WARDEN's index finger. At the completion of the pirouettes he stops himself by quickly grasping the WARDEN's
left hand.

They gaze deeply into each other's eyes and sing together.

WARDEN AND MARK

(in full-throated rapture)

Imagine, for example, an orgasmic Mount Rushmore.
Wouldn't that be so much more inspiring?
Washington, Jefferson, Lincoln, and Roosevelt
Carved in granite *coming.*
Looking out from the Black Hills with these
Contorted rictuses of ecstasy on their faces,
Instead of the stolid, constipated expressions they have.
That would be a great monument.

A monument that actually said something about this
country.

(Chorus)
And I will always love you.
Etc.

M A R K   (voice-over)

I don't know if I buy any of this, especially the
orgasmic-rictus-as-true-self business. I mean, what
makes the expression of someone coming any more genuine than the expression of someone being drawn and
quartered? Or the expression of someone just sleeping
and drooling.
    But the Mount Rushmore idea *is* really cool.

Blood from gash in forehead trickles down MARK's face and
drips onto rug.

W A R D E N

You could probably use a couple of stitches for that.

M A R K

I'm OK. Listen, I apologize for getting so pissed off
before. It's not about you. There's just a lot of shit going
on in my head about my father, and I'm mad at myself
for having waited until the last minute to do the screenplay, and now it's too late to even plagiarize something
from the library, and sometimes DMT, marijuana, white
wine, Demerol, and cough syrup make me a little tense,
anyway. . . .

WARDEN reaches behind her back, unzips her dress, and lets it
fall to the floor. She steps out of her panties and stands naked in
front of MARK.

M A R K

Can I fuck you?

WARDEN

I'm not ready. Do you want to help get me ready?

Now the notorious and achingly beautiful CUNNILINGUS
SCENE.

The scene is notorious because of its extraordinary length—over
three and a half hours; the scene is extraordinarily long for several reasons.

There are a few brief intervals when it all just clicks, and the
clitoral stimulation is perfect—inadvertent perhaps, but perfect—and MARK is this precocious, humming champion, and
the WARDEN whimpers and yelps and nearly growls with
pleasure.

But there are more frequent and more protracted periods
during which MARK earnestly endeavors but, because of his
relative inexperience, endeavors to no discernible effect. The
WARDEN, never turning tetchy or disagreeable, maintains as
positive and encouraging a tone as you could ever hope for—and
this from a woman who brooks neither ineptitude nor careless-
ness from her subordinates. But sometimes her attention does
wander.

In fact, there are stretches where, as MARK heedlessly
works away, his head bobbing incessantly at her crotch, the
WARDEN catches up on neglected paperwork.

During one infamous 95-minute span, amid an endless variety of loud sucking and slurping sounds, with his fingers in her
vagina, and a finger in her anus, and his tongue darting and lapping everywhere at once—the clit, the labia, the perineum—in
a blind, unmodulated fury of licking and trilling and swirling
and churning, with frenzied, accelerating oscillations of his
entire head, the WARDEN is on the phone calmly negotiating
the end to a potentially deadly hostage crisis in Cell Block D.

Later, in a similar 12-minute episode, as MARK lavishes her
pussy with the frenetic diligence of an insect colony servicing its
queen, the WARDEN impassively eats a pretzel.

■

The scene's aching beauty derives primarily from the fact that for over three and a half hours, MARK's face never leaves the vulva of the WARDEN, no matter what she is doing. When she's splayed across the couch, MARK ministers to her from his knees on the floor. When she's seated at her desk working, MARK is under that desk, gripping the steel arm-supports of her chair so as not to be shaken from her pudendum as she swivels one way to attend to a stack of documents and then suddenly swivels in the opposite direction to shuffle through another. And as she grimly paces her office, this naked virago, phone to her ear, struggling to save the lives of several veteran guards being held by a gang of ax- and icepick-wielding psychopaths, MARK at first scrambles crablike between her legs, in an inverted crawl on his feet and palms, and then, finding this too ungainly, he actually dons her in-line skates so his feet can roll across the floor, an arm wrapped around each of her thighs, his mouth pinioned to her genitals.

To achieve maximum aching beauty:
Include frequent CLOSE-UPS of the WARDEN's LABIAL KEY RING—a double-strand gold coil pierced through her upper left labium—dangling from which are the front and back door keys to her condo, the ignition and trunk keys to her Mazda RX-7 rotary twin turbo, the key to a summer house in Belmar, New Jersey, that she shares with two other wardens and the director of a juvenile detention center, and mailbox and safe-deposit-box keys.

Anyone who's seen the infamous video of Richard Speck—pendulous, hormone-spawned breasts swaying back and forth, snorting coke, threshing hundred-dollar bills and getting a blow job from one of his degenerate jailhouse paramours—has to be astonished by the capacity of human beings to enjoy themselves in seemingly infernal circumstances. This is not to say that it would be appropriate in *this* movie to feature a mass murderer sporting a pair of mutant tits, snorting coke as he's fellated by transvestite convicts. (This isn't Joyce Carol Oates, for god's sake.) I'm just trying to locate a certain cinematic *tone*.

In a recent issue of *Harper's Bazaar,* Liz Tilberis writes in her "Editor's Note": "In an issue like this, it becomes clear that we at *Bazaar* set almost unreachably high standards for ourselves. There may be times when we present images and ideas that you are not instantly comfortable with; the idea isn't to shock, but to bring you along with us to the cutting edge of fashion, photography, design, and the arts."

With this scene, you want to position yourself—in terms of cinematic tone—somewhere between the Speck video and *Harper's Bazaar.* As Tilberis says, you want to "set almost unreachably high standards" for yourself. And if a 13-year-old boy, whose father has just survived execution by lethal injection, going down on a warden whose car keys are jingling from a ring in her pussy lips, as she attempts to end a siege by Jheri-Curled homicidal maniacs with ice-picks pressed into the temples of their hostages, as Carreras, Domingo, and Pavarotti sing "White Riot" isn't "the cutting edge of fashion, photography, design, and the arts," then I don't what is.

Tilberis goes on to say: "I liked wearing pastels this summer, and at long last I've had it with black. Brown seems a good way to go instead. Beyond that, I'm thinking it's just a matter of choosing a bag and a pair of shoes or boots to go with everything."

Yes. Totally.

Pledge of Integrity

If the Vincent and Lenore DiGiacomo / Oshimitsu Polymers America Award selection committee is leaning toward giving me the award, but some members are vacillating, and if the only thing holding these members back from unequivocal support for me are qualms about the CUNNILINGUS SCENE, I will remove the scene in its entirety and I pledge never to bring up the subject again.

Up until this point, I've scrupulously refrained from making any appeals that smacked of self-pity, pathos, or groveling. But at this time I wish to make an additional pledge: Because my father has been effectively exiled thanks to his NJSDE sentence,

my mentally infirm and alcoholic mother's financial well-being
is in, like, grave jeopardy. If you, the selection committee,
choose to award me the $250,000-a-year prize (this sum to be
bestowed annually for the entirety of the winner's life), I
solemnly promise to issue my mother a small and time-limited
monthly stipend until she is able to get on her own feet. (I say
small and time-limited—I'm thinking of something in the neighborhood of $300 a month until she secures employment, up to a
maximum of six months—because I don't wish to rob my
mother of her self-esteem by plunging her into an interminable
cycle of dependence and shiftlessness. I love and respect my
mother far too much to do that to her.)

Financing Suggestion

If your producers are depending on rich Persian Gulf backers
for financing, keep in mind that most financiers arrive with a
long list of prohibitions necessary to make any work palatable
back home. (A three-and-a-half-hour cunnilingus scene between
a drugged adolescent and a 36-year-old female prison warden
will probably not be acceptable in a country where it's considered blasphemous to simply show an unmarried man and
woman alone in a room together.) There's also the MPAA
ratings problem back home to consider. And you may be thinking Palme d'Or at Cannes. And what about the possibility that
the movie might someday be selected by the National Film
Registry of the Library of Congress for recognition and
preservation?

Don't despair.

You can delete the footage for general release—I know, I
know, it's a very cool scene—but you can always restore it, in
toto, for the deluxe letterboxed director's-cut laser disc.

And none of this precludes you from simultaneously releasing a straight-to-video *The Vivisection of Mighty Mouse, Jr. (Hard-
Core Mix),* which would be *just* the CUNNILINGUS SCENE.
No establishing zoom from the KH-12 photoreconnaissance
satellite, no Contraband Control Room, no "Gravy" trip, no
white Burgundy, no fiberoptic lapping slurry or endoscopic
pull-back shot, no instant spätzle or in-line nunchakus, and

none of what follows. Just 210 commercial-free minutes of non-stop cunnilingus and music.

There are only two substantive exchanges of dialogue in the CUNNILINGUS SCENE.

In one, after MARK peeks at his Tag Heuer and whines about how he won't be able to get to the library in time to plagiarize a screenplay, the WARDEN advises him to concoct a script "out of this," suggesting that, as soon as he gets home, he type out everything that happened—i.e., everything that's transpired between the two of them in the WARDEN's office—and simply reformat it into a screenplay.

I've decided not to incorporate this dialogue into the screenplay. This colloquy between the WARDEN and MARK in which they discuss how to turn their encounter into a screenplay is essentially an ad hoc story conference and putting a story conference into this movie just seems too "inside Hollywood," too "fashionably self-reflexive," for me. Would Steven Spielberg's *The Harelip of B'nai Jeshurun* be the whimsical delight it is if in the middle of the movie he'd inserted an animated rendition of the development meeting at which Katzenberg first suggested a DreamWorks answer to Disney's *The Hunchback of Notre Dame?* No, that would have ruined the whole spirit of the movie. Same here.

The other exchange occurs during a momentary respite, when MARK asks the WARDEN a provocative question concerning fitness tapes.

I include this conversation in its entirety because I feel that it enables the audience, for the first time, to fully appreciate the WARDEN's erudition, and I think there should be some erudition in this movie, which, in its unflinching verisimilitude, has been so raw and dankly self-abasing. Also, this dialogue provides a necessary segue into the elusive and fleetingly beautiful FUCK scene.

INT. WARDEN'S OFFICE

CLOSE SHOT of MARK

MARK

*(Picks a hair from his tongue and scrutinizes
it between his fingers, like Edison assaying a
test filament for his lightbulb prototype.
Then, looking up at the WARDEN)*

You recently published a monograph in the prison staff
newsletter on the evolution of narrative in exercise
videos, and in it, you argue that early exercise videos
like *Buns of Steel, Kathy Smith's Aerobox Workout with
Michael Olajide, Jr., Your Personal Best Workout with Elle
Macpherson,* etc., were morphologically equivalent to
early pornography, and that with the later introduction
of narrative elements associated with the conventional
film—e.g., plot and character development, measured
pace, laboriously constructed scenes, the story arc with
its conflict and resolution, etc.—the exercise video is no
longer disparaged as a marginal, "specialty" category,
but is now critically regarded as a valid genre. Do you
think that with its new-found respectability, the exercise
video has sacrificed the totally monomaniacal narcissism
that made it such a galvanizing form when it first came
out, and what do you think are, like, the most intense
scenes in the neo-narrative exercise video today? And I
have a follow-up question.

As the WARDEN replies, MARK resumes his marathon oral lovefest.

WARDEN

I think, sure, we've lost some of that exhilaration. I'll
never forget when I saw my first exercise video. I think
it was at the old Film-Makers' Cinematheque at the
Gramercy Arts Theater on 27th Street. One hour of
frenzied, context-less exercise, unencumbered by all the
clunky interstitial devices that are required to move
characters around in a plotted film. It was a revelation.
There was a kind of pure, classical proportion to it, an

Aristotelian unity—men and women in a single room for sixty minutes, laboring, sweating . . .

So, yes, the so-called maturation of the exercise video entails a certain loss—a loss of that formal rigor that was so thrilling. But the recent trend to graft exercise into the structure of traditional movies has resulted in some superb work. There's a richness and complexity that's absolutely new and unprecedented, particularly in the way that the neo-narrative exercise video illuminates the rote narcissism and abject fear of mortality in our most ordinary encounters. As I argue in my monograph, the neo-narrative exercise video is uniquely suited to analyzing the ways in which *all* of our interactions— intimate, social, economic, political—are carried out as a kind of *exercise,* as rites of vanity, and, on another level, as strenuous, albeit overweening, acts of protest against the brute, vanquishing inevitability of death.

As far as most intense scenes, I'd say the scene from the fitness version of Mary Karr's memoir *The Liar's Club* where Mary comes home to confront her fourth husband and former bodyguard after an Italian magazine has published photographs of him cavorting naked with Fili Houteman, a 26-year-old woman who holds the title of Miss Nude Belgium. Mary storms upstairs to their bedroom and finds Peter and Fili on the floor doing abdominal crunches. And instead of denouncing the two of them and demanding that they leave her home at once—which is what we've been led to expect—Mary joins them, and for the next twenty minutes, they take us through one of the most demanding ab routines you've ever seen. Designed to work the upper and lower abs, obliques and intercostals, this killer workout includes front and reverse crunches, incline board and Roman Chair sit-ups, and vertical bench leg raises. It's intense!

And, of course, there's that exquisite, defining scene from the Renny Harlin "Beautiful Backs" version of *Jude*

the Obscure, Thomas Hardy's late-Victorian masterpiece.
The video was shot on location in Great Fawley, the
Berkshire village that is the prototype of Hardy's fictional "Marygreen." Jude Fawley, a rustic stonemason
with aspirations to someday study at Christminster (a
fictional Oxford), is walking hand in hand with his
cousin Sue Bridehead, who's just separated from her husband, the dull, middle-aged schoolmaster, Phillotson.
They're strolling down a forest path, tentatively broach-
ing their love for each other. Just as they reach the end
of the path, Jude looks at Sue and says: "I think and
know you are my dear Sue, from whom neither length
nor breadth, nor things present nor things to come, can
divide me. And because, my darling, I desire nobody in
this world but you, I have gotten you this splendid lat
machine!"

And at that moment, the forest gives way to a daisy-
and violet-dappled pasture in the middle of which sits
this brand-new shimmering lat pulldown machine.

We've all been so culturally indoctrinated to only
expect multistation gym equipment inside a gym, that
to see this lat machine in a flowering meadow, its overhead cable and chrome-plated weight stack gleaming in
the sun, surrounded by the verdant undulations of this
arcadian countryside, is an astonishing epiphany.

Jude, clad in a dark frock, waistcoat, breeches, and
boots, and Sue, in a lavender sunbonnet and mulberry-
colored gown with dainty lace at the collar, proceed to
work their trapezius muscles and latissimi dorsi with an
unbridled enthusiasm that's absolutely contagious!

Later, as the setting sun imbues the landscape with
rich tints of crimson and sienna, Jude spots for Sue, as
the hypersensitive, Swinburne-spouting, sexless coquette
works her lower and upper back, traps, buttocks, and
legs with a five-rep set of 400-pound deadlifts.

And as Jude urges Sue to complete that one last rep-
etition, Harlin wisely sticks to the original dialogue
from Hardy's unbowdlerized final revision:

"It's all you, baby!" Jude exhorted.

Sue Bridehead, her face hideously contorted with exertion, slowly straightened until she was upright, the barbell at her thighs. She sighed and dropped the bar to the thick grass.

"Good set," grunted Jude, their crisp high-five flushing a bevy of quail from a nearby copse of linden trees.

Dude, *that's* an intense scene. I mean, that's an awesome amount of weight for a woman in a Victorian novel to lift. And even on that final rep, she maintains perfect form—back tight and straight, head up. Like so. Check this out—

The WARDEN uses her feet to pry MARK's face from her crotch. She gets up and mimes the starting position for a dead-lift—knees bent, leaning forward over an imaginary barbell, ass canted at about a 45-degree angle to the floor.

This rear view of a naked, partially jackknifed WARDEN inflames MARK's inchoate sense of phallocratic imperialism.

MARK

Can I fuck you now? Are you, like, ready?

WARDEN reaches around, takes hold of MARK's dick in her hand, and guides it in toward her pink, flared orifice. And at the very instant that his penis makes contact with her vagina, MARK ejaculates.

One would have to say that this constitutes a loss of virginity only in the most technical sense. In fact, to ascertain irrefutably whether penetration actually occurred would require such sophisticated equipment—e.g., the femtosecond X-ray photo-electron strobe spectrometer used to aid line judges at Wimbledon and the U.S. Open, which is *très cher* and would send the movie spiraling so far over budget that it would have to gross, like, $300 million just to break even—that it's probably best to simply call it "intercourse" and proceed.

CLOSE-SHOT of MARK making an arrogant, self-satisfied, vacuous face that is so thoroughly ludicrous, given the instantaneousness of the coitus, that it makes you wince with embarrassment. But it's significant because it's the same facial expression that MARK will assume after sex for the rest of his life.

M A R K   (voice-over)

I felt as if my virginity had been a kind of cryonic capsule which encased my childhood. A frozen bubble which maintained my childhood in a perpetual state of suspended animation. And now that bubble had been shattered . . . And I began to feel as if I were bleeding. But bleeding time. Time was flowing from me, inexorably, unstanchably. A hemorrhage of time. I experienced the loss of my virginity as the violent culmination of my childhood, as the beginning of this inexorable hemorrhaging of time . . . but, of course, all I was able to say to the Warden was:

M A R K

That was cool . . . like a video!

The WARDEN repairs to a private bathroom adjoining her office.

W A R D E N   (off-screen)

Remember when I asked you what you'd say at the presentation ceremony if you won the Vincent and Lenore DiGiacomo / Oshimitsu Polymers America Award and you said something about thanking your agents for sticking by you even though you hadn't produced anything except for an imaginary movie review? What was that all about?

M A R K

It's not an imaginary movie review. It's a review of an imaginary movie. I pretended to be a critic who's reviewing a movie I made—well, never *actually* made.

We HEAR a toilet FLUSH and then the spray of a stall
SHOWER.

WARDEN   (off-screen)

*(her voice raised in order
to be heard over shower)*

That's interesting . . . that you've never written a screenplay—in fact, you've never exhibited the slightest interest in even attempting to write a screenplay—yet you've
concocted this ersatz critique.

MARK

I guess I can picture things once they're done—I just
can't picture actually doing them.
    It's not laziness. Concepts excite me. Theory. Form.
But the actual screen*writing* seems so tedious, so superfluous. I'm not into praxis. I'm more a dialectician of
absence. Writing per se always struck me as terribly
vulgar. To actually commit an idea to paper is a des-
ecration of that idea, a corruption of the mind. It's
not laziness. Heavens no. It's simply that I'm loathe
to violate the Mallarméan purity of the blank page.
*"Le vide papier que la blancheur défend . . . Le blanc souci
de notre toile."* And let me tell you, teachers, particularly
in the 7th grade, do *not* appreciate the Mallarméan
purity of the blank page. But I suppose I've always
been rather precocious. After all, I'm only thirteen, and
I'm already a screenwriter-manqué! One *must* resist
succumbing to the blandishments of actual accomplishment.

WARDEN (OFF-SCREEN)

(shouting)

What? I can't hear you.

MARK

(*shouting*)

Sitting down in the morning, sipping coffee, smoking a cigarette, and opening up the newspaper to read a review of my movie . . . that just always seemed like it would be the coolest fucking thing in the world. So one day I just wrote a review myself. I was like, let's just skip the boring part (i.e., coming up with a story idea and a treatment, writing the script, shooting and editing footage, etc.) and go right to the cool part—reading about it in the paper. I figured that writing the review obviated the need to write the movie.

WARDEN   (off-screen)

(*shouting*)

I'd like to read it sometime.

MARK

I . . . uh . . . have it with me.

WARDEN   (off-screen)

(*shouting*)

What?

MARK

(*shouting*)

I have the review here. I carry it with me at all times . . . like a talisman.

WARDEN   (off-screen)

(*shouting*)

You have it with you?

> MARK
>
> *(shouting)*

Yes!

> WARDEN (off-screen)
>
> *(shouting)*

I'd love to hear it. Why don't you read it to me?

> MARK

You sure?

> WARDEN (off-screen)
>
> *(shouting)*

What?

> MARK
>
> *(shouting)*

Do you really want to hear it?

> WARDEN (off-screen)
>
> *(shouting)*

Yes!

MARK locates his trousers on the floor. He reaches into a pocket and retrieves the review, which has been compulsively folded into a compressed rectangle the size of a commemorative stamp. He carefully unfolds the sheet of paper and smooths its creased grid.

DISSOLVE TO:

SOFT-FOCUS MEDIUM-SHOT of MARK at window.

He is naked, seated on sill, holding review, framed by casing and profiled against the vermilion gloaming.

This is *definitely* THE SHOT to use for commercials, print ads, billboards, posters, Web site, and licensed merchandise.

There's a SERAPHIC, almost EPICENE quality to the image that has allure across the demographic spectrum from the CHRISTIAN COALITION to NAMBLA.

INTERSPERSE several single-frame FLASH CUTS of Formula One god Ayrton Senna's blue and white Williams-Renault slamming into a concrete wall at 190 mph on the seventh turn of the 1994 San Marino Grand Prix, in order to SUBLIMINALLY create a disquieting undercurrent of dread in anticipation of this movie's shocking climax.

MARK

(reading aloud)

"There are those who will not want to miss *The Tetherballs of Bougainville* for its opening scene in which two revoltingly sleazy teenagers in filthy, reeking *Terribly Toothsome* warm-up jackets unzipped to the pubes, automobile air-fresheners dangling from cheap gold chains around their necks, cruise the Piazza Navona in Rome, hustling tourists for loose lira and doing grappa shots until they're vomiting into the Fountain of the Four Rivers, as other kids sit around, high on the popular club drug Special K, strumming guitars, singing 'Mandy.' There are many, many more who will want to make sure to miss it. Especially when they find out that this scene—surely unsurpassed in its rapt depiction of emesis—has absolutely nothing to do with the movie that follows—a movie that takes place not in Italy, but briefly in suburban Maplewood, New Jersey, and then primarily in Bougainville, a squalid, war-torn island in the Solomon Sea.

"*The Tetherballs of Bougainville* was written, directed, and edited by 13-year-old Mark Leyner, whose only previous credit is as musical director of a video of the abortive execution attempt of his father, entitled 'I Feel

Shitty.' Extravagantly mannered and constantly undermined by a nose-thumbing nihilism and hollow flashiness that reflect its creator's rock-video affinities, *Tetherballs* is an autobiographical account of the year that follows the sentencing of Leyner's father, Joel, to New Jersey State Discretionary Execution (NJSDE). One can't help but marvel at the sheer chutzpah required to actually base a movie's formal structure on the vertiginous mood swings of adolescence, so that moments of flabbergasting kitsch (the control tower at Bougainville International Airport is a 160-foot statue of Herve Villechaize as Tattoo from *Fantasy Island*) and Grand Guignol sadism (a philandering insurance adjuster, archly played by Charles Durning, is filled with candy, hung from the ceiling like a piñata, and savagely beaten to death by the sugar-frenzied, bat-wielding, blindfolded children at his own daughter's 6th birthday party) alternate with wrenchingly passionate scenes of paternal devotion and filial ambivalence.

"Unfortunately, the movie's self-congratulatory misery, showy camera tricks, and overindulgent, almost compulsive emphasis on medical imaging are frequently unbearable. For example, in what would otherwise have been an extremely poignant scene in which Mark returns home from the New Jersey State Penitentiary at Princeton and attempts to console his disturbed, kamikaze-guzzling, Thierry Mugler–accoutered mother (smolderingly played by Nell Carter, who was absolutely riveting as Madame Verdurin in George Romero's terrifying remake of Proust's *Remembrance of Things Past*), Leyner inexplicably chooses to shoot the scene using a positron emission tomography scanner, emphasizing the glucose metabolism of the characters instead of their emotional interaction.

"With the exception of several Bougainvillean tetherball stars who play themselves—most notably Offramp Tavanipupu, whose sinuous, taunting performance conjures up a Melanesian Adam Ant—the movie's characters are predominantly 13- and 14-year-old kids played by adult actors. Mark's best friend from Maplewood Junior High, Felipe, who suffers brain damage from a skateboarding accident, is played with great magnetism and triumphant bluster by Roddy McDowall. Stellar cameos include Ze'ev (Benny) Begin, son of former Israeli Prime Minister Menachem Begin, as 'Creepy Man at Futon Store' and Tommy Hilfiger as 'Demented Kid on Railroad Trestle.'

"Amazingly for a movie that includes scenes of wild-haired men with bones in their noses eating 'long pig' (cooked human being) aboard the Mir space station; boy soldiers who, having just looted a women's clothing store, lurch down some blighted boulevard in flouncy hats, billowing dresses crisscrossed with cartridge bandoliers, huge spliffs in their mouths, lethal fusillades bursting errantly from their AK-47s each time they stumble in their spike heels; and supermodels Nikki Taylor, Helena Christensen, Carla Bruni, and Yasmeen Ghauri backstroking in an Olympic-size pool filled with gin and vermouth, its lanes demarcated by strings of olives; *The Tetherballs of Bougainville* was shot entirely in Leyner's bedroom in his parents' Maplewood home.

"Although we may deplore the film's scatological language, sexual explicitness and gratuitous gore as seemingly designed only to shock, in the manner of an angry, attention-craving child, we must remember that this movie was actually made by an angry, attention-craving child.

"And if you're an aficionado of witty dialogue, be prepared to find *The Tetherballs of Bougainville* a singularly ungratifying experience. The movie bristles with such urbane repartee as:

'That's me playing Super Mario 64 with this guy in his stepmom's condo in Teaneck.'
'He's all like, y'know, "Tonight you die!" He looks so into it.'

'OK, that's me drinking fermented mare's milk
with this nomadic Mongolian herdsman. That's like
the summer between tenth and eleventh grade . . .
You wanna see another picture of him?'

'That's him? No way.'

'That's him in American clothes. We were so
fucked up in that picture.'

'He looks baked. I like when you look in a guy's
eyes and you can see that he's like totally baked. I
think that's so adorable.'

'I like when you look at a guy who's not high,
but you look into his eyes and it's like, y'know, total
flat-line.'

'What about when a guy's like that, y'know,
really retarded, *and* he's really baked. Both!'

'That's the best! That is *so* sexy! I'd be like: Yes!!'

"I can't think of another recent film so saturated
with fin-de-siècle morbidity. Everyone is perpetually
covered with seabird guano. Almost every single major
character has been left with permanent brain damage
from a skateboarding accident. And those few individuals who haven't suffered from some equally disabling
malady or medley of maladies, e.g., Thereza, a hard-
drinking neonatal nurse, gamely played by Amy Irving,
suffers from epilepsy, Tourette's syndrome, St. Vitus'
dance, and a psychological aversion to infants so severe
that even the whimsical illustration of a baby on a pack-
age of disposable diapers sends her into a murderous
rage that can only be stilled by a self-administered
Thorazine enema.

"During a scene in which an ambulance—siren
screaming, lights flashing, sign on top reading 'Caution:
Student Driver'—plows into a crowd of fans waiting to
purchase tickets for an Offramp Tavanipupu concert, and
one of the mortally injured victims, a dissolute,
syphilitic Dutch aerobics instructor, played with wise-
cracking sangfroid by Joe Don Baker, who recently won

a People's Choice Award for his performance in Jerry Lewis's rollicking remake of Ezra Pound's *Pisan Cantos,* looks up at the camera and rasps: 'Roth . . . Hagar . . . Cherone . . . ,' reciting the succession of Van Halen's lead singers with the portentous gravity of someone intoning the plagues visited upon the Egyptians in Exodus, and then dies, a 15-foot geyser of obviously fake blood shooting from the top of his head, the guy sitting next to me in the theater, Joel Siegel from *Good Morning America,* turned to me and said, 'What the fuck does this *mean?*' and I said, 'I think it has something to do with coming to terms with your father.

" 'But maybe I'm projecting too much of my own filial dilemma onto it. Admittedly, I often see my own life as paradigmatic of the history of mankind, and, inversely, read complex, tragic historical events merely as allegories of my own fleeting, frivolous, trivial contretemps.

" 'And every object, every phenomenon becomes a mirror in this completely claustrophobic, totally solipsistic constellation, e.g., the rain . . . the moss . . . the noodles . . . It's all me! I think that's what Jude meant in Renny Harlin's exercise video when he said to Sue, "It's all you, baby!" Like in the Wallace Stevens song, "Tea at the Palaz of Hoon": "Out of my mind the golden ointment rained, / And my ears made the blowing hymns they heard. / I was the world in which I walked, and what I saw / Or heard or felt came not but from myself."

" 'It's the same with movies. All the movies I find most affecting, like *The Towering Inferno, Dawn of the Dead, Die Hard, Bloodsport, Hellraiser, Speed,* and, most recently, *The Nudniks,* a home-invasion comedy in which a loose confederation of North Korean teenage cyclopes (mutants spawned in the wake of a Yongbyon plutonium plant accident), gold-fanged black superpredator congressmen, and amped-up cannibal models in blood-encrusted New York Rangers jerseys sack Karl Lagerfeld's lavish eighteenth-century residence on the rue de l'Université in Paris, smashing the gold-spouted bidets, mosaic-and-black-terrazzo floors, trellised gardens, and marble fountains with sledgehammers, and then remove Lagerfeld's liver and ponytail and have them FedExed to Ristorante Ai Tre Scalini (on the Piazza Navona), where they're prepared by chefs ("Fegata e tréccia alla veneziano") and served to the ghost of Pier Paolo Pasolini (drolly played by a wizened Paul Sorvino), as meanwhile, back in Amalfi, Lagerfeld's muse and confidant, ex–Hüsker Dü guitarist Bob Mould, is put into a drug-induced coma and kept in a glass sarcophagus à la Snow White, where he awaits the revivifying kiss of the Antichrist, who, according to Nostradamus, will manifest himself after failing the bar exam 666 times—to me, all of these movies are ultimately about the intricate, tangled reciprocations of father-son relationships.'

" 'Through its furious incomprehensibility, *The Tetherballs of Bougainville* radiates a kind of white light. It attains a white opacity toward which sloughed molecules of our own autobiographies float. These are the motes seen drifting in the projector's beam in the darkened theater—the spores of our own autobiographies pulled towards the white, blank screen. And this superstratum of autobiographical spores that colonize the silver media ultimately becomes "the movie." So, in a sense, power accrues to "the movie" parasitically.'

" 'What the fuck does *that* mean?' asked Siegel.

" 'Would you two please shut up?' said Michael Medved *(Sneak Previews),* who was seated in the row directly behind us.

" 'Hey, fuck you!' Siegel shot back, doffing his eyeglasses to add, I suppose, swagger to the macho retort.

"This was a mistake, because then Medved took a purse-size canister of Mace from his jacket pocket and sprayed Siegel point-blank in the face.

"And Siegel lurched out of the theater, howling, 'My eyes! My eyes!'

"I can't say I really felt sorry for the guy. I mean, he

must make like half a million bucks minimum on *GMA* and I write reviews totally gratis for *Der Schweißblatt,* this German armpit-fetish 'zine out of Düsseldorf, and he's like 'What does *this* mean? What does *that* mean?' y'know, pumping *me* for information . . . Let him do his own fucking work.

"*The Tetherballs of Bougainville* first finds Mark (played with pitch-perfect menace by Chandrapal Ram, a 16-year-old contortionist dwarf from the Great Raj Kamal Circus in Upleta, India, who is little known in America, but, if we're to judge by this astonishing, galvanic debut, seems destined for instant megastardom and then an equally precipitous descent into obscurity, impoverishment, substance abuse, a spate of botched suicide attempts, and, finally, a day job) at The Carousel, a topless bar on the outskirts of Princeton, several hours after the failed execution of his father and his subsequent sentencing to NJSDE. The Carousel is a state-operated, officially alcohol-free, topless club for minors. Youthful patrons skirt the booze prohibition, though, by simply going to the 'Gourmet Shoppe' located conveniently next door and purchasing 10-ounce bottles of 'Cooking Vodka,' 'Cooking Beer,' 'Cooking Jagermeister,' 'Cooking Captain Morgan's,' even 'Cooking Robitussin,' and 'Cooking Methadone,' and bringing it back to The Carousel, which provides setups. Designed to simulate an airport baggage carousel, the club features topless women who slide down a long chute and then revolve on a conveyer belt until customers, seated around the belt, signal them for table and lap dances. Mark and his heavy-lidded, barely coherent compadre Felipe are knocking back rum-and-Cokes and puffing cigarettes. Felipe wants to know why the execution took so long, and in a close shot of Mark's face, which fills the frame for some eight minutes as he offers a précis of his day, Chandrapal Ram's virtuosic skills are given full rein. I have never seen such a finely calibrated

choreography of affect, such a deft, protean composition
of smiles, pouts, smirks, winks, and scowls, as he
recounts, in eidetic detail, his attempt to reach 40,000
points in the Game Boy version of *Gianni Isotope*. And
then this physiognomic kaleidoscope of emotion so
vividly manifest as he recounts rescuing future Rock and
Roll Hall of Fame inductees such as Oasis singer Noel
Gallagher, Everything But The Girl's Tracey Thorn,
Shirley Manson of Garbage, and Eye Yamatsuka of the
Boredoms from the gruesome processing plant in the
Lwor Cluster, abruptly (and brilliantly!) collapses into
impassivity when, distracted by the continuous cascade
and slow, mesmerizing orbit of nearly naked women, he
assumes a perfunctory singsong to describe the ensuing
events ('Then he had to tell me this whole long story
about turning a brunette without a cranium into a
blonde, and then they tried to execute him and then he
didn't die, and then I had to go talk to the prison doctor, and then he was resentenced to NJSDE, and then
they had to explain what NJSDE was, and then we had
to pick a song to go with the video, and then we had to
say good-bye all over again, and then I got high with
the warden, and then I had sex with the warden, then I
read my talismanic movie review to the warden. It was
just one thing after another.') and he admits to Felipe
that he's terrified by the prospect of his father resurfac-
ing out of paternal concern for him ('I know how much
he cares about me, man, but those motherfuckin'
NJSDE agents—they could come for him anytime and
they'll take out any sorry assholes who happen to be
around, including us.'). Mark signals one of the strippers
circulating on the baggage carousel, a blowzy woman
with huge, cantilevered silicone boobs, who comes over
and dances at their table, fondling herself, writhing,
moaning, and taunting the young boys, who are
promptly apoplectic with lust. And then Mark espies a
scar on her thigh—the characteristic scar from a
scrimshaw-engraver impaling. 'Daddy!' he screams, a

scream recapitulated from multiple angles to the horror cliché of shrieking strings. 'Dad, it's you!' he gasps, in the first of this movie's numbing succession of epiphanies. Felipe, one of those adolescents who's unctuously ingratiating to his friends' parents, is like: 'Mr. Leyner, sir, those are the most gorgeous fuckin' tits I've ever seen, man. You had that done this afternoon? Unbelievable, dude!' Unbelievable indeed. Sex-change surgery and complete recovery in several hours? 'This is just Plan A,' says Mark's father, Joel (hauntingly portrayed by Gérard Depardieu), cupping his breasts and twitching his G-stringed mons in a campy air-hump. 'I just wanted to make sure you were OK.' He hugs Mark and buries his son's head deep in sweaty cleavage, muffling his plaintive 'Dad, would you *please* get out of here.'

"Suspension of disbelief aside, what the hell are we supposed to make of a scene like this?

"Are we supposed to be moved by this father's extraordinary efforts to keep watch over his young son? Or appalled by the danger in which he (as an NJSDE releasee) heedlessly puts this same child? Or amused by a parody of the typical adolescent's mortification at being seen socializing with his parents? Or are we to read this as a sort of transsexual twist on oedipal conflict?

"Leyner's attention-deficit style of editing gives us scant opportunity to ponder any of this.

"As Mark tries to wriggle out of his father's embrace, The Carousel is hit by several 152-mm howitzer shells, followed by a barrage of AT-3 Sagger wire-guided missiles and rocket propelled antitank grenades, and then several thousand rounds from a turret-mounted .50-caliber heavy machine gun and an M163 Vulcan 20-mm Gatling gun. There's a brief lull, and then a hit team of NJSDE agents appear, some in neoprene rubber wet suits, some in olive green Nomex flame-retardant overalls and bulletproof Kevlar flak vests. They lob in a dozen F-1 antipersonnel fragmentation grenades and then enter, raking the interior with AK-47s and German-made Heckler & Koch 9-mm submachine-gun fire. The massacre inside is luridly illuminated by thin red laser beams from the commandos' aiming devices and the glow of crisscrossing tracer rounds ricocheting off the walls.

"Mark and Felipe—probably because they were drunk and their bodies relaxed—miraculously escape unharmed. Joel, the putative target of this assault, presumably survives and disappears—we don't see his metamorphically full-figured physique among the dead and wounded as the camera slowly pans the smoldering carnage.

"It's worth reiterating—as we ponder this *tableau mort,* in which corpses wheel in a spasmodic, warped orbit on the crippled baggage carousel, many of them headless and gushing great plumes of thin, pink 'blood'—how astonishing it is that the 13-year-old Leyner was able to stage scenes like this in his small, second-floor bedroom in his parents' suburban home, particularly when you consider a production schedule limited to after-school hours and weekends.

"One can't, of course, overestimate the centrality of the male-adolescent bedroom in the history of western art. It is the sanctuary where the maladjusted, antisocial, genius teenage boy seeks refuge from his shallow peers and uncomprehending parents. It is the laboratory where he invents himself. And it is invariably the site of that great initial aesthetic frisson that not only determines the trajectory of his artistic life, but is often its crowning achievement. We rarely surpass in beauty or audacity those first raw, untutored riffs cooked up in the clamorous, totem-packed sancta sanctorum that we (the maladjusted, antisocial, genius teenage boys of America) simply call our 'rooms.'

"It should also be noted that the decapitated torso disgorging a geyser of blood is one of Leyner's signature effects and marks a recurrent, obsessive motif in *The*

Tetherballs of Bougainville. To give just one example: In a scene which takes place during a reading by playwrights David Hare and Wallace Shawn at the 92nd Street Y, the camera scans the auditorium and then stops at a seat occupied by a headless torso, its savagely hewn neck spewing a fountain of blood at least ten feet high. The other members of the audience, including those seated directly next to the spouting trunk and those being drenched by Leyner's egregiously ersatz fuchsia concoction, are absolutely oblivious and listen with rapt attention to Hare and Shawn reading from their own work. Whether this represents some sort of Buddhist memento mori, an absurdist harbinger of the coming millennium, a symbol of how inured we've become to one another's suffering, or is simply an image that the filmmaker finds so perversely satisfying that he can't help but insert it almost everywhere, blithely indifferent to its relevance, one can't say with any certainty. But I suspect the latter.

"It's no surprise that this zeitgeist-savvy film next finds Mark as a guest panelist on a daytime talk show. The theme: 'My Dad Is an NJSDE Releasee.'

" 'Is there anything you'd say to your dad if he were here right now?' asks the host, eyes moist with empathy.

"And Mark responds, 'I'd probably say: "Dad, I love you and I know you love me and want to be near me and watch over me and everything, but please don't come anywhere near me or Mom because they could call in a fucking NJSDE air strike on our house the minute you walk in." '

"The host winks at the audience.

" 'How about saying it to *him,* because he's been listening backstage and here he comes . . .'

"Mark leaps up and tears his microphone off, shrieking, 'Are you out of your mind?! Run! Run, people, run!'

"Panic engulfs the studio audience. There's instant

pandemonium as terrified people rush frantically for the exits.

"Predictably, battered and suffocated bodies soon litter the floor, some pounded and literally flattened into two-dimensional scaloppini by the throng's trampling wingtips and Birkenstocks. (This is far from the only instance of people being trampled to death in *The Tetherballs of Bougainville*. In fact, rarely do three characters congregate in this movie without one of them stumbling and dying under the feet of the other two. Whenever we're shown people emerging from a crowded elevator, we invariably discover, once that car has emptied out, the lifeless body of someone who's been inexplicably crushed to death by fellow passengers. I can understand the Ma Ling Stadium disaster scene in which drunken Bougainvillean tetherball hooligans supporting Wamp Kominika storm the stand filled with Wuwu-Bulolo Puliyasi supporters, and hundreds of people die in the ensuing stampede. But take the scene at the Musées Royaux des Beaux-Arts in Brussels—a group on a museum tour is clustered in front of Pieter Brueghel's *Fall of Icarus,* and when, at the behest of their guide, they continue on to the next painting, we find, remaining at the Breughel—surprise, surprise—the crumpled, broken body of some hapless art maven who somehow fell and was pummeled to death by the shoes of his companions as they scurried off to Hans Memlinc's *Martyrdom of St. Sebastian.* I mean, what's up with that? I've never seen a movie before in which: (a) people can't manage to remain upright for more than several seconds, and (b) when they do fall, passersby can't seem to avoid stomping them into unrecognizable pulp. If scenes like this bother you, you may consider avoiding *Tetherballs* altogether, although the gore is so unrealistic and mannered that I can't imagine anyone finding it really disturbing. We're not talking Industrial Light and Magic here. I don't claim to be a special-effects expert or anything, but I think we're talking raw chicken cutlets, dressed in Ken and Barbie outfits, and then pounded with a meat mallet. Whether this is an improvisation born of budgetary constraints, or a deliberate aesthetic device—a sort of Brechtian *Verfremdungseffekt*—or simply an excuse for the adolescent filmmaker and his crew to bludgeon meat with a hammer, one can't say with any certainty. But again, I suspect the latter.

"Anyway, as he flees this latest disaster, Mark valiantly stops to save a girl who's tripped and fallen under the stampeding feet. The girl's name is Sylvia, and she's played by Reese Witherspoon with equal portions of gamine bluster, little-girl vulnerability, bewitching carnality, and a sort of arid, postwar Gallic Maoist, protofeminist, chignon-wearing hauteur that easily falls away to reveal a kind of Squeaky Fromm— like, giggly, non-compos-mentis 'hey, whatever' insouciance in a performance that marks a stunning comeback from Ms. Witherspoon's disastrous turn as 'Tante Helke' in controversial Austrian director John Jacob Jingle-heimer Schmidt's unwatchable S&M epic *My Name Is Your Name Too.*

"Once safely outside the television studio, Mark and Sylvia sit on the sidewalk and introduce themselves to each other. Sylvia's new in town and, like Mark, about to start the 8th grade at Maplewood Junior High.

"When Mark asks her where she moved from, she hesitates for a long time, I mean a *long* time.

"*So* long that I actually got up, went to the men's room, sat on the john, lit a cigarette, and wrote a poem—a poem whose premise had been in gestation for several days, but the refrain of which had actually suggested itself to me months ago as I gazed down from the Euganean Hills to the plain of Lombardy, with Venice in the distance:

The ground is blanketed with the deciduous wings of
    pupal cicadas.

Two or three lissome, chemically castrated perverts are
    always draped over the railing at the rink.

The corpse has been rotated.
Apply the secretions.

Heathcliffean men wearing two-toned alligator shoes,
    Mirabella baseball caps, and well-pressed military
    attire, with flutes of champagne in their prosthetic
    left hands, trawl the baccarat pits, whispering into
    the ears of scantily clad dowagers, wearing only
    their golden-stringed Venetian tampons.
Florid, hyperbolic allusions to vampiric sex merely
    elicit "been there, done that" rolls of the eyes from
    the dowagers as, meanwhile, miniature
    velociraptors run wild in and out of their profusely
    powdered buttocks.
"Their mannerisms are totally *nha que*," they giggle to
    each other, mixing California syntax with
    Vietnamese slang for "country folk."

The corpse has been rotated.
Apply the secretions.

It's hard to believe that someone named "Gushy"
    Grubenfleisch is considered by so many to be "the
    great genius of our time," that cassettes of his
    lectures in the grand amphitheater of the Sorbonne
    circulate clandestinely throughout the kingdom.
We see him on television in his multicolored Coogi
    sweater and freshly laundered blue do-rag and are
    told to imagine future generations of similar
    "geniuses" spawned from his cryonically preserved
    sperm.
And yet when he opens his mouth to speak, he's
    like . . . way-stupid, totally *nha que*.

The corpse has been rotated.
Apply the secretions.

When rats are threatened, they emit very high
frequency (20,000 to 30,000 cycles per second)
screams.

Emerson said in *Nature:* ". . . my head bathed by the
blithe air."

I'm somewhere in between, I guess, with my own
"Stoned on GHB, soft tiny duck tongues seem to
lave my saddle-scorched perineum."

Strangely, that afternoon's $25.95 All-You-Can-Eat
Foie Gras at Lespinasse doesn't preclude an
overpowering yen, later, for an eggplant parm hero
and Twizzlers.

Oh well . . . soon enough the acacias and jacarandas,
even the shimmering ingots stacked high, will be
replaced by brambles and shriveled, bitter berries.

But for now, to the strains of a scratched, warped 45
of The Boxtops' "Cry Like a Baby" that's been
slowed down to 3 rpm, a springboard diver—*molto
bèllo* notwithstanding a bad-hair day—arcs slowly
through the air and slices through the slime of
filamentous blue-green algae that covers the surface
of the pitiless canal.

The corpse has been rotated.

Apply the secretions.

"I submitted the poem, via E-mail, right from the
stall, to *Logopoeia,* Francis Ford Coppola's new poetics
journal, and sat there waiting for a response. Finally I
got one—a rejection, but fairly encouraging, I thought.
It was from the poetry editor, Sofia Coppola, and it read:
'We went back and forth on this one, but ultimately
decided that all-you-can-eat foie gras at Lespinasse
would cost more than $25.95. Please try us again.'

"When I returned to my seat, Sylvia was still staring
into the middle distance, her eyes misting.

" 'Well, where'd you move from?' Mark reinquires,
thrumming the pavement.

"And finally she says tragically, 'Roquebrune-Cap-

Martin, near Nice.' Then, brightening, she says: 'Well, we lived most of the year in Roquebrune-Cap-Martin, but we spend summers in Seaside Heights.'

"Two quibbles here.

"Her family lived on the French Riviera and summered on the Jersey shore? I don't think so.

"Secondly, I hate to cavil about continuity, especially with a filmmaker this young and exuberant, but inside the TV studio when Mark helps Sylvia in the stampede, she's wearing a sky-blue and black bustier, black satin pants, and a delft-blue jacket. Outside, only minutes later, she's wearing a tailored pinstriped jacket and a leopard-patterned chiffon skirt with ruffles. Hello?

"School begins that September and the plot accelerates.

"Up to this point, *Tetherballs* has suffered from an unaccountable tendency to suddenly lock onto a particularly banal object—a disfigured Nerf ball, a piece of brisket on the highway, a price tag dangling from a bra entangled in a treetop and buffeted by a hurricane—and then subject it to exceedingly minute and prolonged scrutiny. We're talking about a movie in which a peripheral character—a lovelorn quantum electrodynamics professor at nearby Seton Hall University, played by a woefully miscast Willie Nelson—paints a wall in his apartment, and we're then treated to—I kid you not—a one-hour close-up of the paint drying. Although I appreciate the concept of rubbing an audience's nose in its own clichés, and the witty cross-reference to the Musée des Beaux-Arts trampling scene (Brueghel's *Fall of Icarus* is an illustration of the Flemish proverb 'Not a plow stands still when a man dies'), thank God it was a flat coat and not gloss enamel, or we'd *still* be there.

"The junior-high milieu, though, is one in which this filmmaker obviously feels comfortable, and the story line picks up major momentum, each scene invested with kinetic vitality and propelled by split-second tran-

sitions, dizzying montages, and frenetic line readings by
superenergized actors. (Not to harp on the film's ama-
teurish lapses, but there are times when production
assistants' hands are visible in the frame, administering
methedrine suppositories to those actors and actresses
whose recitations have flagged.) By the way, apparently
all of Maplewood Junior High's boys wear Versace
leather motocross trousers and no shirts, and *all* the girls
wear sepia lipstick, plaid skirts, and no shirts.

"Sylvia and Mark become inseparable, with Felipe a
resigned, albeit happy-go-lucky, 'wised-up-about-girls'
third wheel. Mark desperately wants to have marathon
freaky sex with Sylvia, but Sylvia rebuffs him, arguing
that it would jeopardize their friendship. She advocates a
kooky regimen of abstinence and fennel. Crudely updat-
ing an exchange from Michael Curtiz's 1945 classic *Mil-
dred Pierce,* in which Joan Crawford says to Jack Carson,
the horny, cynical bachelor, 'Friendship is much more
lasting than love,' and Jack replies, 'Yeah, but it's not as
entertaining,' Sylvia here assures Mark that 'Our relationship is too precious to be spoiled by a tablespoon of
warm goo,' to which Mark replies mordantly, 'Yeah, but
a tablespoon of warm goo is, like, more entertaining.'
Although Sylvia is resolute in her refusal, Mark's efforts
to undermine her resolve are indefatigable. He's constantly moaning as if in actual physical agony, the pur-
ple head of his raging boner rakishly protruding from
the waistband of his Hugo Boss boxer briefs, and he's
incessantly licking and biting and humping her, and
reading her excerpts from Anka Radakovich's old *Details*
columns, or just turning up on her doorstep naked and
hogtied, but the unflappably good-natured Sylvia's
always like 'Tsk tsk tsk, now c'mon, settle down, settle
down!'

"Sylvia's idea of a good time is to chill on the couch,
munching caramel-covered popcorn and Rolos, and
watch hidden-camera shows like *America's Funniest Viola-
tions of Psychiatrist / Patient Confidentiality.* Mark returns

home from these strictly platonic trysts, and takes out all that pent-up libidinal fury on the tetherball in his backyard. The tetherball scenes are filmed in a bluish haze with severe fun-house mirror distortion that lends them a hallucinatory, ritualistic quality. (These scenes can induce flashbacks of recovered-memory sequences from made-for-television movies with Patrick Duffy and Lisa Hartman, which some viewers may find disturbing.) And then, later, drenched in sweat, his palms and knuckles raw and bleeding, he collapses onto his bed and, as the camera dollies out of his bedroom window and tracks across the moonlit rooftops of Maplewood, we hear his primal howls of onanistic release echoing throughout the slumbering suburbs: 'Aaaaahhhh-ooooo-unnnnng-ohmigod-gh-ghrrr-oh-oh-oh-like-whoa!'

"Whenever anyone says something derisive about tetherball, Mark—who typically employs the impoverished lexicon of his hydrocephalic cronies—quotes ominously from Poe's 'The Masque of the Red Death,' intoning, either in voice-over or *viva voce,* 'Even with the utterly lost, to whom life and death are equally jests, there are matters of which no jest can be made,' and then appending his own patented 'See you in hell, my soon-to-be-dead friend.'

"Sylvia loves Mark deeply, though she limits demonstrations of her affection to hugs and chaste pecks on the cheek, and even these often precipitate the licking and biting and humping. Functioning in loco parentis, she's the only one he can really *heart-to-heart* with about his absent dad, who hasn't been seen since The Carousel. Mark's mother isn't eliminated entirely from the movie's diegetic space, though she is reduced to the by-now-familiar icon of Mom as booze-sodden, semi-invalid. But there's a brilliant scene—a schistlike melange of horror, porn, melodrama, and sentiment—in which Mark opens the door to his mother's bedroom one afternoon and finds her 'partying' with three men. ('Partying' is as delicate a euphemism as I can think of to describe a woman engaging in simultaneous anal, oral, and vaginal sex with three different musicians from a klezmer band that had appeared that morning at the Short Hills Mall.) This scene (which plays to a klezmer version of Sir Andrew Lloyd Webber's 'Close Every Door') powerfully correlates Joel's NJSDE exile and the wife and son he leaves behind in Maplewood with Agamemnon's fabled absence and the more sinister machinations of Clytaemnestra in Aeschylus' stylish shocker *The Oresteian Trilogy.*

"This section of the movie, though more tautly paced than what's preceded, is nonetheless marred by two completely superfluous characters who seem to have wandered in from other films: a crooked boxing manager and a cemetery groundskeeper—a hulking, gargoyle-like mute with a child's mind. Luckily, they are ignored by this movie's cast and eventually leave.

"There's also the de rigueur joyriding/wilding scene. Mark and Felipe hot-wire a jet-powered car they find parked in front of a Benihana. Outfitted with two General Electric J-79 engines from a U.S. Navy F-4 Phantom fighter jet, the 25-foot-long, dart-shaped vehicle, emblazoned with the logo *Spirit of America III,* is capable of reaching speeds in excess of 650 miles an hour. Guzzling small-batch bourbon, they take it out for a spin, careen out of control, the car loses both its wheel brakes and drag parachutes, flips over, and smashes into telephone poles at 400 miles an hour before sinking in a salt brine pond. Mark and Felipe walk away unharmed, all giggles and high-fives. After smoking a blunt and swigging a bottle of Bailey's, they set off on a mini crime spree that I can't begin to describe in detail here; suffice it to say that it begins with targeting yuppies in Burberry raincoats and injecting them with the drug Versed, a central-nervous-system depressant that leaves a person conscious but paralyzed; negotiating to buy a bottle containing about an ounce of liquid VX nerve gas (an amount that, if released in a crowded area, could kill 15,000 people); a clumsy, halfhearted attempt at sodomizing a police horse; the vicious, completely unprovoked beating of a waiter outside Osteria del Circo; shooting a neighbor's seeing-eye dog because, the day before, the woman had casually remarked that Naomi Campbell 'looked bloated' on Leno; and culminating with spraying graffiti on Memorial Sloan-Kettering Cancer Center including swastikas, slogans praising cancer, and gruesome, smiling 'oncogenes' with obscenely misogynist speech balloons.

"Predictably, reviewers have criticized this scene as 'irresponsible,' 'morally reprehensible,' 'pernicious,' etc.

"I disagree. An unintended consequence of liberalism has been to deprive sullen, alienated adolescents of a language or iconography of transgression, forcing them to turn to ever more blasphemous rhetoric and imagery, and, when these are invariably co-opted, to sociopathic behavior, and then, when even these modes of behavior are appropriated by the entertainment and advertising industries, to increasingly deviant and destructive acts. So I actually don't see what choice Mark and Felipe have *but* to behave precisely as they do. And as far as the woman with the seeing-eye dog goes, what does she mean Naomi Campbell *'looked* bloated' on Leno? I thought she was supposed to be blind. So, apparently, what we have here is some lowlife pulling an insurance scam that's going to mean higher premiums for the rest of us. So why *not* shoot her fucking dog? But let's say, for the sake of discussion, that the behavior depicted *is* 'vile and repugnant.' I think that's exactly what makes this scene such an intrepid act of filmmaking—the adamant refusal to airbrush, candy-coat, or sentimentalize reality, however unpalatable.

"Let's not be naive. Kids are going to experiment with drugs and alcohol, vandalism, callous violence, semiautomatic handguns, chemical weapons, and neofascist hate crime—it's inevitable behavior for adolescents

trying to determine what 'truth' is in a world torn
between the self-replicating apocrypha of the Internet
and the info-hegemony of Eisner-Murdoch-Turner. We
did it when we were kids, our kids will do it, their kids
will do it, their kids' kids will do it, etc., etc., until the
end of the world. And surely that's how the world—or
at least the human species—is going to end. I don't care
what lofty endgame scenarios the pundits concoct: asteroid collision, global warming with melting polar ice-
caps, biosphere toxic shock, iatrogenic plague, the
ultimate Darwinian triumph of Artificial Intelligence,
cosmic entropy, etc. The end will lack any such
grandeur. It will be undignified, banal, and breathtakingly stupid. The world is going to end because, one
night, a carload of solvent-sniffing 15-year-olds from
Long Island mess around with something they shouldn't
have messed around with. Take all your unsolved disas-
ters from history—mass extinction of the dinosaurs,
Pompeii, the Black Death, the great Siberian explosion
of 1908, the *Andrea Doria,* the Triangle shirtwaist factory fire, the Lindbergh baby, the *Hindenburg,* Amelia
Earhart, JFK, Hoffa, the *Exxon Valdez,* Bhopal, Chernobyl—ultimately there's only one consistent explanation for each of these—a bunch of skanky, dyslexic
adolescents, high on drugs, looking for trouble.

"Ironic, isn't it, that the civilization of Dante, Car-
avaggio, Keats, and Einstein will end with some fried,
feebleminded kid breaking into a Level 4 maximum-
security biological weapons facility, mumbling 'Yo—
what the fuck . . . ?'

"And so, eighth-grade transpires. Wracked by his
unconsummated passion for Sylvia and the loss of his
father, Mark is a surly, apathetic student. The only class
in which he pays the slightest attention is 'The Punic
Wars,' a seventh-period elective taught by a Ms.
Hogenauer (Steven Dorff, for all intents and purposes,
reprising his role as transvestite superstar Candy Darling
in Mary Harron's *I Shot Andy Warhol*). Hogenauer, a vet-

eran of the downtown performance-art scene, has relocated to Maplewood after a series of disastrous marriages with Mafioso restaurateurs, and moved in with the director of a Satanic day-care center in neighboring Milburn, played with over-the-top lesbian-supremacist fervor by Kyra Sedgwick. This section is firmly in the *To Sir with Love, Dead Poets Society, Mr. Holland's Opus,* pedagogue-as-charismatic-hero tradition with scenes like the one in which Hogenauer shimmies up the down escalator at the Virgin Megastore in Times Square on a purple-and-aquamarine ACG snowboard with a big stuffed Dumbo draped across her back, symbolically reenacting—I assume—Hannibal crossing the Alps with his elephants, and lines like: 'Gosh, Ms. Hogenauer, nobody ever made the Carthaginian victory at Cannae come so alive before!'

"In all his other classes, though, Mark sulks and daydreams, filling his notebooks with drawings of grotesque heads.

"Sylvia is continually preaching this nauseating Anthony Robbins, *Awaken the Giant Within*–style self-empowerment, and urging him to accomplish something, *anything*—to actually start a project and finish it. Mark insists that he wants to write and direct a film that will do for tetherball what *The Poseidon Adventure* did for synchronized swimming. But, of course, he never does. He's too busy getting fucked up with Felipe. Finally, disgusted with his inertia and excuses, Sylvia takes matters into her own hands. Through some relative's friend of a friend, she's able to finagle Mark a summer internship with *Game Face,* an inane MTV-style cable sports show whose target audience is 12-to-14-year-old boys, and which entails going to—guess where?—yes, Bougainville!—and gathering information, maybe even writing and producing a short feature about the glamorous and bewilderingly arcane world of Bougainvillean tetherball.

"The day before he leaves for the Solomon Islands,

Mark makes a last-ditch plea for the ever-unattainable marathon freaky sex. 'I may never see you again,' he says gravely. 'Nonsense, silly boy. It's merely a summer internship. I'll see you in September,' says Sylvia, deftly parrying his grubby little hands.

"In desperation, Mark scrawls the following in the margin of Sylvia's *New York Review of Books*:

" 'Are you a petite, buxom, free spirit with liquid-food-secreting glandular ductules and a piezoelectric ceramic-fiber fecundating cleft who's interested in romance, egg creams, Glenfiddich, the Cirque du Soleil, '31 Duesenbergs, Newports, forties, blunts, GHB, khat, keepin' it real at Rancho la Quinta, Bauhaus furniture, Janet Jackson, quiet walks in the Everglades, ceviche, and fiery curry, and who has the self-confidence to feel just as feminine and desirable in a cranial halo, nasogastric tube, and cervical collar as she would in a Hervé Leger evening gown, and who wouldn't mind occasional binges that end with the two of us stinking-drunk, incoherent, and penniless in the offal-strewn gutter of some squalid equatorial port? Extremely attractive, slim, 5'1", athletic, vivacious, affectionate, intelligent, down-to-earth, erudite, warm, upbeat, energetic, sincere, loyal, evolved, solvent, nurturing, 13-year-old mensch wants to come on your tits.'

" 'Settle down,' chides Sylvia.

"That night, we see a close-up of Mark's open mouth and vibrating uvula, as we hear his long onanistic howl, and then a match sound-cut to what is discernibly someone else's open mouth, with corresponding vibrato of the uvula, as whoever it is sings 'Aaaaahhhh-ooooo-unnnnng-ohmigod-gh-ghrrr-oh-oh-oh-like-whoa-di spela pisin savvy tok bullseet!!' The camera pulls back to reveal the bushy-haired Melanesian megastar Offramp Tavanipupu on a video screen in a multimedia information kiosk at Bougainville International Airport.

"And at long last, we have arrived at our eponymous destination.

*"Bougainville . . . Volcanic island in the Solomon Sea . . .
3,880 sq. miles . . . Population 150,000 . . . First explored
in 1768 by the French navigator Louis de Bougainville,
namesake of the vine . . . Declared independence after seceding
from Papua New Guinea . . . Major exports: copper, ivory
nuts, green snails, copra (dried coconut meat), cocoa, tortoise
shells, and trepang (sea cucumber).*

"All according to the info-kiosk touchscreen.

"Mark encamps in Kieta, the island's main port, and
sets out the following day in his rental Jeep with driver
to interview the venerable coach of the national junior
tetherball squad. Not far from his hotel, the Jeep is
forced off the road by a Cherokee Chief full of
Bougainville Treasury Police—a sextet of surly, Uzi-
toting motherfuckers, wearing San Jose Sharks caps
and chewing wads of the narcotic leaf khat. The
Cherokee's license plate number is 77 R-K5.

"I mention this only because in the very next shot of
the car, the license reads 78 KxP and in the next, 79 R-
KKt5, and then successively 80 R-KB5, 81 RxP and 82
R-K7. There was something so familiar to me about this
alphanumerical series, yet, as I watched the scene, I
just couldn't put my finger on what it was. Then it hit
me . . . Of course! These were Alexander Alekhine's final
six moves (playing the white pieces) in the 34th and
conclusive game of his world championship chess match
against José Raul Capablanca, which took place in
Buenos Aires in 1927.

"And at about the same time that *I* realized the
source of the license-plate sequences, there were
corresponding murmurs of recognition throughout the
theater.

"Capablanca resigned on his eighty-second move,
giving six wins and the championship to Alekhine, who
was renowned for the brilliance, viciousness, and zeal of
his attacks on the board, and for the heavy drinking,
sadism, and phallo-narcissism that characterized his
social behavior.

"Clearly, a correspondence is being drawn here between Alekhine's psychopathology and Mark's burgeoning emotional disorders. I found the use of chess notation on license plates to elucidate the psychology of this movie's 13-year-old protagonist to be an especially effective device and not at all cryptic.

"One of the goons casually shoots the driver in the head (*ars longa, vita brevis*) and then hands Mark an embossed invitation that reads:

> Col. Nusrahana Vanipapobosa Alebua
> requests the pleasure of
> Mr. Mark Leyner's
> company at luncheon
> on Tuesday, the Twenty-sixth of June
> at one o'clock
> The Presidential Palace

"Now, I've always been amazed at how long written material is kept up on the screen in theaters—whether it's a no-smoking announcement, one of those cinema trivia quizzes, or some piece of text in the movie itself. And this particular item is no exception. I mean, c'mon, how long does it take to read those seven lines? And yet as I sat there in the theater, I could hear people all around me struggling out loud to phonetically decipher the words: 'ree-kwests th-th-thuh ple-ah-zhoor . . . kum-pah-nee at lun-chee-on.' Sadly, today, even people who are capable of picking up sophisticated cultural references, such as Alekhine's last six moves in his 1927 match with Capablanca, have terrible difficulty reading simple text. Surely this is further proof of the deteriorating literacy of our intelligentsia.

"While the invitation is on screen, we hear Wu-Tang Clan's vertiginous remake of the old Chinese Cultural Revolution standby 'Sailing the Ocean Depends on the Helmsman.' Dissected and reassembled by Wu-Tang production wizard the RZA, and brought back to life like some Red Guard Frankenstein defibrillated with jumper cables, this hortatory Maoist classic never sounded better. If this deranged sonic vortex of stuttering revolutionary dogma, wafting samples, and interlacing, static-drenched beats is any indication, we can only look forward to the entire Clan or individual MCs—the Method Man, Ol' Dirty Bastard, Genius, Raekwon—deconstructing more vintage funk from the Cultural Revolution like 'Liu Shao-chi Is a Deviationist-Clique Reactionary,' 'Long Live the Third Corp of the Rebel Army of the Shanghai Artisans' Apprentices,' and, of course, 'Those Who Want to Damage the National Economy by Sabotaging Production, Opposing Chairman Mao and the Great Proletarian Cultural Revolution, and by Corrupting the Revolutionary Will of the Masses with Material Interests and Letting Bourgeois Ideas Run Amok Must Be Arrested Without Delay by the Ministry for Public Safety and Severely Punished (I'm Talkin' 2 U, Bitch).'

"Mark looks at his watch and, seeing that it's already 12:50 P.M., Tuesday, June 26, realizes that no RSVP will be necessary, and he accompanies the thugs to *chez dictator.*

"Colonel Nusrahana Vanipapobosa Alebua (played by a bewigged and artificially dusky Chaz Palminteri) is the despotic junta leader who engineered Bougainville's bloody secession from Papua New Guinea. Hamstrung somewhat by having to battle internal opposition groups—groups that receive political and material support from Papua New Guinea—Alebua nonetheless endeavors to amalgamate a 'Greater Bougainville' by capturing the neighboring islands of Choiseul, New Georgia, and Ysabel. A draconian autocrat, the Colonel is committed to lining his pockets and those of his cronies—the scions of Bougainville's oligarchic families who were Alebua's classmates at the military academy. What distinguishes Alebua from the Papa Doc Duvaliers and the Idi Amins, from the Jean-Bedel Bokassas,

Mobutu Sese Sekos, and Macias Nguemas, and from the paradigmatic caudillos of Latin America, is that Alebua was raised on satellite feeds of American educational television and is a wild aficionado of the Public Broadcasting System (PBS). Given to squandering millions on grandiose monuments, his palace is an exact replica—down to the andirons, breakfront hinges, and toilet-tank float balls—of Brideshead, the great country house from the lavish and lengthy 1980 *Masterpiece Theatre* adaptation of *Brideshead Revisited*.

"His shapely 16-year-old daughter (*Baywatch Nights'* Donna D'Errico) is named Lehrerasha, after *NewsHour* anchor Jim Lehrer.

"Lunching with Alebua, Mark is confronted with an unnerving hybrid of feral tyranny and chuffing Edwardian pretension, as Alebua—in bowler hat, sunglasses, fatigues, a brace of ivory-handled pistols holstered at his hips, and a raised-welt lightning bolt on either cheek—washes down tinned kippers and crisps with a magnum of kava, the official intoxicating beverage of the South Seas. Alebua breaks into a betel-stained grin as he discusses his ruthless suppression of tribal minorities and a cooking show he hosts, which is devoted to the preparation of dissidents. This is all something of a stretch for Palminteri, who seems confounded by his own minstrel pigmentation.

"Meanwhile, members of the elite Palace Guard wander in and out, their TEC-9 assault pistols slung in WNET and WGBH tote bags. (One of the first edicts issued by Alebua upon his ascension to power was a decree mandating that each and every man, woman, and child on this impoverished island contribute to PBS fund drives. Bougainvilleans who neglect or refuse to make these donations are 'kabobbed'—groups of five are lined up in single file, run through with eight-foot skewers, marinated in kava, grilled, and sold by vendors at tetherball tournaments. Bill Moyers said at the time, 'Although I don't necessarily condone kabobbing, I think it's an understandable reaction on the part of a government that believes very deeply in public television.')

"The Colonel knows who Mark is. He's seen the 'I Feel Shitty' video on which Mark was musical director, and he *loves* that video—he's, like, a *huge* fan. That's why he had him abducted. He needs the dude's help.

"See, Alebua has an image problem. He has garnered a dreadful international reputation. The poor man can't clap-on his 60-inch Hitachi Ultravision without seeing that brazen Christiane Amanpour incriminating his villainous regime, or some sanctimonious Amnesty International spokesman bellyaching about death-squad atrocities, or some sallow IMF wonk carping about ruinous economic policies. So he asks Mark to write a series of VNRs—video news releases—that will recast his despicable government in a more flattering light. ('Mi wanem numbawan bullseet!')

"Mark is fully aware that Alebua is a homicidal megalomaniac. He weighs the moral opprobrium that he'd incur working for a brutal, conscienceless dictator against the prospect of finally having some produced work to show around. He considers Pirandello, Marinetti, and Ezra Pound, Riefenstahl, Céline, and Paul de Man, and finally assuages any lingering qualms of conscience by reasoning that just as every defendant is entitled to effective counsel, every despot is entitled to a creative public-relations consultant.

"He calls Heather Schroder, ICM foreign-rights specialist (Gwyneth Paltrow in an impish cameo reminiscent of her ebullient walk-on in Kenneth Branagh's *The Porcine Mammary Gland as a Bioreactor for Complex, Therapeutic Proteins*), brings her up to speed, and then hands the phone to Alebua, who screams in unintelligible but pugnacious pidgin for several minutes before handing the phone back to Mark.

" 'Well, what's the deal?' Mark asks.

" 'Here's what we got,' says Heather. 'You do the

work, you get 15,000 Bougainvillean kipas per video,
unlimited expense account, sumptuous living quarters.
You don't do the videos, you're kabobbed. My inclination is to take it.'

" 'Fifteen thousand kipas . . . is that good?'

" 'It's pretty standard for a coerced VNR.'

" 'What about a kill-fee?'

"Heather reviews her notes.

" 'If your video is not acceptable for release, they
will give you an opportunity to revise it. If the revised
video is likewise unacceptable, they kill you.'

"Mark accepts the job after Heather is able to cajole
Alebua up to 15,500 kipas—because he *loves* that video
('Mi laik lukim "I Feel Shitty" mas time. Sena bwoyna!
Numbawan!').

"The Colonel forsakes his Melanesian pidgin only
once in the course of the movie. While playing minia-
ture golf with Mark and Admiral Elmo R. Zumwalt
(portrayed with unexpected gravitas by Charles Nelson
Reilly), Alebua, who's about to putt into the mouth of a
political prisoner, looks up solemnly from his ball and
says, apropos of nothing in that sunny afternoon's affa-
ble, inconsequential banter, and in crisply enunciated,
declamatory English: 'The world, which seems to lie
before us like a land of dreams, so various, beautiful, so
new, hath really neither joy, nor love, nor light, nor cer-
titude, nor peace, nor help for pain; and we are here as
on a darkling plain swept with confused alarms of struggle and flight where ignorant armies clash by night.'
Zumwalt says nothing in response, impassively plucking
shreds of artificial turf from the honed crampons of his
miniature-golf shoes. After a time, though, Mark, visi-
bly discomforted by this brooding silence, weighs in
with: 'Sometimes I feel like I don't have a partner.
Sometimes I feel like my only friend is the city I live in,
the city of angels. Lonely as I am, together we cry . . . I
don't ever want to feel like I did that day. Take me to
the place I love. Take me all the way.'

"The three of them then stare blankly in different directions for several minutes.

"Summoned to the Presidential Palace at dawn the following day, Mark immediately starts peppering Alebua with ideas: 'One—if you're gonna do the whole cult-of-personality, ubiquitous monument thing, I'd spend a few extra kipas and go with Portrait of Dorian Gray Statues. They're piezoelectric polymer animatronic figures. The more vile, ruthless, and paranoid you become in your murderous drive for absolute power, the more horrifically scabrous the statues of you become. They'll scare the living shit out of your population. Two—you know what most dictators do that's really stupid? They're too secretive about their medical condition. That's exactly the wrong way to go. Absolutely everything about you—from the consistency of your bowel movements to your HDL count—should be announced in shrieking front-page headlines. The daily vicissitudes of your dermatologic health should be treated like biblical events. If you have an ingrown hair on your ass, I want to see flags at half-mast, I want to see endless streams of grief-stricken workers and school-children converging on the Presidential Palace, singing dirges, laying wreaths, weeping, throwing themselves onto their knees, beating their brows against the ground until they're bloody and unconscious. Three—you gotta start licensing merchandise. You come up with a logo— say, six intellectuals en brochette. You grant manufac-turers the right to incorporate it on their products. We're talking royalties of, like, 7.5 percent on the wholesale price. I'm telling you, chief, in terms of mer-chandising, Bougainville could be the Oakland Raiders of the new millennium. Every homey, wannabe, slacker, club kid, yuppie, and soccer mom in the U.S.A. is gonna want to wear Bougainville caps, Bougainville insulated parkas, Bougainville windbreakers, T-shirts, and boxer shorts. And you do, like, baby bibs, toothbrushes, sheets, lunch boxes, drink coasters, chip-and-dip bowls, kids' vitamins. And you do a rotisserie chicken and a book club. Four—you absolutely, positively, must do a scent. I'm thinking a mass class fragrance at around thirty-five bucks for a two-ounce eau de toilette spray. We call it *Génocide* (zhen-o-sid). The name's got a kind of goth panache to it, and it focus-groups exceptionally well with your target audience—18-to-35-year-old married working women with dashed expectations. For top notes, I'm thinking, like, nuoc mam, bull semen, halvah, and Altoids. Tag line: 'The acrid aroma of savage machtpolitik and unwavering intransigence gives me goose bumps . . . It's *Génocide*.' Herb Ritts does the campaign. Print ads, outdoor posters, television . . . I see a whole id-driven barbarian stud-muffin-conqueror creamy European chattel-concubine concept. The whole 'pillage our city, burn our library, take me with you' fantasy. I see a couple—you and maybe, like, Claire Danes—caressing in the sea against a limitless sky, tinted crimson to match the bottle and packaging. The idea is Clean, Fresh Romance, and the Annihilation of the Civilized World. It's like Ralph Lauren meets Pol Pot, if you will.'

"Lehrerasha saunters in, sipping Cherry fX Bomb, a popular kava-based soft drink. She and Mark exchange smoldering looks of sexual communion, winking, pouting, and flaring their nostrils at each other with a frenetic, almost Tourette's-like intensity that portends an imminent liaison.

"We're never told which, if any, of Mark's canny marketing gambits Colonel Alebua actually employs. But he obviously admires the kid's extemporaneous verve, because he installs him in an opulent apartment of the sort reserved exclusively for junta families, plutocrats, and tetherball stars. The elegantly appointed three-bedroom duplex is in the ultra-prestigious Adam and Eve Towers, two 115-story, anthropomorphic, anatomically correct, and transparent edifices built by a fabulously wealthy and fanatically evangelical, born-

again copra exporter. Realistically depicting the prelap-
sarian Adam and Eve in an act of upright sexual congress, the structure's interior architecture also maintains
strict fidelity to human anatomy. Elevators travel up and
down the two spinal columns. A 'coital concourse' con-
nects the towers with a moving walkway and shopping
arcade that run through the conjoined genitalia.
Although *New York Times* critic Herbert Muschamp
assailed the Adam and Eve Towers as 'the single most
egregious act of pornographic kitsch in the history of
architecture,' many critics judge the Towers more favor-
ably, finding antecedents in Tantric sculpture and the
celebrated erotic carvings at the 13th-century Temple of
the Sun in Konarak, India. Of course, the Towers have
no prurient connotation for Bougainvilleans, a simple-
hearted and spiritual people, who see only a sacred and
engendering act of union, and not two 1,500-foot freaks
fucking the living shit out of each other in broad day-
light. Mark's condo, which is in Eve's pancreas, puts him
in giddy proximity to the tetherball superstars he's idol-
ized his entire life. Ataban Tokurapai lives down the hall
in Eve's spleen, and Ezikiel Takaku owns an apartment
two flights down in her duodenum. Wamp Kominika
lives in Adam's left eyeball, which affords a spectacular
view of downtown Kieta and the harbor. Lyndon
Kakambona and Fagi Pinjinga own magnificent suites
in Adam's medulla and cerebellum. And Offramp Tavanipupu occupies a palatial, 15,000-square-foot penthouse that he created by knocking down the wall
corresponding to the central sulcus between the frontal
and parietal lobes, and which was recently featured in
the Style section of *Der Schweißblatt*.

"The public-relations campaign is a stunning success. Mark's video news releases are regularly featured on
CNN, C-SPAN, MSNBC, FOX NEWS, etc. Efforts to
ostracize Colonel Alebua and his clique from the community of nations abate, as Mark is able to reposition
Alebua as an emancipator and populist, defending his

fledgling nation against the imperial predations of Papua New Guinea. With the assistance of ILM, Digital Domain, Sony's Image Works, and Pixar (which did *Toy Story*), Mark shrewdly restages recent history to portray Alebua as an indispensable player on the world stage. Utilizing sophisticated computer graphics technology— akin to that used to digitally transplant Paula Abdul into a pas de deux with Gene Kelly in the Diet Coke ads and make possible the Kennedy cameo in *Forrest Gump*—Mark produces a fiendishly brilliant series of VNRs that not only place Colonel Alebua at the side of eminent Johns Hopkins neurologist Dr. Jeffrey Roth- stein as they work together on an experimental drug, riluzole, that slows the deadly progress of amyotrophic lateral sclerosis, but that also show him assisting Richard Jewell in his lawsuit against NBC and anchor Tom Brokaw; as a pallbearer at Dean Martin's funeral; carousing at Club Macanudo with New Edition mem- bers Bobby Brown and Ronnie DeVoe, Chinese Defense Minister General Chi Haotian, and former Arkansas governor Jim Guy Tucker; and stoning an adulterer to death with Taliban militiamen in Kabul, Afghanistan (Alebua is seen throwing three stones: the first one, delivered from a full windup, misses high; the second, a slider, is just outside; on his third rock, Alebua— from the stretch—comes with his split-fingered fastball, and nails the unregenerate fornicator flush in the forehead, receiving a standing O from the turbaned fundamentalists).

"Although the campaign succeeds in rehabilitating Alebua's image abroad, his job ratings at home remain dismally low.

"There are daily assassination attempts on Alebua and his associates. Dissimulation, treachery, and paranoia are pervasive throughout every echelon of society. The 'enemy' is everywhere, and there's no certainty whose side anyone is on at any given moment. In one particularly disturbing scene, babies with bloated bellies, covered with flies, and sprawled listlessly in the dust, suddenly produce assault weapons, leap to their feet, and rake a passing motorcade with automatic gunfire. It's chilling to see a gaunt, glassy-eyed infant, who's apparently starving to death, peel off its full-body latex mask to reveal a sneering, heavily muscled, 6'2" mercenary commando.

" 'My people despise me,' the subtitled colonel concedes. It appears as if he hasn't slept for days—dark rings circle puffy, bloodshot eyes. His speech is slurred.

" 'Tennesseeans love Senator Fred Thompson. Why? Because, as baby-sitting adolescents, they spent thousands of hours in front of televisions watching movies in which he was an almost imperceptible presence, and he subliminally insinuated himself into their subconsciousnesses as an avuncular icon,' continues Alebua, a perceptive student of American politics. 'I've been reviewing the entire Fred Thompson oeuvre—everything from *Curly Sue, Dayo,* and *Unholy Matrimony* to *Aces: Iron Eagle III*—that's why I haven't slept for days. And I've come to the shattering conclusion that having failed to subliminally insinuate myself into the pubescent psyches of my people, I will never have their love.'

" 'Au contraire, Mein Führer,' says Mark coyly. 'I have an idea. I will create a retroactive canon of movies for you. You'll star in them all. We'll get the most beautiful women in Bougainville—those cigarette girls from the trepang hatcheries you love so much—to co-star with you. We'll churn out product like the great studios of Hollywood's Golden Age. And we'll flood the video stores and fill all the time slots on the classic-movie channels, so that people will actually begin to believe that they originally saw the movies long ago, and they'll feel this nostalgic fondness for you, and they'll even develop false memories about where they were as children when they first saw such-and-such a film, and

they'll come to cherish you with a love as innate
and unconditional, as ardent and as unfathomable,
as the love they feel for their own mothers and
fathers.'

" 'Good,' says Alebua. 'Pitch me some ideas
tomorrow.'

"Although Mark knows that the Colonel has been
delighted with his VNR work, he's somewhat apprehen-
sive when he arrives at the pitch meeting the following
morning. There are skeletons manacled to the walls—
apparently screenwriters who've made unsuccessful
pitches to the Colonel and his Minister of Culture, a
sallow, hollow-cheeked, pockmarked, acromegalic
degenerate (played by the formidable Derek Jacobi) in a
sleeveless flak jacket and domino mask, who spends the
meeting shooting up speedballs and fondling his 'wife,'
a cardboard cutout point-of-purchase display of the Oak
Ridge Mountain Boys. (Dental records would later identify the skeletal remains as notorious Euroschlockmeister
Joe D'Amato, and Americans Ethan Coen and Todd
Solondz.)

" 'You're on,' says the Minister.

" 'OK . . . this is, like, completely off the top of my
head, but . . . We do the life of Leonard Gutman, the
great signage copywriter. I see a full-blown, lush, 70-
millimeter artist-hero biopic—a kind of signage *Lust for
Life.* Maybe we call it *Gutman*—y'know, kinda like
Basquiat. We start back when he was a little boy,
because the interesting thing is that Len Gutman grew
up with all these legendary jazz musicians hanging
around the house—all these jazz greats used to just drop
in. It wasn't unusual for Len to come down to dinner
and find, like, Eddie Vinson, Johnny Hodges, Coleman
Hawkins, and Jo Jones seated at the table. Or to wake
up and find Ben Webster, Jimmy Heath, Roy Eldridge,
Charlie Christian, Milt Jackson, and Fats Navarro in the
living room, jamming late into the night. But no one
could figure out why, because apparently neither Len nor

his parents knew any of them. So one day Mr. and Mrs. Gutman have one of those "I thought they were your friends"–"I thought they were *your* friends" conversations, and Mr. Gutman asks the jazz musicians to please leave, which they do, cordially and without incident. This entire episode has absolutely no effect whatsoever on young Len, who never had and never would have the slightest interest in jazz or any other kind of music.

" 'That summer, Len's parents take him on a vacation to Wiseguyana.

" 'Hundreds of years ago, Mafia turncoats—mobsters who'd "rolled over" and testified for the prosecution—were put into the federal witness protection program and exiled to an isolated region of a country on the northern coast of South America—what is today called Wiseguyana. And over the generations, as the ex-Mafiosi interbred with the indigenous population, they gradually devolved into a primitive tribe of hunter-gatherers. And although today they depend on very basic means of sustaining themselves—spears, blowguns with curare-tipped darts, and manioc cultivation—they retain a number of cultural vestiges of their forebears. They wear loincloths made from their ancestors' $3,000 double-breasted Brioni suits, for instance. And the shaman keeps the tribe's sacred amulets in the last surviving monogrammed sheer Gucci sock. But this culture's fascinating lineage is most conspicuous in its speech patterns and idioms. Here's a young hunter as he trusses a wounded tapir in the moonlit forest: "You don't stay still, I'm gonna whack you in the fuckin' mouth, you scumbag. I don't need this shit. You think I enjoy this? I could be at the track or with some broad, but no, I'm here so you can break my fuckin' balls? You piece of shit, nocturnal, ungulate cocksucker." Here's the tribal headman, a wizened elder in feather headdress and ornamental earsticks, pacing in front of his palm-thatch clubhouse, concerned about the outcome of the tapir hunt: "I send this bum out for tapir . . . this Johnny

Butterass, Johnny Blowjob, whatever the fuck his name
is. Where the hell is he? I'm like a fish in the desert
here, for Christsake! I gotta read the *New York Post* to
find out how he fuckin' made out? I hate this [*inaudible*]
with a fucking passion!"

" 'After two weeks of boogie-boarding, snorkeling,
golf, and sight-seeing in Wiseguyana, the Gutmans are
in a taxi on the highway en route to the airport and little sunburnt Len sees a billboard at the Convention Center that reads: "Due to Plane Crash, Buddy Holly,
Richie Valens, The Big Bopper, Patsy Cline, Jim Croce,
and Lynyrd Skynyrd Will Not Be Appearing Tonight."
Now, not only should this be an extremely compelling
scene because of how powerfully it will resonate in the
audience's collective memory of that ill-fated flight,
which was piloted by 7-year-old novice aviatrix Jessica
Dubroff, but in terms of the plot, this is *the* pivotal
scene in the entire movie. This is the precise moment at
which young Leonard Gutman realizes his almost mysti-
cal affinity for signage copywriting. From that moment
on, Gutman studies and rewrites every single marquee,
billboard, and sign he encounters.

" 'And, basically, the rest of the movie deals with his
teenage years, which are uneventful except for an
uncharacteristic, albeit tragic, indiscretion; his long,
illustrious career and unparalleled accomplishments and
awards; and finally his controversial death at the hands
of New Jersey cardiologist and Tae Kwon Do black belt
Dr. Richard Cuozzo.

" 'Obviously I see you, Colonel, playing Gutman,
but I also thought—and tell me if this sounds crazy—
that maybe you could play Cuozzo, too—y'know, do a
sort of Alec Guinness in *Kind Hearts and Coronets,*
multiple-role, tour-de-force thing.

" 'So, what do you think?'

"Alebua grins broadly.

" 'I think it could be huge,' he says, greenlighting
the project on the spot.

"But Mark is desperately worried, of course, that he won't be able to actually write the screenplay."

"One day in his trailer on the lot, he meets Polo.

"Polo—who's come in to interview for a position as a dialogue writer—is a completely hairless, chain-smoking Bonobo chimpanzee. Shipped, as an infant, from a research facility in Kinshasa, Congo, to a bio-medical laboratory in Bougainville, where he spent much of his adult life, Polo is cross-hatched with vivi-section scars, his health ravaged by pharmaceutical experimentation. But he's been taught a vast and erudite vocabulary of sign language by the researchers who abandoned him when they fled Bougainville's civil war. Melancholic, physically decrepit, squinting through the smoke of a ubiquitous cigarette, Polo is a sort of simian Dennis Potter.

"With Mark serving primarily as Polo's amanuensis and occasional junior writing partner, they complete the script for *Gutman* in less than a week. This becomes the first of scores of movies that they write, direct, and pro-duce for the Colonel. (These are perhaps less 'movies' than the ultimate product inserts—Alebua being the product, of course.) It's common for security guards, passing by Mark's trailer late at night, to see through the window the glowing ember of Polo's cigarette trac-ing irregular shapes in the darkness as he signs, with Mark struggling to keep pace with his shorthand. The studio becomes a huge, thriving enterprise, employ-ing the finest actors, actresses, stuntmen, cinematogra-phers, choreographers, grips, gaffers, and best boys in Melanesia.

"In addition to their working partnership, Polo and Mark develop a close personal relationship. Polo exhibits a keen sensitivity to Mark's conflicted feelings about his missing, NJSDE-releasee father. Grateful for the empathic companionship, Mark keeps a Louis XIV porcelain candy box (with zaftig shepherdesses cavorting

on the lids) continuously stocked with panda nuts,
sugarcane, and sun-dried termites for his dissipated,
four-foot confidant/mentor, and makes sure that he has
the latest downloaded issues of German and Turkish
pornography specializing in explicit photos of estrous
female Bonobos.

"In addition to screenplays, Polo 'writes' novels.
Same modus operandi: Polo signs, Mark takes dictation,
offering the odd emendation and bon mot. Polo has an
astonishing capacity to write proficiently in *any* style—
techno-suspense, New Age inspirational, Sadean transgression, high lyricism, faux-naif ebonic, slacker
confessional, magic realism, cut-up, avant pop, trailer-
park minimalism, neo-gothic southern, you name it.
And his novelistic output is prolific—some sixteen novels so far, ranging in length from several hundred pages
to over a thousand.

"One afternoon, Polo and Mark decide to fabricate
noms de plume for their novels by making anagrams out
of the surnames of Bougainvillean tetherball players.
Determining it wise to avoid the better-known players
like Offramp Tavanipupu, Wuwu-Bulolo Puliyasi, and
Onguglo To'uluwa, they select the last names of minor-
league players who appear in the back-page box scores of
that day's sports section: Mafuta Mel'Chachanibo, Yam-
abola Trantando, Udang Gascand-Pupulolo, Waso Libré-
El'Fennjé, Moses Nirrshinca'olo, Paza Christifebro,
Ushaga Eresed-Yeffé'Jingu, Hazu Tonnra-N'JenFhaza,
Bonabuzo Tsirinamma, Ng'ombé Tandizüjo, Elijah
Tetsi-Lélé'Bona, Sr., Mühür Nampinsomso, Xavier
Tergheepo, Ali Falla'd-Certdevi-Waso, Ozzy Emshamo,
and Satmak L. L.'Herbé-Tetziwuza.

"This is an extremely long scene, during which a
coffee-guzzling, Liquid Paper–huffing Polo and Mark
endeavor long into the night, endlessly rearranging and
re-rearranging letters in order to anagrammatize the
players' surnames into appropriately authorial-sounding

pseudonyms. By early morning, Mel'Chachanibo has been transposed into 'Michael Chabon.' Tranttando has eventually been worked into 'Donna Tartt.' Gascand-Pupulolo is anagrammatically reshuffled into 'Douglas Coupland.' Libré-El'Fennjé becomes 'Jennifer Belle.' Nirrshinca'olo becomes 'Colin Harrison.' Christifebro—'Tibor Fischer.' Eresed-Yeffé'Jingu—'Jeffrey Eugenides.' Tonnra-N'JenFhaza—'Jonathan Franzen.' Tsirinamma—'Martin Amis.' Tandizüjo—'Junot Díaz.' Tetsi-Lélé'Bona Sr.—'Bret Easton Ellis.' Nampinsomso—'Mona Simpson.' And Tergheepo—'Peter Hoeg.' Some of the concocted pen names go through scores of iterations before a suitably literary sounding version is achieved. Falla'd-Certdevi-Waso provisionally becomes 'Darlesca "Lew" D'Fatvio' before 'David Foster Wallace' is deemed more urbane. Emshamo is 'Amos Hem' before one last reshuffling into 'A. M. Homes.' And Mark and Polo almost settle on 'Walter Huzzbeitle' as the final anagrammatical product of L. L.'Herbé-Tetziwuza, before several more reconfigurations yield 'Elizabeth Wurtzel.'

"It's also tricky deciding which pen name to assign to which novel. The novel about the yuppie serial murderer is originally attributed to 'Mona Simpson,' the novel about the terrible father who owns a biotechnology company to 'Bret Easton Ellis,' the one about the middle-class, 19-year-old drama student who moonlights as a $1,000-a-night prostitute to 'David Foster Wallace,' and the hefty opus about the tennis academy and 12-step programs to 'Jennifer Belle,' before Mark and Polo decide that these are not felicitous pairings.

"Some reviewers have remarked that the pseudonymous anagrams constitute *The Tetherballs of Bougainville*'s major artistic achievement. Snideness aside, they *are* impressive. After seeing the movie, I spent three days checking the noms de plume to confirm that they transpose back into the Bougainvillean surnames. They do.

"I've previously discussed how the phenomenon of

the male-adolescent-sequestered-in-his-bedroom is fundamental to this movie. Surely, anagrammatizing the names of tetherball stars is the obsessive activity par excellence of the druggy 13-year-old ensconced in his lair.

"Mark considers these novels to be the best collaborative work he's done since the paper on fraternity-hazing deaths at the Fashion Institute of Technology that he wrote with his dad.

"And he sends the completed manuscripts—now attributed to the fabricated noms de plume—to various agents and publishers in New York.

"Meanwhile, Mark begins dating Lehrerasha. And they become the toast of the Bougainville *beau monde,* fawned upon by the supercilious sommeliers at La Petite Sangsue, club-hopping through the shantytowns of Kieta, necking in the backseat of her Toyota Land Cruiser as drovers pass by, switching the rumps of their oxen—Lehrerasha naked except for her vibrating beeper and the Breathe Right nasal strip across the bridge of her nose. They party with the tetherball superstars, and become, along with Offramp Tavanipupu, official co-cynosures of Kieta's cultural vanguard. And during the Ma Ling Masters, they swig Cherry fX Bomb in the luxurious sky-box used by Oshimitsu Polymer execs. Oshimitsu Polymers is, of course, the world's leading manufacturer of tetherball tether.

"Thanks to Mark and Polo's success in marketing Colonel Alebua and his regime, dictators, warlords, corrupt corporations, and criminal cartels from around the world seek out their services and become clients. Tyrants, despots, and terrorists of every nationality, ethnicity, and ideology; Cosa Nostra families, yakuza clans, and Hong Kong triads; chemical and metallurgy companies that pump dioxins and PCBs into reservoirs and aquifers; rapacious mining and logging conglomerates; makers of tainted baby formula, botulism-contaminated vichyssoise, and mercury-laden facial creams; fast-food chains whose burgers are saturated with E. *coli,* shigella, and necrotizing fascitis Strep A; athletes who habitually molest, defenestrate, crucify, and then bury alive their wives, children, and in-laws; etc.

"They post $677.3 million in billing for the first quarter.

"It's *Heart of Darkness,* and Mark is Kurtz.

"But it's Kurtz as Maurice Saatchi.

"They expand into a full-service agency. Their 'manpower' agency, which has been providing temps for governments that need, say, an agent provocateur for entrapping members of an opposition group, evolves into a full-fledged talent-management company with a comprehensive roster of mellifluous BBC-accented foreign ministers, venal judges for annulling presidential and parliamentary elections, and pliant figureheads for giving your regime that imprimatur of legitimacy.

"They even take Colonel Alebua and members of his junta to the mountains one weekend for a synergy- and trust-building training retreat.

"The evolution of The Bougainville Group into the world's largest mercenary advertising and infotainment company is more than the world's traditional ad agencies can stomach. They begin to fund a coalition of armed groups dedicated to the violent overthrow of the Alebua government.

"The first to open their coffers to the insurgents are McCann-Erickson, J. Walter Thompson, and BBDO Worldwide, jointly underwriting a full armored division, a dozen helicopter gunships, a Medevac, a twin-rotor Chinook, and an amphibious assault ship.

"At Young and Rubicam, a volunteer brigade, made up of passionately committed mail-room clerks and entry-level copywriters, sets out for the Solomon Islands. The war in Bougainville is, for these brave and idealistic Y&R volunteers, what the Spanish Civil War was to the generation of Hemingway—the defining moral conflict of its era, a conflict for which many give their lives.

"Each week another agency aligns itself with the rebels: Ogilvy & Mather, Grey, Chiat/Day, D'Arcy Masius Benton & Bowles, Ammirati Puris Lintas, Wells Rich Greene BDDP, Leo Burnett, DDB Needham, Foote, Cone & Belding in Chicago, Fallon McElligott in Minneapolis.

"Weapons, ammunition, combat vehicles, logistical support, and advisory personnel pour in; sophisticated real-time satellite surveillance is provided.

"The tide of the civil war begins to turn. The Alebua regime begins to crumble.

"The rebels gain control of the outlying provinces and advance on Kieta. In broadcasts from their clandestine radio station (a 'lite' rebel station—more music, less inflammatory rhetoric) and in a front-page editorial in *Advertising Age,* it's announced that, if they aren't captured, Alebua and Mark will be tried *and executed* in absentia.

"With the rebel troops some 48 hours from the capital, Colonel Alebua prepares to flee the country.

"Lehrerasha asks Mark to come live with her in Europe.

" 'Daddy has a chateau in Luxembourg. We could be so happy.'

" 'I can't,' Mark says. 'Look, Lehrerasha, it's been a great summer, but . . . I've gotta get back to Maplewood. School starts soon . . . and, y'know, I miss my friends—Sylvia and Felipe and everybody.'

"He drapes a lei of frangipani blossoms around her neck and kisses her.

" 'Good-bye . . . it's been, like, really, really great. *Really!*' he calls to her, as she sashays across the tarmac and boards the cargo transport plane that her father's bodyguards are loading with $66 million in gold bullion and the original prints of all their movies.

"Polo is presumably dead. He's reportedly last seen

knuckle-walking disorientedly through a mine field and into a free-fire zone.

"Mark manages to escape, hidden on a fishing trawler, the night before the country falls to the rebels. As the vessel pulls past boats swaying languidly in the soporific heat, and the menacing, blackish-purple palisades and jagged promontories of Bougainville recede in the distance, the rhythmic thud of mortar rounds is a lulling accompaniment to the khat he chews.

"(The fact that khat, a shrub cultivated exclusively in the Middle East and Africa, appears to be widely available in Bougainville, is one of several ethnobotanical incongruities in this movie. This is either a deliberate allusion to an active, multilateral global marketplace in indigenous intoxicants or simply the result of lazy fact-checking. I suspect the latter.)

"Arriving in the United States, Mark makes the appalling discovery that impostors are claiming to be the fabricated authors of all the novels that he and Polo wrote. Who these people are, Mark has no idea—out-of-work actors, streetwise professional con artists, perhaps even disillusioned and cynical young editors or agents. Whoever they are, they have successfully assumed the identities of each and every anagrammatized nom de plume, and secured fat six-figure book deals. The novels are published with intense media buzz, and launched with glittering, bibulous parties at the trendiest boîtes in Manhattan. The sham 'novelists' are feted and photographed by the intellectual, fashion and entertainment magazines, rocketed off on whirlwind 15-city national book tours, interviewed on *Fresh Air, The Today Show, Charlie Rose,* etc. A number of the books have become huge best-sellers, several even hit movies.

"And if this isn't dispiriting enough, all efforts to get in touch with Sylvia are futile—she seems to have disappeared off the face of the earth. And he realizes that he misses Lehrerasha desperately.

"Deeply depressed, he abandons Maplewood and takes a suite at the Mondrian in Los Angeles.

"It's a Saturday night. Mark is watching a re-edited version of *Gutman* that's being shown on the Sundance Channel. The first movie he and Polo wrote and directed for Colonel Alebua, this searing portrait of a tortured signage genius has been turned into a mawkish musical starring Tony Danza and Dixie Carter. He flicks off the television, disgustedly hurling the remote against the wall. He crumples onto the couch and thumbs absently through magazines fanned out on the coffee table—*Buzz, Wired, Harper's Bazaar, New York.* But there, in glossy shot after glossy shot, brooding theatrically, mugging with haughty smirks and moues, are the very impersonators masquerading as 'Jennifer Belle,' 'Elizabeth Wurtzel,' 'David Foster Wallace,' 'Junot Díaz,' etc.

"It's all too much for him to bear. First, his movies gelded. And now these phonies, these rank pretenders, defrauding him of *his* critical acclaim and *his* royalties.

"He decides to ingest a huge wad of khat he salvaged from the trawler.

" 'Perhaps,' he thinks to himself, 'I'll sleep for a day, for two days, for a thousand days . . .'

"He's just about to swallow the revolting bolus, when . . .

"There's a knock on the door.

" 'Who's there?' he asks.

"There's another diffident knock.

"Mark gets up from the sofa, walks to the door, and opens it.

"There, trembling before him, is an exhausted, gaunt, dehydrated Bonobo chimp, wearing a pair of frayed Hugo Boss boxer shorts, his hairless body splotched with impetigo and covered with ticks, an unlit cigarette in his cracked lips.

" 'Polo . . . you're alive!'

" 'Got a light?' the chimp signs feebly, whereupon he collapses across the threshold of the suite.

"After resuscitating him with food, drink, and a hot bath, Mark tearfully explains to Polo how their novels have been stolen by the pseudonym impersonators.

" 'We'll never get credit for our work, Polo. It's hopeless. It's . . . just hopeless.'

"Polo slaps Mark across the face, and then slowly and emphatically signs the following words: 'Any asshole with a Master of Social Work degree can put on a turban and start issuing fatwas about whom you can and whom you can't send meat to, but it takes real balls to turn a brunette without a cranium into a blonde.'

" 'What did you just say?' a stunned Mark asks.

" 'I said, "Any asshole with a Master of Social Work degree can put on a turban and start issuing fatwas about whom you can and whom you can't send meat to, but it takes real balls to turn a brunette without a cranium into a blonde." '

" 'Dad . . . ?' Mark asks tremulously.

"And then, in full-throated astonishment: 'DAD!!!! DAD!!!! IT'S YOU!!!!'

"This, of course, is attended by the shrieking violins that accompany any even mildly unexpected plot contrivances in this movie.

"At the screening I attended, this scene, in which Polo is revealed to be Mark's father, was greeted in the theater by a mixture of gasps and embarrassed laughter—some viewers seeming to experience a profoundly cathartic epiphany, others finding this latest revelation to be bathos bordering on farce.

" 'I did it all for you, son,' says Polo/Dad. 'I had to be there for you in Bougainville. Just like I was during the school year.'

" 'What do you mean, *during the school year?*'

" 'I was Sylvia.'

"More shrieking violins.

"And another proportional outburst of tears and titters in the audience.

" '*That's* why Sylvia wouldn't ever have sex with me!' says Mark. 'Because . . .'

" 'Because it would have been *so* wrong,' signs Polo/Dad. 'See, I had to stay near you, son, but I also had to alter my DNA in order to elude the NJSDE boys.'

" 'How, though? How did you do it?'

" 'Chemical mutagens, irradiation, viral agents—the standard transgenic protocol. You target specific genes and then specific sites, known as codons, on a gene's DNA sequence, and basically, you transpose the sequence. It's like a genetic anagram. You reshuffle the code. For instance, *Sylvia* was homozygous for the amino acid methionine at polymorphic residue 129 of PrP . . .'

"Polo/Dad's explanation of how he was able to genetically rearrange himself first into the stripper at The Carousel, then into Sylvia, and finally into a Bonobo chimpanzee runs some 90 minutes, and although personally I found it easy to follow, it's so thoroughly larded with arcane jargon, biotech neologisms, and unexplicated acronyms as to be completely impenetrable to the average layperson.

"In the ensuing weeks, Mark nurses Polo/Dad back to health, and persuades him to allow Mark to act as his attorney in a lawsuit against the phony authors *and* their publishing companies.

"It's the Trial of the Century. A legally intricate— and, from a dramatic perspective, almost unbearably intense—maelstrom of concepts and case law ranging from the Scopes Monkey Trial to the Janet Malcolm– Jeffrey Masson and Joan Collins litigations to, of course, the Milli Vanilli case.

"Chandrapal Ram—whose rendering of Mark has heretofore been almost Noh-like in its sullen laconicism and choreographic rigor—explodes here, giving one of the most uninhibited, convulsive, transformative, and courageously over-the-top performances I have ever seen.

"Stalking the courtroom shirtless and in his signature Versace leather motocross trousers, he combines not only the tenacity and snarling, ruthless brilliance of Barry Scheck and the majestic oratorical abandon and mesmerizing, free-associative whimsy of a young Muammar Qaddafi, but the taunting, gutter sexuality of a Susan Dey.

"During the climactic closing arguments, the courtroom is overflowing with spectators and press. The fake 'Chabon,' 'Tartt,' 'Coupland,' 'Belle,' 'Ellis,' et al., sit together in a specially reserved section of the gallery. David Levine is the courtroom sketch artist. The publishing executives and their attorneys occupy the defense table. Polo, of course, sits slumped at the plaintiff's table.

"Mark prefaces his summation by thanking the judge (played by a somnambulant Lou Diamond Philips) for his equitable and expeditious rulings and the jury (one of whose female members wears a T-shirt throughout the trial that says 'Men Suck') for its patience and sacrifice.

"And he begins by rephrasing the opening line of Stéphane Mallarmé's beautiful poem 'Brise Marine' (Sea Breeze), which originally reads *'La chair est triste, hélas! et j'ai lu tous les livres'* ('The flesh is sad, alas! and I have read all the books').

" 'Ladies and gentleman of the jury,' he intones, 'The flesh is sad, alas!' And then pointing to Polo, 'And he has *written* all the books.'

"At first he affects a casual, amiable, at times intimate manner—seeking to connect personally with each member of the jury. He jokes about a newfound interest in petit-point embroidery. He shares odd, seemingly irrelevant bits of gee-whiz scientific trivia ('Most things swell in the heat, right? Well, zirconium tungstate *contracts* when warmed!') and then a strange anecdote about being chased through the Museum of Natural History by a girl with webbed fingers. He launches into a long, pointless digression about Seattle Supersonics point guard Gary Payton and Los Angeles Laker Nick Van Exel. And then he relates a dream he says he had the previous night ('There were these aliens, female aliens in, like, Carmelite nun headgear and long silver Gore-Tex capes, and they had these Super Soaker water guns filled with stagnant vase water and they were forcing these real narcissistic musclemen to whack off—y'know at, like, gunpoint—and then all the female aliens turned out to be, like, all my teachers from school and stuff . . .').

"At this point, the jurors are frantically scribbling notes.

"An arm draped casually over the railing of the jury box, as he swirls water in a plastic cup, Mark confides that he was mortally hydrophobic as a small child. He then tells a story about how once a day-camp counselor playfully tossed him into a swimming pool. Mark's feelings were hurt terribly, and he put a Satanic curse on the counselor, who, the next day, was mysteriously scalded to death in his own shower.

"Whether or not this is a cryptic attempt on Mark's part to intimidate the jury is furiously debated by legal analysts in television studios across the country.

"Following another personal aside ('I don't know about you, but I hate the goddamn beach. I lie there, I feel like a fucking cutlet—drenched in oil, coated with sand, and frying. That's a vacation?'), he maneuvers deftly into the heart of his summation by reading to the jury, in a lilting singsong, the entirety of Baruch Spinoza's *Ethics* ('For no one has acquired such accurate knowledge of the fabric of the body, as to be able to explain all its functions; nor need I omit to mention the many things observed in brutes, which far surpass human sagacity, and the many things which sleep-

walkers do, which they would not dare to do when
awake: this is sufficient to show that the body itself,
merely from the laws of its own nature alone, can do
many things, at which the mind marvels, etc., etc.').
"He then pauses dramatically.
" 'These people you see seated there in that row in
this courtroom are not authors, they're impersonators.
Actors! Straight out of central casting! They're impostors! They're garden-variety lowlife scamming slacker
scum! "Elizabeth Wurtzel," "David Foster Wallace,"
"A. M. Homes" . . . these people don't even exist! There
are no such people. THEY DO NOT EXIST!'
"The courtroom at this moment is hushed and
absolutely still. The only sounds are the scratching of
David Levine's sketch pen and the sobs of the jurors.
" 'Polo and I fabricated these names from the sports
pages of a Bougainville newspaper. You all remember
when I had that refrigerator brought into court and I
showed you with the magnetic letters how easy it was
rearrange the names, to concoct "Jennifer Belle" from
Libré-El-Fennjé, and "Douglas Coupland" from
Gascand-Pupulolo. His Honor let you play with the
letters and you saw for yourselves how simple it was to
make the anagrams. And we even had some of the
players—Mafuta Mel'Chachanibo and Ozzy Emshamo
and Satmak L. L.'Herbé-Tetziwuza brought all the way
from Bougainville to present their birth certificates and
testify in this courtroom, under oath, as to their given
names.'
"Again he pauses dramatically, and then walks
slowly past the defense table.
" 'This trial is a search. A search for a writer. The
writer of all those books,' he says, pointing to a huge
mounted display of enlarged glossy dust jackets.
" 'But, ladies and gentleman, these are not writers,'
he says, gesturing contemptuously at the row of impersonators.

" 'These are merely . . .' he hesitates, as if groping for the most precise way to articulate his disdain. 'These are merely *the tetherballs of Bougainville!*'

"There's a buzz throughout the courtroom.

"He strides back toward the plaintiff's table.

" 'This is *the writer*,' Mark says reverently, with a sweeping flourish of the arm, indicating Polo, and then a deep genuflection.

" 'No one wants to believe that *Microserfs* and *Infinite Jest* and *Prozac Nation* and *The End of Alice* were all written by a Bonobo chimp and a 13-year-old boy smoking weed and drinking forties in their bedroom! No one wants to believe it! No one wants to believe that those assholes over there didn't write these books. Throughout the 1930s, American physicians routinely prescribed potassium cyanide as a palliative for headaches and menstrual cramps, even though it inevitably resulted in the death of the patient within minutes of ingestion. But doctors continued prescribing it, and people just kept on taking it. Because they couldn't deal with the truth. And they can't deal with the truth here. No one can deal with the fact that a drunk, stoned Bonobo chimp and a 13-year-year-old boy actually wrote every single one of those novels. It just shatters everyone's cherished notion of the great, exalted, hallowed *Author.* Right? It just can't possibly be. How impudent to suggest that this is how these books were written. But it is! It's true. You've seen that demonstrated beyond a reasonable doubt in this courtroom. And you know something? Any inbred, paint-chip-munching, goat-bonking pinhead retard they put on this jury could see that. Because it's the truth! It's the goddamn irrefutable truth!! And in your hearts you know it is! You can't lie to yourselves! *You* know who wrote those books!! WE *ALL* KNOW WHO WROTE THOSE BOOKS!!!' he raves, froth appearing at the corners of his mouth.

" 'And now you have an extraordinary opportunity to redress this foul, unconscionable injustice. You can

make it right! Do it, my fellow Americans! Do it for
every adolescent anomic skank genius cloistered in his
room, getting cranked, rabidly humping his sampler as
he confects some heretical, monstrous persona for himself and dreams of an orgiastic, blood-soaked apocalypse.
Yes, the *impudence!* We have *nothing* in this life of suffo-
cating obligation but our motherfucking impudence!
For God's sake, give us this day our motherfucking big-
dick impudence!!'

"In a volcanic recitative, with venomous, profanity-
laced fury, he continues to exhort the jury to render the
correct verdict. It's a febrile, histrionic, spellbinding
masterpiece of demagogic virtuosity: the carefully practiced threatening and imploring gestures, the calculated
hysterical climaxes, the modulations of the voice—one
moment, shrieking and gesticulating, and in the very
next, whispering urgently and with hypnotic persuasion.

"He concludes with the final stanza from Mallarmé's
'Sea Breeze': 'An ennui, bereft of cruel hopes, / Yet
believes in the ultimate farewell of handkerchiefs! / And,
perhaps, the masts, inviting storms, / May be those a
wind bends over shipwrecks / Lost, without masts, nor
masts nor fertile shores . . . / Still, O my heart, hear the
seafarers' song!'

" 'Ladies and gentlemen of the jury, I am confident
that, having considered the evidence we have presented
to you in this trial, you will sing that seafarers' song,
and you will find in favor of my client.

" 'Thank you.'

"The jury responds with convulsive emotion—many
are weeping, others have swooned, several rise to their
feet, shaking their fists in the air, some are simply paralyzed in their chairs, slack-jawed with astonishment.

"Mark returns to his seat, exhausted, his eyes glazed.
He is soaking wet, having lost five or six pounds.

"The jury takes only 45 minutes to deliberate before
rendering its decision.

"In a stunning, landmark verdict that fundamentally

and irrevocably changes the relationship between the publishing industry and brachiating primates, it awards Polo $10.5 million in compensatory and punitive damages.

"And the counterfeit 'authors' are utterly discredited and exposed as the scheming con artists they are.

"In the final scene, we see Mark and Polo seated next to each other in the first-class section of a plane to Luxembourg. Sipping Cristal, the hitherto hairless Polo wears an expensive, custom-tailored, full-body Bonobo pelt.

"After the plane takes off, Mark stares contemplatively at the clouds for a while and then turns to Polo.

" 'Dad, do you know when I first realized how much I really love you?'

" 'When?' signs Polo.

" 'When you danced for me and Felipe at The Carousel. Maybe you don't really appreciate your father until he has huge tits.'

" 'Y'know,' Polo signs, embracing his son, 'maybe you're right.'

"Passengers and flight attendants break into applause, stanching their happy tears with cocktail napkins.

"The music swells (Offramp Tavanipupu's searingly unapologetic cover of the Jim Nabors' elegiac smash classic 'Oh My Papa') as the plane disappears into the distance, and credits roll across the azure screen.

"To me, this ending represents something of a squandered opportunity. We have the protagonist Mark—who, having spent most of the movie shunning his father out of fear for his own safety, has been as much a target for the audience's opprobrium as he has for its sympathy—finally redeemed by his passionate and courageous courtroom advocacy. We have the

ancient archetype of the hero reckoning with his patri-
mony—going through a series of ordeals culminating in
a crisis in which he and his father are atoned. And we
have five million years of hominid evolution telescoped
into two generations. And the best they can come up
with as a conclusive, overarching declaration is 'Maybe
you don't really appreciate your father until he has
huge tits'?

"This is all the more perplexing, in light of asser-
tions by individuals with intimate knowledge of the
movie's genesis, that this very line—'Maybe you don't
really appreciate your father until he has huge tits'—is
the end product of a succession of extravagantly expensive rewrites by script doctors including Richard Price,
Callie Khouri, and John Gregory Dunne, each of whom
purportedly received a seven-figure paycheck for tweak-
ing this single sentence of dialogue.

"But that line is, in essence, *The Tetherballs of
Bougainville*. This is a movie that consistently subordinates meaning to titillation. And it is a movie that perpetually teeters between puerile perversity and puerile
sentimentality.

"But between the perversity and the sentimentality,
like a gleaming sliver of light emerging from between
abutting slabs, there is—dare I say it—an element of
grace.

"*The Tetherballs of Bougainville is rated PG-13 (parents
strongly cautioned). Although it contains incessant profanity;
graphic and extraordinarily gruesome violence; explicit heterosexual, homosexual, transsexual, and hermaphroditic sex; and
constant on-camera drug use; the only scene which teenagers
may find disturbing is the 'klezmer orgy,' which, although
brief, is unusually intense.*"

CLOSE SHOT of MARK meticulously folding review back into
compressed rectangle. (When he's finished, this rectangle should
be exceedingly tiny, almost an origami microchip.)

MEDIUM SHOT of WARDEN emerging from steamy bathroom with one towel wrapped turbanlike around her head and another wrapped around her torso.

> MARK

So, what did you think of the review?

> WARDEN

Unfortunately, I had trouble hearing a lot of it because of the shower.

> MARK

Well, what parts did you hear?

> WARDEN

Basically, the part about something emerging from between two abutting slabs.

> MARK

That's it?

The TELEPHONE RINGS on Warden's desk.

The WARDEN answers.

> WARDEN
>
> *(covering receiver with hand)*

It's for you.

MARK takes phone.

> MARK
>
> *(into telephone)*

Hello? Dad? Your voice sounds kinda funny. *(Covers receiver, whispers to Warden)* He's dusted. *(Back into telephone, to father)* Where are you? . . . Uh-huh. *(To Warden)* Where's the Princeton Marriott?

WARDEN

The Marriott? It's only about ten minutes from here.

MARK

(into telephone)

Dad, don't you think it's sort of, like, *dangerous* for you to be so close? . . . Uh-huh. OK. I *know* it's due tomorrow. I will, Dad. I *know* I should have started it earlier. I will. I'm gonna go home soon. OK. OK, 'bye.

WARDEN

Your father cares very much about you, doesn't he?

MARK takes the WARDEN's hand and playfully tugs her away from the desk, to the far end of the room, across from the windows affording a view of the gazebo.

Standing directly under one of the suspended speakers (from which we now hear Offramp Tavanipupu's "Mi Laik Kai-Kai Dim-Dim," as sung by Vanessa Williams), they embrace each other in an oblique column of moonlight.

MARK

Listen, if I'm going to win that award, I guess I better get going pretty soon and start working on this screenplay. I just wanted to tell you that this afternoon and this evening—hanging out with you and everything—it was really, really great. *Really.* And . . . I want you to have this.

MARK removes the ring from his finger—the oval Burmese sapphire flanked by heart-shaped diamonds that his father had given him just prior to the abortive execution attempt—and he slides it on the WARDEN's left-hand ring finger.

EXT. THE SKIES OVER THE PRINCETON MARRIOTT

Three NJSDE F-117 stealth bombers swoop down over the hotel, each delivering a 2,000-pound, laser-guided bomb.

Several moments later, from high altitude, an NJSDE B-52 Stratofortress delivers its devastating 70,000-pound bomb load on the Marriott.

We HEAR the THUNDEROUS, EAR-POPPING BOOMS of the shells hitting the hotel and its environs.

Towering black plumes of smoke and shafts of brilliant orange flame shoot into the sky.

INT. WARDEN'S OFFICE

Shock waves from the NJSDE air strike on the Princeton Marriott are causing the prison to shake violently.

The gigantic Meridian DSP-8000 speaker is swaying back and forth over MARK and the WARDEN, who are kissing passionately and feverishly caressing each other.

Suddenly, THE FOUR LENGTHS OF OSHIMITSU SYNTHETIC SPIDER-SILK SPEAKER-SUSPENSION LINE SNAP, IN RAPID SUCCESSION, WITH FOUR DISTINCT *TWANGS*—a grotesque pizzicato comprising the first four notes of "When the Saints Go Marching In."

The 300-pound SPEAKER PLUMMETS to the ground, CRUSHING the WARDEN and MARK.

The WARDEN is killed instantly.

MARK has suffered massive head trauma and internal injuries.

SOFT-FOCUS CLOSE SHOT of NAKED, HEMORRHAGING MARK lying pinned beneath the huge speaker.

> M A R K
> Yo—what the fuck . . . ?

He dies.

FADE TO BLACK

ROLL CREDITS OVER BLOOPER OUTTAKES